The SWEET *and* BITTER TASTE *of* Moonshine

a novel by

ANDREW ROSS

Palmetto Publishing Group, LLC
Charleston, SC

For information regarding special discounts or for bulk purchases, please contact Palmetto Publishing Group at
Info@PalmettoPublishingGroup.com.

ISBN-13: 978-1-944313-17-3
ISBN-10: 1-944313-17-6

Dedicated to my wife Maggie, who embodies the strength of Boadicea with the love of Penelope.

Chapter One

AMBROSE WELLS SAT IN THE FRONT SEAT of his aging Ford Bronco, staring across highway 174 through a dusty haze of South Carolina red earth. Light filtered through the slowly falling dust, and gently settled on a palmetto bush that grew under the shade of a massive, old live oak, and all Ambrose could think of was how beautiful it all seemed. In the back of his mind, in that deep, dark singularity where nightmares are born, he sensed that it was odd that he should think about this. Of all possible emotions that might be coursing through his rigid, aching body right now, it was this one—this appreciation of the ephemeral beauty of light passing through the drifting, sparkling particles of floating earth on a hot August evening— that had taken precedence. After all, the dust had been kicked up by his own tires as his truck had spun around on the soft, grey asphalt, and had come to rest on the dirt shoulder of the road. His vehicle was now facing ninety degrees to the right of its intended direction. In what must have been no longer than five or ten seconds, Ambrose's Bronco had narrowly missed an oncoming, top-of-the-line Mercedes, spun around with startling speed, and slid to a violent stop on the curb he now found himself upon. As he realized this, the whole accident was replayed in his head with dazzling clarity.

He closed his eyes and saw himself driving down 174, a trip he'd made many times in the past, though it had been years. For the life of him, he couldn't remember one damned thing he'd been thinking about between gassing up near Walterboro, and then nearly hitting the Mercedes here on Edisto Island. Almost an hour of time had elapsed, and he couldn't remember what he'd done, seen, or thought of. He vaguely had the impression that maybe he'd been thinking about Big John Connolly, his boss up in Columbia who'd sent him down here on what seemed like a fool's errand, but he wasn't entirely sure. He hazily remembered going over the impressively arcing McKinley Washington, Jr. bridge that gracefully passed over the Dawhoo River like the curved neck of a swan, but other than that, he couldn't be sure of what he'd thought about or seen while driving for the better part of an hour at roughly fifty-five miles per hour. But suddenly there had been a remarkable flash of brilliant green that had darted across his field of vision, almost simultaneously followed by a jarring, baritone thump as if something heavy had hit the windshield, and finally the sickening realization that his truck was halfway in the other lane, careening toward a light blue Mercedes.

The thunk of whatever he'd hit against the windshield seemed to have snapped him out of his reverie, and from that moment on, Ambrose experienced everything that subsequently happened with exquisite detail and crisp sensory recall. He'd looked up and seen the Mercedes rapidly approaching. He could see the driver, a young woman with light, sandy hair and a blue bandanna around her neck, tensely gripping the wheel and screaming, as if she were in a silent movie, for he could not hear her. He watched as she pulled hard to the right, and he felt amazed in an almost out-of-body way as her side mirror was violently sheered off by the front of his car. By now, he had automatically reacted himself, and he pulled his wheel hard to the right. He could hear the grinding of his wheels against the uneven dirt on the side of the road, and feel the rough bumps as they transmitted up through the chassis and into his seat.

Overcorrecting (and feeling somewhat ashamed about it now), he'd then turned the wheel hard to the left in order to return to the pavement while simultaneously slamming on the brakes. He felt the stress on the car, and the tension in his right calf as he pushed with tremendous effort against the poor brake pedal. The back of the Bronco by then had started to swerve around to his right as the wheels had trouble finding purchase on the softer earth. He remembered spinning a full 360 degrees, the back half of the car crushing a few unfortunate palmettos, and one very immature crepe myrtle that hadn't stood a chance against the mass and velocity of the back half of his steel, 1992 Bronco. As the car swung around, Ambrose felt amazed that it had not yet flipped, and he even had time to wonder about how that was even possible—until he saw the Mercedes, whose side mirror he had violently freed, crash headfirst into a wooden picket fence. He sat staring ahead, transfixed at the scene unplaying before him, gripping the wheel with Herculean strength, and continuing to jam the brake against the floorboard. Wooden beams flew up above the Mercedes, came down on its roof, and landed on the road to the car's left. Before he could fully process this fact however, his car—miraculously still not airborne—had continued to swing around from the back, crossed the road, and had come to a hard stop on the left shoulder, which left him staring incredulously at the beauty of early dusk sunlight filtering through the slowly falling dust he had so spectacularly lifted against gravity.

He then suddenly felt the ache in his right calf, and a squeezing tightness in the small lumbrical muscles of his fingers. He realized that he was still driving the brake pad home and gripping the wheel with all of his might. Slowly releasing his grip, he felt his stiff fingers relax as he exhaled, and only then did he realize that he'd been holding his breath throughout the whole ordeal. As everything slowed down, he quickly came to his senses. *Am I hurt?* he thought suddenly, and was briefly panic-stricken. He moved his feet, and brought his hands to his face. *Thank God!* He could move everything, and instead of feeling pain, he felt intense joy, as if he'd leaned over the precipice and stared in to the deep, black stillness of death, only to be pulled back at the last minute by some angel of deliverance. He realized he had tears in his eyes, and he inhaled and exhaled deeply several times, thrilled that this simple exercise could still be done.

"Holy Moses! God in Heaven! You okay, son? You alive and well in there?!"

Ambrose opened his eyes and turned his head left to see an old black man struggling to run on tired, stilt-like legs, his shabby, button-down shirt mostly unbuttoned and partly untucked from his equally ancient jeans, flailing in the wind behind him as he half-jogged, half-ambled up to the driver's side window. Ambrose could see the old pickup truck. *Even older than my Bronco,* he thought. The man had jumped out of the driver's side door, which was encrusted with flaking rust, and was still wide open. Two youthful faces were staring out at the scene in front of them from within the cabin, and their small grubby hands were plastered against the main windshield.

"You okay, young man? That was a hell of a thing to see. I can't believe you didn't flip over. I just can't believe it!"

By now the man had almost reached the driver's side door to the Bronco, and Ambrose wanted to say something to him through the open window, but as he opened his mouth nothing recognizable as English came out, and sensing the awkwardness, he simply shut it again. The old man made the final steps approaching the door at a much slower pace. Ambrose watched the concerned lines on his forehead melt away to a look of relief.

"Well, you ain't talking, but you're moving and breathing. Thank the good Lord for that. Yes, sir."

Before Ambrose could generate a response, the old man continued to speak as though the two were engaged in conversation.

"You don't move from that seat there, sir. I'll be back in just a minute. Gotta check on that other car. Yes, sir. Hit the fence at a good clip—Lord—a good clip. I sure do hope everyone's ok. Gotta see about that. Be right back."

The old man ambled off with his awkward gait, continuing to speak to nobody in particular, and made a beeline for the Mercedes that was now parked on the side of the road, about twenty feet into what had recently been a wooden picket fence. Turning his head to the right, Ambrose saw the trail of destruction the Mercedes had wrought upon the fence before it had finally come to a hard stop halfway on the shoulder of the road, halfway on to someone's previously well-demarcated property line. Several shattered pieces of wood were strewn all over the road, with one particularly large splinter that lay directly on the roof of the car, and several smaller fragments that rested on the trunk.

Holy shit, he thought to himself. Taking it all in, he suddenly thought about the panicked woman with the blue bandana screaming like the lead in a Charlie Chaplin flick, her face wrought with sheer panic, yet not a sound reaching his ears.

"Holy shit!" He suddenly cursed aloud as he wondered, panic-stricken, if he hadn't just killed a woman. He rapidly went to unclick his seatbelt, his shaky hands suddenly functional again as the shock of the accident wore off like a nightmare in the morning. He then pried open his door, and stepped out on to the shoulder of the road. His calves, especially the right one, protested the sudden movement, but he forced himself up. He quickly followed after the old man, who was now at the Mercedes door, peering inside the car, and either talking to himself or to the driver.

"Please be talking to that lady. Please be talking to that lady." Ambrose repeated this to himself nervously, an edge of terror to his voice, as his legs quickly covered the two hundred feet or so that lay between their vehicles.

"I'm okay, Mr. Dawes. Thank you. I'm fine. I've just hit my wrist against the dash, that's all."

A wave of relief flooded over Ambrose as he approached the driver's side door and heard—who he assumed was the driver—speaking, with evident familiarity, to the old man.

"Oh, thank God. You're okay!" He heard himself speak out loud, but almost didn't recognize his own voice—high-pitched and rushed, as the words tumbled out in an exhalation of relief.

The young woman looked over her left shoulder to peer behind the old man's shoulder at Ambrose, who was staring back at her with what she initially thought was a wild, almost panic-stricken look. She grimaced in obvious discomfort, and Ambrose could see that she was holding her right wrist, cradling it between her left hand and her chest.

"Well, I don't know who you are, sir, but I am most definitely not all right. My wrist feels like it's on fire. I don't suppose you've noticed, but there's a large piece of Mr. Dawes' fence extending halfway through my windshield. I was nearly impaled to death thanks to that fool of a driver in the Bronco."

She looked down at her injured wrist, and composed herself.

"I suspect he was drunk," she continued. She suddenly glanced cagily up at Ambrose.

"Well, I suspect you are that fool, aren't you Mr...?" She trailed off, a look of contempt in her eyes that pierced Ambrose's soul, and caused him to forget all about the relief he felt over her being okay—not to mention his own near-death experience. He looked down at his feet, unsure of how to reply.

"Yes. Now, Ms. Hampton, he was the lucky fella in the truck back there. This here's Mr…" The old man trailed off. "Well, I'm sorry, sir. I don't believe I caught your name."

Ambrose looked up at them both, feeling horribly guilty. He noticed a large pylon of wood literally sticking through the front windshield of the woman's car, stopping within an inch of the steering column. She had been nearly impaled to death, and it was all his fault! Wanting to speak, but uncertain of what to say in such a situation, he stammered softly, "My God, I'm sorry, ma'am. I hit…something green."

It sounded patently absurd, and Ambrose knew it. Unable to bear the silence any more, he followed this up quickly by inquiring about her wrist.

"My name is Cora Hampton. Thank you for askin'," she replied. "And my wrist feels like it's been stung by a yellow-jacket. I slammed it against the damned radio."

She flexed the fingers of her right hand against her chest, and winced.

"I think I'm gonna need a trip downtown to see about this," she concluded.

Looking down at her seated in the car, Ambrose felt like he wanted to do something—anything really—to help rectify the situation.

"Can I take you down to Charleston to get it looked at? I think my car's okay, and I feel awful."

She laughed unexpectedly.

"I think I've seen enough of your driving, sir."

Mr. Dawes laughed as well.

"I had Johnny call the ambulance. They should be here soon."

He nodded over to his pick-up truck where the two children Ambrose had seen earlier stared out the front window at the three of them.

Ambrose blushed, and muttered, "Of course. I am sorry, Ms. Hampton." He suddenly realized he hadn't yet introduced himself. "My name is Ambrose Wells. Let me help you out of the car."

Mr. Dawes beat him to it, opened the door, and unbuckled Cora's seatbelt. Gingerly taking her good hand in to his, she slid her upper torso past the large stake pointing menacingly at her sternum. She stepped out of the vehicle using Mr. Dawes as support, and kept her injured right wrist close against her chest. Her beauty struck Ambrose as she stood up. She was almost as tall as he was, and he was no slouch at six feet one. She was lithe and graceful, even with an injured wrist, and as she stepped out of the car, Ambrose noticed her riding boots and chaps that hugged her hips. She had a red, button-down shirt tucked in to tan riding pants, with the blue bandana he'd seen earlier tied around her neck now pinned against her shirt underneath her injured right wrist. Her eyes were light blue, and complemented the bandana, and Ambrose thought their softness made her look kind, especially framed as they were by her long, chestnut-colored hair, tussled some after the accident. She had a small nose and thinner lips than most people, but this simply drew people to her eyes, which had a tint of melancholy to them. They added softness to her every look, even when angry or hurt, just as she seemed to be right now. Ambrose felt his heart quicken, and he caught his breath. Not only was she striking, but the horrible thought raced through his mind that he had almost killed her five minutes ago.

Mr. Dawes stepped back so that she could fully escape from the vehicle. Cora walked around to the front of her car, taking in the extent of the damage and wincing whenever her wrist moved the wrong way against her shirt.

"Well, it certainly appears to be destroyed, Mr. Wells. I hope you have a decent insurance plan." She looked at him angrily, but yet again he saw a sweet sadness in her eyes that seemed to soften even her most scornful expression.

"Of course. I'll just go to my car, and get the information for you, ma'am."

Ambrose excused himself, and walked back to his car. He hated to think what this would cost him, but even while worrying about the inevitable consequences of this wreck, he couldn't keep himself from looking back at Cora several times.

After the necessary insurance information had been exchanged, Mr. Dawes let his grandchildren out of the car, and they ran over to see the wreckage for themselves. Johnny and Rose—their names as Ambrose discovered—quickly lost interest in him and Cora, and started to fence each other with epees made from the remains of Mr. Dawes' railings. Making use of the limited sunlight that was left to them, they parried and dove around the crepe myrtle that clung to the side of the road just beyond the remaining fence that was still intact. They laughed and squealed at each other in obvious delight, and took advantage of what was—for Ambrose, Cora and Mr. Dawes—a less than ideal situation. Several cars slowed down to offer assistance, but Cora waved them off, and after another ten minutes or so, a Charleston County ambulance arrived, its lights and sirens flashing. The medics briefly checked Ambrose out as the sun lazily set, and then turned their full attention to Cora.

Gently evaluating Cora's injured wrist, the EMS crew

immobilized it in a temporary splint, and then wrapped it in a bandage. She seemed a little unsure whether to accept their offer for a ride downtown to get an evaluation at the medical university, so Ambrose—partly out of guilt, and partly out of an opportunity to spend more time with her—offered a ride for a second time. She graciously demurred for a second time, politely said goodbye to Ambrose, and gave Mr. Dawes a quick hug, apologizing for his fence. She then climbed in to the back of the ambulance for the trip downtown.

As the ambulance pulled away, a dark and dirty tow truck, with multiple fishing-related bumper stickers, showed up, and a grease-covered, rotund man in well-worn Carhart overalls stepped out. Mr. Dawes and Ambrose watched as he grunted an acknowledgement, and then hitched the remains of the Mercedes to the large metallic hooks that extended from the back of the tow truck. Hauling the vehicle up in the deepening twilight, Johnny and Rose were repeatedly warned about straying too close to the driver and his monstrous truck. It's tentacle-like hooks appeared to—in the eyes of the children—snare the Mercedes, and draw it slowly closer toward the truck. It resembled a massive, metallic Architeuthis squid, dragging its prey toward its beak. It cast a menacing, yet attractive, spell over the children.

"I am sorry about your fence, Mr. Dawes," Ambrose said to him as the tow-truck driver finished his lonely work. "I want you to know I'll come and call on you to help with any costs you might incur to repair it. I'm staying down at the Anhinga Motel near the beach for at least this week." He paused, and then softly added, "I'm here for work," as if an explanation for his presence on the island was required.

Mr. Dawes glanced over after warning Johnnie to stay away from the tow truck for at least the third time. He smiled warmly, as if to give the receding indigo remains of daylight another minute or two of brightness.

"That'd be nice, Mr. Wells. My drive is just around the curve, over beyond them oak trees," he said, pointing off in the direction Ambrose had been driving from before the accident. He paused then for a second, before he continued. "I hate to be a busy-body, Mr. Wells, but aren't you Davey Wells' boy? I used to work with him, you understand, and you look just like that little boy, all grown up. I say, lookin' at you is like going back in time!"

Ambrose felt a little taken aback that anyone on the island would recognize him. He hadn't been there in roughly seven years—not since Christmas break his freshman year at the University of South Carolina, and prior to that, he'd only been there sporadically. He'd spent large portions of his childhood there, and had grown up with pluff mud—that primordial Lowcountry ooze that seemed to be the very clay God made men out of—stuck between his toes and in his ears. His later adolescence had brought about a lot of tension between he and his father, David Wells, and that chilly Christmas holiday was the last he'd seen of his father or of his property—despite the fact that, after his father's untimely death, the property had been willed to him in full as the only son and last remaining member of his family.

He had missed the land, but it was also painful in some inchoate sense that was hard to identify. He'd had an elderly tenant for a while, who served as caretaker of the old home, but after she'd moved out, a large summer storm blew through, and an ancient pine fell on the equally ancient house. Both entities had been destroyed in what seemed like a suicide pact they'd made between the two of them. Ambrose had been told that the remains of the home were still there, along with the kitchen and south wing, the back porch, and a few minor exterior buildings that were still apparently intact—though Father Time and Mother Nature continued to pound it all back into the soil from whence it had come. Ambrose had been thinking about going to visit, but hadn't come down firmly on a decision one way or another, prior to starting his trip back to Edisto.

He looked down at his shoes, regained his composure, and forced a smile.

"Yes, sir. He was my dad. Folks always said we never looked much alike, that I must have been my momma's son. I'm hoping I don't have many of his genes. He had a poor heart, if you know what I mean."

Mr. Dawes leaned back on his heels for a moment, his hands behind his back, and smiled broader than before, though Ambrose had not thought it possible.

"Ah ha, I knew it! I knew it before you even said anything to Ms. Hampton. I thought to myself, 'Now that there is Mr. Wells' boy in the flesh. Yes sir, in mind, body, and spirit, or I'm not Willy Dawes!' But you know what? You don't worry about your daddy's poor heart. I think you got a strong one, Lord, yes. And that type of problem, it'll jump right on over you. I can see it clear as the sun in the morning." He started laughing again. "But I sure am glad to see you, Mr. Wells!"

Ambrose briefly wondered how the old man could have recognized him, as he looked nothing like his short, wiry father. He figured the old man must have seen him running around as a child, and guessed that he must have been one of a few that had worked alongside his father doing odd jobs around the island for Edisto's wealthier residents. Ambrose was tall. At six feet one, he was head and shoulders above his father, and not unattractive, with broad shoulders and a robust physique. He'd always considered his natural athleticism to be a wasted gift—something like Cassandra's prophecies—as he had no innate inclination for sports whatsoever. Continually disappointing his high school football coaches, he'd set his mind on classic literature, ancient history, and more scholarly pursuits in quiet libraries, yet somehow his physicality had never abandoned him. He had a square jaw, and light, grey eyes that women seemed to gravitate toward. He'd enjoyed their attention, but after the pleasantries of a first date had finished, he'd never been able to entertain them with his academic interests, and they bored him with small talk about sports and trips to the bars.

His few friends told him he dated the wrong girls. They were probably right. Women in college mistook his quiet nature and lack of more mainstream interests for vanity, and, ironically, stupidity. None of it had bothered him, but now, out of college and in the real world, it was even more difficult for him to meet people. Yet Ambrose didn't worry too much about it still. There was a comfortable and regular security in his solitude, and his old soul quickly fell in to a pleasant rhythm, interrupted only occasionally by a lonely squeeze of the heart whenever he saw people happy in the presence of loved ones. Burying such disruptive thoughts deep in his psyche was easier than reflecting on them, and so life had darted along with every lonely year building upon the previous one, creating a stronger foundation for him to retreat behind. *You'll be a recluse one day,* an ex-girlfriend had once told him. *Who's to say I'm not already?* he'd replied. She'd run off to rejoin the world, shaking her head all the way. Ambrose never blamed her.

Willie reached out to shake Ambrose's hand again, now with both hands, and continued to smile, chuckling to himself. Ambrose felt surprised at his kindness, but reacted well, and extended his own hand to shake Mr. Dawes'.

"Thank you," he replied softly. "But your fence. I feel awful."

"Don't you worry about no fence! I'll take a look at it, and you swing by sometime this week. We'll figure all that out. You said you'd be here this week, is that right? Staying at the Anhinga down on the water?"

"Yes, I'm here on business." He paused for a moment, and thought of something suddenly. "Hey, Mr. Dawes."

"You can call me Willie, son. We old friends, but you just didn't know it!"

Ambrose smiled, feeling the contagious warmth of the old man who just kept on holding his hand with both of his.

"I'm sorry, Willie. I'll call you Willie if you'll call me Ambrose."

"Yes sir, Mr. Wells. Ambrose it is. Yes, Lord." He released his hand, and stepped back.

"Well, Willie." Ambrose paused. "I was thinking, I'm here for work, and I gotta take a look at the property out on Wellspring Island. I need to talk with the owner, a Mr. P.F.—" he stopped short, apparently tongue-tied. "Shoot, I can't think of his name. For some reason, it's escaped me, but I have it in my car. Let me just show you. I'm not sure how to reach him, see. He's got no phone number, no cell. How does one even get to the—"

Ambrose stopped speaking when he noticed that Willie Dawes was no longer smiling. The old man looked shaken, like he'd witnessed something unnatural take place. Ambrose suddenly felt cold and awkward, as if he'd just made a grave faux pas.

"Don't you go out there, Mr. Wells. No reason to show your good heart at that wicked place. I'll take you anywhere you want to go to on Edisto, but I won't take you there, not for anything. You'd best just turn around and head back to the city if it's Wellspring you trying to get to."

He turned around, and ominously yelled at the purple sunset.

"Johnny! Rose! You two stop messing around with my busted up old fence posts, and get in the truck!" He turned back around, his smile now only a faint wisp of what it had been.

"Come on by the house anyway, Mr. Wells. I can tell you more about it later, but not with the sun going down, and you and I just sitting here in the middle of the road talkin' like it's Sunday after church. Just don't be going out there until we can chat, you hear? Ain't no use in a good man like you going out to a place like that. That's an old man's learning, and it's better than all your fancy city schooling."

He hobbled off after the two children who had run back to the pickup truck, opened the door and helped them clamber in. Ambrose didn't know what to say after such a marked change in the man's otherwise warm demeanor, but he called after him.

"Thank you, Willie! I'll swing by on Monday!" He tried to feign enthusiasm, but felt chilled as he watched the old man wave one last time in response, hobbling into the pickup truck, and then turning the lights on. The engine coughed twice and turned over, and Willie Dawes pulled out with his grandchildren waving enthusiastically at Ambrose from the backseat. The pickup swung off the shoulder of the road, and slowly moved around the bend, disappearing out of sight.

Suddenly, the gloaming was a darker, lonelier place, and Ambrose shuddered a little despite the warmth of the evening. What had caused such an abrupt volte face in the old man, he wondered. It seemed as if the very mention of Wellspring Island had made Mr. Dawes extremely uncomfortable. Ambrose, having practically grown up on Edisto, knew about the rumors that swirled amongst his boyhood friends regarding the place. It was the Devil's summer house. It was a portal through time and space. It was kept by an old murderer who got off on a technicality. It was the final resting place of a particularly restless Gullah witch, still practicing dark juju at midnight. So on and so forth. Stupid tales from his youth, as far as Ambrose was concerned, and if Willie Dawes believed in some of them, well, then, that was on Willie Dawes. He had a simple job to do: assess the property for state tax purposes. Speak to the owner—if he was even still alive—get some copies of the deed and architectural blueprints of the property if possible, send them onward to Big John up in Columbia, and then get the hell out of Edisto. Whether or not he visited the old homestead while he was in town was yet to be determined.

Suddenly, something green caught his eye for a second time that evening. He'd been thinking about Willie, Wellspring Island, and Big John as he walked back to his car that was still awkwardly perched perpendicular to the highway along the shoulder of the road. He'd almost reached the passenger door that was facing him, when he saw it again. In the gloom, the object seemed less brilliantly green than it had when he had struck it with his windshield, precipitating the evening's unfortunate accident. Ambrose knew it had to be the same thing, whatever it was. He turned, and walked five feet off the shoulder to further investigate. Squinting his eyes in the almost near darkness of the early night, he still couldn't make out what it was. He fumbled for his cell phone, and turned on its flashlight, suddenly illuminating the object in a flash of harsh, almost fluorescent, light. He caught his breath in amazement.

Beneath the bright light of his cell phone lay a fairly large, radiantly green bird with a bright yellow head that morphed into a deep burnt orange near its large, prominent beak. Its neck was unnaturally twisted, clearly broken, and the luminosity and beauty of its plumage made its death seem all the more tragic. It would have merely been sad had it been an ugly bird, but it's showy, gorgeous feathers made its ill-starred, sudden, and violent death seem all the more deplorable. Ambrose sighed, and looked away briefly with a guilty conscience.

Turning back, he tentatively reached down, and gently poked its wing, as if it might still contain an ember of life, but the bird lay there, dead on the side of the road, motionless, it's vacant eyes staring up at Ambrose, causing him to recoil at the death of such a fine creature. At first he thought of leaving the bird there, but the thought of abandoning it to rot like all the other carrion on the side of highways seemed like an unbecoming death for such a fair animal. He decided then and there that he'd take it, and dispose of it properly at his first opportunity.

Running back to his car, Ambrose pulled out an old plastic bag from Harris Teeter that had held an empty Powerade bottle. He threw the bottle in the back seat, and ran back to the dead bird. Sliding the bag under its beautiful corpse, he managed to get the bird inside of it, and then gently placed it in the back seat. He was unsure of what he'd do with the bird, but the more he thought about it, the more he considered burying it back at his old house—if he could summon the courage to visit. *Yes*, Ambrose thought, *maybe I should bury it out on the creek.* For the first time since the accident, he felt a little better about the situation, having resolved to do something small but something he felt was right, and to go home to do it.

Chapter Two

THE REST OF HIS DRIVE lasted a mere fifteen minutes, but seemed like it was taken directly out of *A Midsummer Night's Dream,* or a scene from one of the classic Romantic poets—perhaps from a Byron or a Wordsworth piece. The moon had risen in the east, and as he had driven down the mostly deserted country road, its silver light had glistened off the tops of the stately, large live oaks that lined the road, shimmering off the Spanish moss in an almost melancholy way, giving the entire scene a poignant and pastoral tranquility. The night birds had awoken, and started to stir, and Ambrose, reflexively driving slowly after the recent accident, could hear the occasional spectral call of the barred owl chanting, "Who cooks for you" in between the constant chirps and croaks of the tree frogs. They called to each other from across the marsh, with a constant, sonorous rhythm. Lightning bugs had taken up their nightly summer courtship ritual, setting the woods aglow with their amorous display, reminding Ambrose of carefree summer nights, running down toward the marsh with an empty mason jar in hopes of capturing his own private show. Rounding a curve, a skittish doe and her spotted fawn ducked into the undergrowth, but not before having their eyes lit up by the headlights, which eerily gave them an otherworldly appearance as they dashed out of view. A fat, nearly corpulent raccoon, most likely planning a midnight foraging raid on the nearby campsites, trundled across the road fifty feet in front of his car. Finally, gliding across the causeway toward the beach, now surrounded by marsh on both sides, Ambrose couldn't help but wonder how many alligators slid into the muddy water amongst the crabs and oysters that were hiding in the abundant Spartina grass that dominated the estuary.

He'd felt infinitely better about the entire accident after he'd resolved to bury the beautiful, green bird at home. It seemed like the right thing to do. It felt as if his running in to it had some type of cosmic significance; as if it was a way of forcing him to a place he'd long neglected. Now, having made the decision, he felt at peace with it. He'd briefly considered that perhaps the bird was a house bird that had escaped its cage, only to quickly find that freedom could be fatal in the harsh outside world. As such, he'd debated about bringing it to the animal hospital tomorrow to see if anyone had reported it missing. He'd read that those types of birds could live for decades, and the owners might be very distressed about their loss. But ultimately he concluded that even if that were the case, what comfort would its death be to them? And after all, he'd decided to bury it at home. It just felt intrinsically like the right thing to do. His almost magical late night drive somehow confirmed the decision in his mind.

He'd made it to the Anhinga Motel, checked in, thrown his bags in the room, and then wandered over to the Lusty Crab, the bar and restaurant that was attached to the establishment. He'd been unsure of what to do with the bird. Would it smell in his room? Unsure, he'd tied the plastic bag around it tightly and left it in the back of the Bronco with the windows down an inch or two. He would settle the issue definitively tomorrow. His family's place was only about ten miles back the way he'd come, sitting there in the sultry night like a forgotten sentinel on the marsh. A quick drive back, a quick burial, maybe he'd try and see if the old keys still worked, and see if time and looters had left him anything of value in the place.

Sitting at the outdoor bar now, finishing dinner and looking out over the bay, he could see a tiny pinpoint of light flashing intermittently in the distance, as if desperately trying to prove to the rest of the world its existence out there on the water. He knew from his boyhood days that it was the old dock for Wellspring Island, jutting out from the island's northern point in to the bay. He'd never been there in person, but he knew of the island, and he figured that was one prominent reason why Big John Connolly had pushed him out of the office and down to Edisto. *Hell, you grew up there, Ambrose! If anyone can do this, it oughta be you!*

Rather than protest the idea, Ambrose had gone through his usual routine of ignoring the entire concept for weeks, hoping it would disappear like most of his responsibilities did in the state office after a long enough period of willful ignorance. Eventually, however, the problem proved to be of enough importance that he found himself surprisingly driving down to make an assessment. He smiled to himself as he took a swig from his sweating Budweiser. After all, he'd been afraid of all the rumors about the place when he was a boy, and he wouldn't have gone near the island then. Now here he was, trying to figure out how in the hell he was supposed to make contact with the owner.

"You want another one, darlin'?" asked the attractive, though somewhat past her prime, bartender, disturbing his reverie. He had been staring at the repetitive, distant flashing light, beaming at him from the mouth of the bay. Looking up suddenly, he felt briefly confused by the question as his mind was startled back to reality.

"Yes, ma'am. That'd be nice." he said. "Hey, have you ever heard of Wellspring Island? Out there, near the entrance to the bay?" He pointed out toward the faint, flashing light in the distance. "You see," he continued before she could reply, "I have some business out there, but I don't know how to get there from here. Do you know the owner, or know how I might be able to call him? His name is P.F…" He paused for a moment, and pulled out a folded, dingy piece of paper from his back pocket. He unfolded it to see Big John's scrawling, arrogant cursive. "A Mr. P.F. Grimball."

She stared at him for a moment, almost absently Ambrose observed, before turning around and reaching into an ice bucket behind her and pulling out a fresh beer.

"Honey, I ain't never heard of no Grimball, and I ain't never been out on that island. And from what I've heard slingin' booze at this shithole, maybe you ought to reconsider. Here's your beer. That'll be eighteen dollars total. You want me to run it on the card?"

Ambrose sighed dejectedly while simultaneously nodding in affirmation. He had no way of contacting this "Mr. Grimball," and, as far as he was aware, no way of getting to the island. Would he troll the shrimp boat docks tomorrow morning to see if someone would drop him off and pick him up? It didn't seem like a promising proposal. Perhaps he could drive in to Charleston and see the lawyer who apparently represented Mr. Grimball's interests. He had been given the name by Big John prior to leaving Columbia, but figured he'd find a way to get to the island and contact the actual owner first. That just felt more honest. Now he wasn't so sure about his well-laid-out plans.

The waitress brought the bill and Ambrose's card back, and dropped them both unceremoniously on to the bar in front of him. He quickly calculated the tip, and, after signing the bill, he looked up at the waitress again.

"So what did you hear?" he asked suddenly, as he slid the bill back over the table into her waiting hands.

"I'm sorry. What did you say, sweetheart?" she asked. She was looking at him now as if she suddenly remembered he existed.

"You said, 'From what I've heard slingin' booze at this shit-hole, maybe you ought to reconsider.' What did you hear?" Ambrose asked. He took a long swig of his cold, fresh two-dollar bottle.

She looked down at him, and a smile faintly tried to beat the odds on her face, curling her right upper lip just enough to see her canine tooth and giving her the appearance of a snarling animal. It was not a complimentary look, thought Ambrose.

"All sorts of things. I heard the guy's been dead for years, but nobody wants to turn the power off out there. I heard he killed his wife and children, but got away with it when the DA fucked up the evidence, and now he's just waitin' for God knows what out there." She paused for a moment before she leaned in a little and began to speak slower and more softly.

"And I've heard a lot worse than that," she said.

"Ah, Mable. That's bullshit! Don't listen to her, man. She's got the mouth of a pelican, and the brain of one, too."

Ambrose looked up from the bartender, disappointed and somewhat annoyed to not hear her secret revelation about to be revealed, and turned his head to the right to see the old man who had interjected. The old man sat at the last bar stool underneath the television, sipping on a shot of dark-looking liquor.

"Yeah, do you know how to get out there?" Ambrose asked somewhat confrontationally.

"Well," said the drunk man, slurring his words incontinently from across the bar. "You could always fuckin' swim." The man laughed to himself, and then took another sip from the shot glass in front of him.

Ambrose sighed. He didn't miss the local boozehounds.

"Thank you," he replied. "I'll take that under due consideration."

"Or you could always ask Charles. Cost you a couple of coins though…" The drunk man replied as he stared into space.

"Charles? Who's Charles?" Ambrose asked. "Does he know Mr. Grimball?"

The drunk man was now grinning, clearly enjoying Ambrose's consternation through the fog of his own intoxication.

"Charles? Charles is a goddamn drunk!" He laughed riotously and suddenly, and almost scared Ambrose, though Mable the bartender seemed less than surprised. She mumbled something that sounded less than courteous under her breath as she poured hot water over the grate underneath the beer taps, and began to close the place down.

Ambrose, however, was intrigued. He took leave of his seat, and walked over to the drunk man who was wearing a filthy Pabst Blue Ribbon trucker's hat and who smelled of raw fish and cheap bourbon. Ambrose took a seat that was a safe distance from the old man, one barstool in between the two of them. He took another swig, and looked at the amused older man in front of him.

"How do I find that drunk? And how does he know Mr. Grimball? You see, he lives on that island." He pointed out into the bay again. "And I need a boat."

The drunk man leaned back and almost fell as he gave a booming laugh and wiped tears from his eyes.

"Good news for you, son. You're surrounded by them!" He gesticulated wildly with his arms, as if to suggest there were boats everywhere, and in doing so, he fully stressed the two hind legs of his bar stool, which were already struggling against all odds to keep the man from flailing backwards. "But Charles—Charles, my friend—actually *goes* there."

The drunk man suddenly leaned forward, and became intently serious. Ambrose could smell the cheap rum oozing from the man's pores as he stared at Ambrose from across the space of the extra bar stool between them. He said nothing, as if he intended to draw emphasis to his last sentence.

"Does he?" Ambrose said. He suddenly felt a little alone and intimidated. Mable had gone into the back room, and it was just the two of them, sitting one bar stool too close Ambrose thought now. "Why?"

"He signed a deal with the devil, that's why!" howled the drunken man, slapping his thigh enthusiastically. "I told him to stop goin' out there. But Charles...Charles..."

The drunk man stopped slapping his thigh, and stared at Ambrose once again with serious intent, which made Ambrose immediately uneasy.

"Charles," said the drunk man, continuing now with the corners of his lips curling upward and with slurred speech, and almost intoxicating breath, "Charles is a real drunk." He laughed riotously again, and Ambrose shuddered as Mable returned to her spot behind the bar. She began yelling at the drunk man—whose name was Leroy it turned out—to stop scaring the paying customers and to get the hell out.

Leroy continued to laugh hysterically as he clumsily got off of his bar stool, once again almost falling to the old wooden floor. He told Mable to "put it on his tab", and started to wander off out the back door toward the dock and the marsh. Ambrose, recovering quickly from his initial trepidation, suddenly realized that he might never find this mysterious—apparently drunk—Charles.

"Wait, Mr. Leroy! How do I find him? Charles, where does he live?" He got off of his bar stool, and started to follow Leroy out the back door, but Leroy suddenly stopped short and turned around.

"Charles shrimps outta Edisto. He captains the *Flying Horse.*

She's upriver a bit, but not hard to find." Leroy waved his arms toward the Edisto River through the door. "But don't go out there, kid. Charles signed a bad deal."

Leroy stumbled out the back door down the dock to his own boat, the *Gullah Girl*, and Ambrose watched after him as Leroy nearly fell in to the river making his way on board. How the man hadn't drowned during one of his nightly trips to the Lusty Crab, seemed a miracle. But Ambrose felt good about the whole day suddenly, despite the accident and the dead bird and the discomfiting drunk. He had a clue, and maybe a way to get out to Wellspring Island.

Returning to his room for the evening, Ambrose felt a little better about his odds of making it out to Wellspring soon. He found his mind traveling back to happier days—his boyhood adventures on the marsh, his college days studying English literature and history at USC, and his friends, most of whom had moved on to big careers in bigger cities. He wistfully remembered a few ex-girlfriends who had run off to New York City or Boston, places that seemed too big to be real in Ambrose's opinion. Their enormity intimidated him, and he'd always avoided visiting as a result, though he knew this reason would sound ridiculous to others so he kept it to himself. He thought of his ex-roommate, Pete Myers, who'd moved off to DC and taken a job working as a biologist at the National Zoo. It had been a year or so since he'd spoken with Petey, but they'd always been on good terms. And then it suddenly dawned on him.

Rifling through his pocket past his car keys, he pulled out his cell phone. It showed he had one bar of service, and Ambrose felt his heart sink a little. He quickly returned to his car in the gravel lot, opened the door, and grabbed the plastic bag with the green bird in it before walking back to his room. Closing the door behind him, he turned on the harsh, bright bathroom light, and tentatively opened the bag. He prepared himself for an awful smell, though he wasn't sure if that would be the case or not. He gasped a little, and was taken aback at the bird's condition.

Its sparkling green feathers, that had earlier appeared almost bioluminescent in their brilliance, had lost their magnificence. They appeared wilted, and many had fallen off the bird's corpse. Its eyes had sunk into its head a little, and one of its toes, or perhaps toenails—Ambrose couldn't really tell which because he wasn't sure which of the two birds actually had—had completely come off, and was lying at the bottom of the bag. Its yellow neck and orange feathers near the beak coalesced into an unattractive mustard-brown color, and Ambrose considered whether he would have left the bird on the side of the road had it been in this condition just a few hours ago. He had never known animals to decompose so fast, but he also knew that he didn't know the first thing about ornithological decomposition rates. Best to bury it first thing tomorrow, or it would probably stink up his car.

He gently picked up the bird, amazed again by its size, and laid it on one of the towels on the bathroom counter. He took note to definitely not use that particular towel after he showered later. Placing a pen he found on the bedside table next to the bird for scale, he then took several photographs with his phone, and returned the parrot to the plastic bag. During this transition, he felt a little sick to his stomach when a clump of green feathers fell off. He tightly wrapped the bag up again, and placed the morbid package back in his car for the night.

After he'd returned to his room, he lost his cell phone signal altogether, and, therefore, decided to walk to the main lobby to use the Wi-Fi. He signed on, and looked at his phone for a moment, trying to decide what to type. Finally, he texted, "Pete, I hope you're doing well, man. This is a little weird, but I have a question for you. I'm down at my folk's old place on Edisto, and I hit a large bird with my car, caused an accident, and damn near killed myself and another lady. We're both okay, though she hurt her wrist. Reason I'm texting you is that I found the bird on the side of the road, and I've never seen anything like it down here—not in all my years growing up on the island. It's big and green, and I figure it must have been someone's pet. Do you know what it is? Not the end of the world if you don't, really, but I was just curious. Thanks, man, and give me a call soon!"

He then uploaded the pictures he'd taken in his bathroom, and sent them along behind his text message. The Wi-Fi signal was pretty weak, but after about forty-five seconds, his texts went through. Ambrose waited several minutes to see if Pete would respond but, not having received any word back, he sighed, and then returned to his room. It was getting late, and Ambrose remembered that his friend usually worked early mornings. He glanced at his watch. 11:43 p.m. It had been a long and strange day, and tomorrow was feeling like it might be just as long, and definitely a little uncomfortable. He anticipated having to ask strangers about finding a drunk man named Charles, captain of the *Flying Horse*, and then returning home for the first time in years, only to possibly meet an island recluse people seemed a little scared to even talk about. The day promised to be, at the very least, quite unusual, perhaps even quixotic, and Ambrose had an anxious feeling he would be far outside his comfort zone.

He quickly got ready for bed, and as he tried to read Churchill's *A History of the English-Speaking Peoples*—as was his routine lately—he found his mind wandering back to the old house. Feeling anxious and unable to concentrate on Palmerston or Peel, he shut the book, set an early alarm, and closed his eyes. Strange, dark dreams followed, of voodoo curses and murderers, of his ancestral home, boarded up and imposing, with rattlesnakes and wasps nests hiding behind the half-rotten planks and lurking near the tidal creek, where even the music of the frogs seemed to be warning him to stay away. When the alarm went off at seven o'clock, Ambrose woke up feeling on edge, like he'd under slept, though he was unable to recall with any clarity the disturbing visions of the night that rapidly dissipated in to the morning haze. He'd sweated through the sheets, so he quickly got up, and went to turn the shower on. He stepped in to the shower, and gratefully let the cool water wake him, and wash away his lingering misgivings.

Chapter Three

THE DOCKS WERE MORE OR LESS DESERTED by the time Ambrose arrived at a quarter after eight in the morning. Even the *Gullah Girl* had somehow made it out at the crack of dawn in search of the millions of small crustaceans that made the humid South Carolina coast their home. How Leroy had ever gotten over his hangover to turn the motor over and glide out to sea in search of them was a mystery to Ambrose, but he figured that old Leroy was probably well practiced. He had cursed himself as he pulled in along the gravel parking area, and saw that most of the shrimpers had taken off much earlier in the morning. He should have known better. Putting the car in park, looking out over the harbor far past the Anhinga and the Lusty Crab, the morning's haze melded into the horizon, and blurred the distinction between the firmament and the sea. Sighing, Ambrose took another swig from the extra-large black coffee sitting in the cup holder, and swept his eyes over the docks in front of him. There were three old boats still tied up. It seemed unlikely that any of them might be the *Flying Horse*, run by some mysterious drunk named Charles, an apparent colleague of the upstanding Leroy. *But what the hell,* Ambrose thought. *I got up, and I'm here. Might as well check it out.*

He left the Bronco in the gravel lot, grabbed his rapidly cooling coffee, and then walked down the gangplank to the dock. The first boat was labeled the *Dory Anna,* and seemed to be absolutely forsaken. The second one, a little further on, looked like it hadn't actually been off the dock in over a decade, and the lettering on the stern was almost indecipherable. Ambrose stopped and tried to make out the boat's name. The word "the" had been completely worn away by time and brine, and the exposed wood underneath was showing through the aged white paint. The second word looked like it could be "lyin," with the F and the G missing on either end, and replaced with what looked like more rotting wood. After that, what appeared at one time as scrawling cursive, was "hor," badly damaged with age, with the last S and E missing, apart from a small spot at the end of the E. This gave the unfortunate appearance that the *Flying Horse* had the errant name *Lyin Hor.* It was an inauspicious start.

"Hello? Mr…" Ambrose paused suddenly, realizing that he had no idea what Charles' last name was. "Charles?" He felt immensely stupid, and heard nothing but the wind in the harbor and the old boat groaning against the fenders on the dock.

"Hello? Charles?" he repeated, louder now hoping there might be an inkling of an answer that might escape from the cabin.

Hearing nothing, Ambrose looked up and down the forlorn dock. Hesitating for a moment, he took a deep breath, stepped over the gunwale, and called out Charles' name once again. Silence followed, and the gulls perched in the old rigging eyed him imperiously from above. With trepidation, he walked toward the closed door that led down into the main cabin, and went to knock.

Suddenly, just before his knuckles hit the battered wooden door leading into the main cabin, he heard a low growl that slowly grew in volume and pitch. Ambrose hesitated, unsure of how to proceed or who or what exactly was making such an unnatural noise.

"Who in God's name is on my boat?!"

The voice had come from inside the cabin, no doubt about it, thought Ambrose. He unconsciously recoiled, and walked backwards toward the wheel. Suddenly, the low door was flung open, and out stepped the wildest looking old man Ambrose had ever laid eyes upon. He looked to be about sixty years old, with wild, unkempt gray hair matted down over a forehead that looked as if it had seen a century's worth of sun and wind. His eyes were bleary and bloodshot, and his mouth, grimacing, revealed cracked lips and several missing teeth. His tattered t-shirt hung on just barely at the shoulders due to the multiple rips it had suffered while servicing its owner. The man himself could not have been much taller than five foot eight, but his limbs were muscular, like cords of wood wrapped in cellophane. His fingers gripped the sides of the entryway as he leered menacingly at Ambrose—who had nearly fallen into the transom in shock. The man's appearance was alarming enough; however, the pungent smell of rum and body odor released when the doors were swung open, caused an immediate visceral reaction, and were it not for a slight breeze that helped clear the air, Ambrose may have vomited right then and there.

"Who the hell are ya? And what are ya doin' on my boat?" yelled the old man. Presumably—and hopefully, thought Ambrose—this was Charles, the drunken shrimp boat captain. Stunned for a moment, now leaning against the front of the wheel, Ambrose tried to gather his thoughts while simultaneously attempting to stand upright. Charles lurched forward, and Ambrose slipped a little once again, grabbing on to the binnacle behind him, and using it as support to finally stand. Despite his distinct advantage in height and size, Ambrose felt keenly aware that he was trespassing on the man's boat, and that this particular man could provide a thorough beating should he choose to do so.

"I'm sorry, sir," Ambrose was finally able to get out. "My name is Ambrose Wells. I'm looking for a man named Charles who skippers the *Flying Horse*."

"Yeah? What d'ya want him for?" The man growled, took a final step up toward the main cabin, and was now firmly standing on the deck. Ambrose quickly stepped away from the wheel and on to the locker to his right, closer toward the small stepladder that had allowed him entrance on to the ship to begin with.

"Well, I need to get to Wellspring Island. For work, you see. I need to speak to a Mr. Pey…"

"Drime! I don't believe ya! Ain't nothin' up there worth seein'. What are ya? One of them ghosthunters I seen on TV? Always tryin' to get to places ya ain't got no good reason to be goin' to. Get outta here!"

The old man, suddenly quite nimble, bounded across the deck, and Ambrose quickly jumped back on to the dock, scaring away several seagulls nearby.

"I'm not a ghosthunter!" Ambrose replied, and almost laughed for making what sounded like such an idiotic declaration. "I'm here for work. I need to speak to a Mr. Peyton Grimball who lives out there. A Mr. Peyton Farquar Grimball. I was told you could get me to the island. That you know the owner."

The old man paused, and quizzically looked down at Ambrose. He ran his calloused hands through his greasy hair as if he were thinking profoundly. Ambrose was taken aback by the man's vitality. He looked like he should have been falling down, wracked by alcohol and time, hard work and hot sun, and yet, as he stood there with his hands on his head peering down at Ambrose, he appeared the picture of strength. He had one leg up on the gunwale and the other back on the deck, and the morning sun beamed down to reveal a man who had lived hard but who seemed oblivious to that fact—one of those rare breeds who seemed to only grow stronger over the years, even as the work became harder. Ambrose was in awe looking at him, and despite the age difference, he believed right then and there that he had made the right decision to get off the man's boat quickly. Height and age difference aside, Ambrose wouldn't want to tangle with a man like that.

"You ain't some city dingbatter comin' down here cause you heard stories 'bout the place, are ya? Cause there ain't nothin' to 'em. Mr. Grimball enjoys his privacy, and I help him out, see. That's all there is to it. The rest of the time, I shrimp!" He laughed, as if that was the height of comedy, and then suddenly turned to head back into the cockpit, their conversation apparently concluded.

"Wait! Wait, Mr..." Ambrose paused again, frustrated with himself for not extracting Charles' last name from Leroy.

"My name is Charles Delacroix. My family was French, but I never knew it. Grew up on the outer banks, on the ocean. Maybe one day I'll head back."

Ambrose could no longer see the man once he'd continued to descend back into the main cabin, but his voice rung out strongly from below, and again, Ambrose got a sense of vigor coming from the old fisherman.

"I'm sorry, Mr. Delacroix!" Ambrose yelled, a little louder now so that his voice would carry into the boat. "I work for the state of South Carolina. I've come to assess the property. For tax purposes. I just need to meet with Mr. Grimball, and see the property. It won't take more than a couple hours, but I need a lift! I was told you were the man to talk to."

"Yeah," Charles said, as he stuck his head out of the cabin door again. "And who told you that, might I ask? Was it that drunken fool Leroy? You know, he's an all right guy, but he's a bit of a drunk. Not to be trusted."

Ambrose did everything he could to keep from rolling his eyes. "Maybe so, Mr. Delacroix, but that's the word on the street. Can you take me there?"

"Maybe," he said, again from deep within the boat, the sound of bottles clanging around as if he'd strewn them about the cabin. "I'll tell you what, Mr. Wells." He suddenly appeared again, Lazarus-like, thought Ambrose, and stood on the starboard deck for the second time now. He peered down at Ambrose with a cockeyed look.

"I'm headed out there tonight on business. I'm not to bring just anyone out to the island, but I'll ask the man himself when I'm there. Meet me here tomorrow. 'bout this time if it suits ya, and I'll let you know. May cost you a few bucks, though." He laughed in such a way that Ambrose could tell he meant what he'd said, and then started to head back in.

"Okay," Ambrose replied. "I'll be here. Tell him my name, and why I'm here, please. It's important."

"Yeah, yeah. Ambrose Wells. Some dingbatter from the city. I'll be sure to let him know. See ya later then."

Charles was already raising Cain back inside the boat, and Ambrose, not sure if their meeting could have gone better or not, turned and walked back up the gangplank toward his car. There was nothing more he could have done, and he felt lucky to have at least found the crazy old coot, who apparently didn't take shrimping seriously enough to get up before the crack of eight in the morning.

Leaving the pier, Ambrose drove out of town, and stopped at the local hardware store to pick up a shovel before he then headed back down the same state road he'd come in on the night before. He passed the scene of yesterday's accident, and felt a twinge of guilt as he eyed the remains of Mr. Dawes' fence, still scattered across the shoulder of the road. Slowing down after a couple more miles, he scanned the brush for a nondescript dirt road that would be nearly completely invisible to the average motorist doing 50 miles per hour on the way to the beach. Spotting a familiar old oak tree, he slowly turned right, drove about thirty yards, and stopped at a rusted old gate. He caught his breath. It had been a long time since he'd been home, and memories—both good and bad—threatened to overwhelm him.

Pausing for a moment, he killed the engine and took his keys out of the ignition. Looking down at them now, he found three separate keys on their own ring that he had not used in years. Fingering the smallest one, a flimsy, silver little thing that would hopefully open the padlock for the gate, he smiled as he opened the car door. How bad could it be? The place was deserted, and had been for years. Perhaps this little field trip for work would allow him to assess his own property, and put it up for sale with one of the local realtors. It was probably worth a lot, given its impressive acreage, river access, and proximity to the beach. A nice country house for some Charleston doctor or lawyer, he mused as he stuck the little key into the rusty padlock.

Holding his breath, he turned the key, and after a moment's hesitation, the tiny lock, groaning with rust and age, begrudgingly clicked open. The gate swung wide with a high-pitched squeal of protest, and Ambrose propped up an old stump against it. Returning to his car, the positive feelings generated from thoughts of selling the old family estate quickly withered away into the shade of the magnificent oaks and stately pines that lined the path and kept it in perpetual darkness. The rutted track seemed to envelop him as he slowly drove for about half of a mile. Just before the final turn that led to the main house and grounds, he found his way obstructed by a large tree branch that had fallen on to the road, obstructing his path forward as if telling him that his abandonment of the place hadn't been forgiven.

Sighing, Ambrose stepped out of the car, and grabbed the shovel and the bag containing the dead bird from the back seat. Stepping over the large branch, he walked down the hot and dusty road, and he felt more and more claustrophobic, like he was being watched. Several times, he turned around to see nothing but the thick palmetto brush and old moss hanging from every conceivable branch in the thick trees. Cursing himself for feeling jumpy, he picked up the pace despite the humidity, and found himself perspiring through his shirt. Mosquitoes began to buzz around him despite his best one-handed efforts to destroy them all. Finally, at long last, he could see the remains of the old house, still gracefully seated along the banks of the beautiful, black South Edisto River. He stopped walking, and nearly dropped his shovel.

Ambrose didn't know if he should cry or cheer. The north-facing part of the house had indeed been crushed under what had been the largest, most ancient oak on the property. The main entranceway, living room, and two of the upstairs bedrooms were demolished, and even the oak tree itself had been slowly destroyed by erosion and time. He could peer directly down the main hallway toward the still-intact kitchen. Walking around the east end of the house, he approached the river, and could see part of the dock had been swept away. The kitchen and back deck were still standing, but Ambrose thought the old homestead was a lost cause. His love of history mourned the loss. It had been a beautiful antebellum home, though the late nineteenth and twentieth centuries had not been kind to the

Wells, and the home had suffered from neglect long before the oak tree had performed its coup de gras.

His recent thoughts of selling the place notwithstanding, Ambrose felt a deep pang in the pit of his stomach, and he turned from the house, unable to look at it any longer. It was a strange thing, coming home like this. It forced him to think of things he'd become quite good at putting away—his stormy relationship with his father, for one, and their last argument. *You'll come to nothing, Ambrose.* The last words of a man who had lived on the efforts of his ancestors, and who had contributed nothing to the world. That had been Ambrose's reply, and he regretted it still. His father dying suddenly thereafter had been hard, but not being able to take back the malignant final conversation between the two of them had been the cruelest twist of all.

Swallowing hard, as if to consciously force those bad memories back where he'd buried them, he turned, and began walking to the river, determined to do what he had set out to do, and to then get the hell off the property. He found a pretty spot about a hundred feet downriver from the dock he'd enjoyed coming to as a boy to try and throw rocks clear across to the marsh on the other side. He stopped, and took in the view. It hadn't changed at all, though he reflected, he certainly had.

Suddenly, he heard a rustling in the underbrush behind him. He turned, and saw nothing but the overgrown front yard, the hot, parched road, and the woods. He felt like he was being watched again. He turned and started digging, determined to finish the job so he could leave. He dug a small hole just above the high-water line, sending fiddler crabs scampering sideways to darker places, and threw the shovel on the grass above him. Soaked in sweat now, he bent down, and picked up the bag. Unraveling the knot in the bag, he opened it, and then suddenly gasped.

The bird was hardly recognizable as such. The green feathers were almost completely gone. A skeleton of light, porous bones was still there, partially buried within fine, grey dust that seeped out when Ambrose had opened the bag, which had almost caused him to drop the bird in order to avoid getting it stuck to his sweaty fingers. Peering back into the bag, he felt a moment of revulsion as he noticed the large beak that was now completely detached. He thought he could make out traces of larger organs that were still partly intact, but he couldn't be sure. The bird had almost completely decomposed.

"But in twenty-four hours?" Ambrose heard himself ask, a reply to his own silent questions. "What the…" he trailed off. He was stunned. He'd never known anything to do that, but, then again, he wasn't a biologist by any stretch. Maybe that happened with birds? Maybe this bird was special in some way? Or perhaps it had been diseased?

Not sure of what else to do, he emptied the contents of the plastic bag, and what had once been one of the most beautiful birds he'd ever laid eyes upon, into the small hole along the river bank, and got the fine, gray dust everywhere in the process. Cursing, he stepped away to let it settle, and grabbed the shovel. He didn't want to breath it in. What if it had been sick?

Hearing something else move, but now much closer, over by his left foot, he looked down, and jumped hysterically into the muddy riverbank. A large, fat cottonmouth slithered by as if he were nothing more than just another palmetto brush. Grabbing the shovel, he thought about decapitating it on the spot the way he'd watched his father do when he was young, but the snake was already ten feet away now, and it slithered toward the dock, down underneath it, and disappeared into the dark water.

"Jesus Christ!" Ambrose yelled aloud. Now that his initial shock and fear had dissipated, he was angry. "Let's just bury the damn thing."

He now felt like it had been a bad idea to come back. It wasn't his anymore. Maybe it never was. He didn't feel welcome, he thought to himself as he finished burying the bird, and it was high time he left again. Grabbing the old bag and slinging his shovel over his shoulder, he walked double-time back down the road, and kept a sharp eye to the ground for any more unwelcome surprises. Despite the heat, he had the unpleasant sensation that someone, or something, was panting hot, fetid breath on the back of his neck, steadily urging him to move along, faster and faster still. He turned once when he knew himself to be out of view of the ramshackle old house, but of course there was nothing there but woods and mosquitoes. *And damned copperheads*, Ambrose thought.

Walking onward, he continued to sense that something was watching him from the woods, urging him to leave forever. He could almost smell the rancid breath of some malevolent entity wafting down across his nape. Off in the distance, the shrill cry of the cicadas echoed amongst the long leaf pine like a warning siren. He felt nauseated, and his pulse quickened as he hurried toward, and finally saw—thank God—his old Bronco parked where he'd left it, beyond the fallen tree, a symbol of familiarity in an otherwise strange and seemingly hostile environment. Almost jogging now, he leaped over the fallen trunk in one bound, and flung his door open.

He jumped in the car, and threw his muddy shovel in the passenger seat next to him as he simultaneously slammed the door shut. Immediately, he felt better. That awful smell was gone, and despite the heat in the car, it felt better than the heat outside, and that terrible suffocating presence with that moist, putrid panting he'd felt on the back of his neck.

He found his keys, turned on the car, and happily left, feeling a huge sense of relief as he locked the padlock again and turned on to the sunny main road. Rolling his windows down, the cool air washed over him like a benediction, and he sighed a great exhalation of relief. He'd been home again, and it hadn't seemed to miss him. He'd be sure to call the realtor.

Chapter Four

HAVING NOTHING FURTHER PLANNED FOR the afternoon, Ambrose had driven back to the Anhinga and cleaned up. He'd ignored a few angry text messages from Big John up in Columbia, changed into fresh clothes, and felt infinitely better bathing in the fresh southerly breeze blowing in off the water, which kept the sea island tolerable despite the afternoon heat. With the rest of the afternoon free, his mind kept wandering back to the splintered fence that belonged to Mr. Dawes, and he'd resolved in the shower to pay a visit to him a day early so he could apologize once again. Perhaps he could get an estimate on the costs for repair, and rectify the damage done. That damned green parrot would likely cost him in the long run, he thought ruefully.

Once set upon a course of action, he wolfed down some barbeque at the local lunch counter, and returned back the way he'd come for the second time that day. After several miles, he came across the devastated fence, slowed down as he rounded the curve in the road and searched for a nearby driveway that might point toward the Dawes' home. He followed what fence was still intact to beyond the scene of the accident, spotted a dirt driveway on the right, and brought the car to a near halt. The faded and peeling stickers along the side of the mailbox read "Dawes," though the S had almost completely peeled away. Ambrose swung the vehicle right, and slowly continued down the rutted track. Angry thunderheads started to gather as he drove down the road toward an old doublewide trailer that sat in an open clearing, behind which stood several large fields with various crops. Willie Dawes' old pickup was parked on the lawn out front, and as Ambrose drove up to park next to it, he recognized two small figures—Johnny and Rose from the accident scene. They tumbled out from the screened porch, and ran out to the yard to see who was visiting. Looming from within the framed doorway, painted blue, along with the borders of the rest of the trailer, was an old woman who tried to be kept hidden within the confines of the dark entranceway. As Ambrose put the Bronco into park, he could not easily distinguish her features.

"Rose! Johnny! Don' be runnin' up in duh yad on dat man! You don' know who he be! Unnu come back up on de do'step wit me now!" Ambrose heard—who he presumed was the woman in the doorway—yell out to the children as they spilled out of the trailer, and he debated whether he'd perhaps made a mistake in driving out there after all.

"Hey! Hey, man! You the man who made that lady knock the fence down!" Johnny yelled almost joyously while Rose laughed uncontrollably behind him and shyly kept to the passenger's side so that Ambrose could not get a good look at her either. Smiling, feeling somewhat abashed at being called out by the boy so publicly, Ambrose waved and thought that he might as well see if Mr. Dawes was home.

Ambrose stepped out of the car and Johnny ran around the back of it laughing with Rose again. Together they rocketed back up the steps toward the dark figure still standing in the shade of the doorway. Ambrose took a few steps toward the trailer, not wanting to offend anyone.

"Hello?" he called out tentatively. "My name is Ambrose Wells. I'm here to see a Mr. Willie Dawes? I'm sorry to just show up unannounced, but I wanted to see what I could do to make amends for the broken fence out front." He wasn't sure what else to say, or to whom he was even speaking. There was a pregnant pause. Ambrose could hear the wind through the magnolia tree that stood behind the trailer, and the hushed giggling of the children who'd disappeared behind the dark figure at the top of the steps. Unsure of what else to say Ambrose was about to turn around and get back into the Bronco when suddenly the old woman broke the silence from the top of the porch steps.

"Yeah, you at Willie Dawes' place. He out in duh field doh'—, workin', see. You gwine fix duh fence ya broke?"

Ambrose approached the trailer steps, and he began to make out a large, older black woman in an ancient apron standing defensively in the entranceway. The two children— grandchildren, Ambrose presumed—peered out from behind her thick legs. Her lips were set, with the edges of her mouth curled down, and her brow was furrowed with lines so thick Ambrose thought her face resembled a woodcut. She had an old bandana wrapped around her head, and was smoking a large pipe, with its sweet-smelling blue smoke wafting out from the doorway and disappearing into the fluttering breeze. She stepped out into the daylight, and Ambrose noticed her bloodshot eyes, as if she'd spent too much time indoors around smoke.

"Yes, ma'am," Ambrose stuttered, after pausing for a moment. "I wanted to talk with Willie—er, Mr. Dawes—about that today. That's primarily why I came by. I am sorry to have bothered you without any warning." Unable to look at the old woman directly, he stared down at his feet, feeling very out of place.

"Hmm," the old woman pondered, as if all her suspicions had just been validated. Ambrose briefly thought about leaving a message with her, and for the second time was about to turn around, get back in his car, and then leave, when suddenly he saw Willie walk up from behind the trailer. Willie approached him from the side, and smiled widely, as only he could do it seemed.

"Mr. Wells! Yes, sir! It sure is good to see you again, Mr. Wells. Lord yes, it's good!" He walked toward Ambrose in his crooked yet brisk manner—quick for his age—his right hand outstretched. Ambrose couldn't help but return the man's infectious good cheer, and reached out to shake Willie's hand.

"Mr. Dawes! I'm glad to see you too. I came by to discuss the fence with you. I have good insurance, and wanted to make sure this didn't set you back any. I feel awful about the whole thing."

"Ain't nothing about no fence, Mr. Wells, Lord no! I know we'll get that figured out," Mr. Dawes replied. He finished vigorously shaking Ambrose's hand. "Auntie, this here is Mr. Wells

I told you about—Davie's boy, from over on Store Creek. Had that accident, but thank God, he's ok! Ms. Cora swung by today, too. She's got a broke wrist but she's gonna live, yes Lord."

Ambrose did not think Willie could have smiled any wider, and he wanted to reciprocate in kind, but felt as if the old woman standing above them was silently judging him.

"Well, I'm glad to hear Ms. Hampton is okay. I feel awful about her wrist and her car. Perhaps I could swing by her place with some flowers or something, and apologize."

Ambrose did feel damned awful about the accident, and he wanted to apologize in person; however, he knew he'd be lying to himself if he tried to believe there weren't ulterior motives behind him wanting to pay her a visit. She had been one of the most captivating women he'd met in a long, long time.

"Oh yeah, I'm sure you could, Mr. Wells. She lives not too far down the road, just a little further on up that way," Willie replied, waving his right hand in a vaguely western direction. "Can't miss the gate. Big, metal one, with two large egrets on the top of each door, yes Lord. Big old gate for the big house, about a half-mile down the road."

"Really?" Ambrose replied, and took a mental note of the vague address. "I'll be sure to swing by—maybe tomorrow or the next day—to offer my apologies. Her car took a beating, and her wrist…" he paused for a moment. "Well, I'm glad it's only her wrist that was injured."

"Yeah, she'll be okay, Mr. Wells, but it's you I'm worried about. I told my auntie you're heading over to Wellspring Island, and she thinks like I do. Ain't no good can come from that wicked place."

Ambrose smiled a little. Here he'd come to help with the fence he'd had a hand in destroying, and was instead getting local advice steeped in superstition.

"Mr. Dawes, I appreciate your concern, but I have to. It's why I'm here! It's for work. I'm sure it's not such a bad place."

"Why you wantuh go dat wickit place? You a soonman, ain't ya? Ain't no good comin' from dat place!"

The woman on the porch forcefully interrupted him with evident concern.

"Come'yuh in duh house, and we talk'um," she said, a little more softly than before. Ambrose, not sure what to do, glanced up at her, and then over to Willie, as if seeking confirmation it would be okay to go in. He nodded, smiling, and waved him up the steps as the older woman began to retreat into the entranceway. Ambrose felt as if he didn't even really have much of a choice.

The interior of the trailer was dark, with the blinds drawn, and it took Ambrose a minute for his eyes to adjust. He felt Johnny and Rose brush by his legs, like giggling phantoms, and push through the screen door again, which briefly allowed bright squares of light to permeate the inky darkness. The place reeked of pipe tobacco, which was the first thing Ambrose noted as his eyes tried to adjust, and coming from the back of the trailer through the open bedroom door came the sound of a television set on low. The blue light of the TV filtered through from the back, and gave his eyesight some purchase to focus on. The large, aged woman walked in front of him, and then sat down heavily on a bench that lined the wall before squeezing her thick torso between the wall and the kitchen table.

Searching through the pockets in her dress, she pulled out a book of matches, and in one quick movement, lit one up.

The bright flash of light gave Ambrose a brief moment to grasp the layout of the structure. Across from the woman, to his left, was the main kitchen sink, and a small oven. Directly in front of him, there was a long, main hallway that led to the room with the TV on in the back, with several other doors that lined the hall. The old woman had lit two blue candles that were on the table, and then used the match to relight her pipe. Rapidly inhaling, the contents of the pipe glowed orange. She then sat back a little, and exhaled more smoke into the air as she made a gesture with her left hand to indicate Ambrose should sit across from her.

Sensing that Willie was behind him, Ambrose took a few tentative steps forward, and heard Willie's reassuring laughter.

"It's okay now, Mr. Wells. You go ahead and sit down on the bench there. My auntie wants to tell you about that island you're trying to get yourself to. If you still wanna be heading out there after, we won't stop you—no, Lord—but we think you oughtta know what you're getting into. Lord, yes, I was a friend of your daddy's, and that makes us friends, too, you see. I ain't much of a friend if I just let you run on out there without talking with you first."

Willie gently pushed Ambrose forward through the cramped kitchen, and Ambrose sat down across from the old woman who continued to smoke her pipe with obvious pleasure. Ambrose was alarmed to realize that the walls were lined with what looked like old newspaper, and he was thinking that this fact—in conjunction with the candles and the woman's pipe—made the dwelling seem inherently unsafe.

"Willie ses hunnuh gwine Wellspring Island fuh wu'k."

Ambrose paused, not sure how to respond. It was difficult for him to understand the old woman. It had been a long time since he'd heard any Gullah spoken. Willie, he could understand, no problem, but his ancient auntie was much more difficult for Ambrose's unaccustomed ear.

"Um, yes ma'am. I'm on Edisto for work. I need to assess the property's value," he replied. He began to feel more and more uneasy in the dark, cramped trailer. Willie had sat down next to him, though, which seemed reassuring, and he could hear the children laughing outside in the bright sunshine. He felt the urge to run out and join them.

"Duh buckruh libbin' out dere ain't no man. He gotta daak cuss on 'im. He older den dem oak trees out dere. Older den muhself!"

Auntie Dawes, as Ambrose had taken to thinking of her in his head, laughed at this to herself. It was a deep, guttural laugh that seemed to start somewhere down in her abdomen, and swell and grow as it climbed through her chest before it exited in a breath of blue smoke. Her whole body shook a little under the apron and dirty shirt she wore. The few teeth she still had were noticeable, like yellowed tombstones projecting at unfortunate angles from behind her dark lips.

Ambrose, again, didn't know how to respond. That was, after all, absurd. He turned to his left to look at Willie for reassurance, but Willie was now—for once—not smiling. He looked deadly serious as he stared at the candle flame flickering in front of him.

"I'm not sure he's that old," Ambrose replied. He laughed awkwardly to try to ease the tension, but his laugh sounded hollow to him. "I mean, to be honest, I don't know his age even, or really much about him at all, other than his name: Mr. P.F."

"Don' hunnuh talk'um 'bout dat cuss'd name!" said the old woman suddenly, cutting Ambrose off mid-sentence, startling him in the process. "Hunnuh jis' lissin, now! Hunnuh went down to duh old house at middleday, and duh spirits chase hunnuh away, yes Lawd. Like a chil', you's skay'd away by duh boo hag. Dat place ain't b'long to hunnuh chil' now, and it ain't nebbuh did! Dat's why hunnuh skay'd and run off. It ain't dat hunnuh don' lub duh lan' but duh lan' don' lub hunnuh!" She cackled again, as Ambrose sat, dumbfounded, across from her. How had she known he'd been down to his old house just a few hours before? He looked at Willie again, who continued to stare resolutely at the candle. Ambrose looked back at the old woman who now had an almost triumphant look on her face.

"How did you —" he started to ask, but stopped again. He felt uncertain, and even more uneasy when he thought about the awful presence he'd felt at his father's home. "Were you following me?" he asked.

The old woman gave a deep, unsettling laugh once again, and each time she'd done so, it seemed like more hot, blue smoke came pouring out of her, and added to the haze that wafted throughout the house and along the ceiling, which was also covered in yellowed newspaper print.

"Hunnuh mus tek care ahde root fah heal duh tree! Yo farruh ain't yo farruh, an yo murruh iz dead, po chil'. If hunnuh mus' go out on duh island, den hunnuh won' be comin' back duh sem way." The old woman took another long drag from her pipe, and sat back against the wall—smugly, thought Ambrose, who was now beginning to feel angry.

"What do you know about my parents? They don't concern you, and they certainly don't have anything to do with Wellspring Island." Ambrose stood up, backed away from the table, and prepared to leave the gloomy trailer. He felt as if he could hardly breathe, and, suddenly becoming lightheaded, he turned toward the screen door.

"Now, Mr. Wells, ain't no need to get upset now. Auntie's just," Willie began, before the old woman across the table cut him off.

"I laa'n 'bout en'ting on dis island, chil'. I know 'bout yo farruh and yo murruh, and I know hunnuh's full'up wit' anguh! Yes, lawd, full'up wit bex vex, but he don' know duh half of it, see. Lawd, no he don'! I know 'bout duh plat'eye dat be gyaad'in duh secret out dere," she said quietly. She purposefully stared directly at Ambrose through the blue haze, like she was attempting to penetrate his soul. "I know 'bout duh debbleman who lib wit' it too. Dat man ain't no man at all! Not like hunnuh is. He brings 'strucshun on eb'ryting dat he tet'chum. He be a unnat'ral ebil haant. Hunnuh goes out dere, hunnuh tuh'n bahd, Lawd yes, it tuh'n hunnuh ebil too." She set her pipe down on the table, and started to reach into her apron again, but Ambrose had heard enough. He waved his hands at her, and then went to make an escape through the screen door, and was blinded by the sunlight.

He nearly stumbled down the front steps as he made a beeline for his car, feeling angry at the old woman, and for some reason—which he couldn't lay a finger on—he was embarrassed. Johnny and Rose watched him from behind Willie's old pickup truck as Ambrose got inside his trusty, familiar Bronco, and then slammed the door shut.

"Wait one minute, Mr. Wells! Just a minute!"

He looked up to see Willie bounding down the steps now, no longer smiling, with an anxious furrow to his brow Ambrose had never seen before. It made him pause, and he took his hands off the car keys that were already in the ignition.

"Damn it, Willie! I came to offer to help pay for your busted fence, not get sermoned to by some voodoo grandmother of yours! I don't need this shit! And what the hell does she know about my parents anyway?"

"I'm sorry, Mr. Wells. I'm sorry if she upset you, see. She's old school, and that's just her way. She don't know no other way. She wants to help you, Mr. Wells. So do I."

By this point, Willie had reached the Bronco, and through the open passenger window, he held out his right hand. In his hand was a small, dingy-looking, brown burlap pouch. A small piece of twine ran through the top of it, as if it was meant to be worn around the neck. Ambrose looked down at it quizzically.

"What the hell is that, Willie?"

"It's to help you. I know you gonna' head out to that island no matter what we say. I'm sure you think we're just crazy, old superstitious country folk, but I really did know your daddy, Mr. Wells. He was a friend of mine, and I don't wanna see you get hurt out there, is all. This here will help protect you. Lord knows, it'll help you."

"What is it? Some type of amulet?" Ambrose asked. He took it from Willie's outstretched hand, looked at it, and then brought it closer to his face. It gave off a pungent odor of old spices and manure.

"Ugh, Willie! It stinks to high heaven!" He immediately held it away from his face. "I'm not wearing this thing under my shirt, if that's what you were thinking."

"That'd be fine, Mr. Wells. Just put it in your pocket if your headed out that way. That's all we ask." Willie made a backwards gesture with his head, and Ambrose then looked up to see the old woman standing on the porch again, smoking her pipe as if nothing bizarre had just occurred. Rose and Johnny had ambled up the steps, and were now peering out from behind her thick legs, just as they had when Ambrose had first arrived.

"Jesus, Willie," Ambrose sighed. "Fine. I'll keep it on me if that's what y'all want me to do. Just call me with an estimate for the fence. I'm at the Anhinga all week." Ambrose went ahead and turned the car on, and put it in drive, eager to leave the place.

"Yes sir, Mr. Wells. I'll let you know, but it ain't so bad. We'll get it taken care of. But Mr. Wells?" Ambrose had almost started to drive off, but he hit the brake again, hearing his name.

"Yes, Willie?"

"Your daddy was a fine man. He just loved your mama too much. When she died having you, it broke him up good, and he wasn't ever the same. But he was a good man, yes Lord. One of the best."

Ambrose, for what seemed like the twentieth time that afternoon, was unsure how to reply.

"Yes. Well thanks, Willie. I wish I could've known him like you did. And my mother too, for that matter." Ambrose didn't like talking about his mother who he'd never met. "I'll see ya around, Willie."

"Take care now, Mr. Wells. You be careful, and find me if you need any help with anything—anything at all, now!"

Ambrose waved, slowly pulled away, and drove back down the ancient, dirt driveway. He was exhausted all of a sudden. He fingered the strange, malodorous bag in his hand, and pushed it deep down into his pocket. The old woman had left him feeling unsettled. A late afternoon thunderstorm began to rumble above him. The sky darkened, and as he pulled into the Anhinga's gravel parking lot, the rain came down in ominous buckets, and the wind tore at the once-calm harbor.

Chapter Five

THE FOLLOWING MORNING, after the storms had blown themselves out over the Atlantic, the sun rose over the water, casting rose and purple hues on to the calm bay. The seagulls had chased the shrimpers out early in the morning, cackling and cawing in their wake, hoping to scavenge whatever they could per their usual raucous sunrise routine. After the shrimpers had passed by, the sun had climbed a little higher, and the morning haze had quickly burned off. The sea was so calm that it seemed like one could simply walk out upon it, and without any whiff of an apparent breeze, it was destined to be a long, hot day.

A tall man, the lone resident of the island, stood at the end of the sturdy little dock that jutted out into the harbor facing the mainland. He stared out to the point where the South Edisto River emptied its cool—now brackish and slightly less tea-colored—water into the briny sea. He'd always loved that river, from its source in the rolling Sandhills area in the middle of the state, down to the Lowcountry swamps and marshes. It was one of the last undammed sources of blackwater along the East Coast. Its meandering course wove through small, colonial towns, ancient farms, and woods that had once been tall and deep, then cut down, then allowed to grow again as the whims of men changed over the course of decades and centuries. Every oxbow had its story to tell, of Indian canoes long removed from the scene, of bison and bear and catamount—long hunted away and vanished—of early explorers who had faded into the mists of history just as their descendants had done. Soldiers, slaves, plantation owners, freedmen, railroad men, and a whole line of humanity, all melted away after their time on this mortal plane, only to leave nothing more substantial than an old foundation or shallow rice canal as testament to their existence.

Yet if the old, flowing river could speak, the man thought, it would tell a grand and aching story, full of tragedy and loss and victory and joy. Sometimes he thought, traveling along its banks in the quiet of a canoe, he could almost hear its murmuring tales bubbling up in the gurgling current, and in the easy wind rustling through the tall grass of the marsh.

Off in the distance, a small but steadily growing object—very familiar to the man's keen eyes—made its way toward the very dock he stood upon. He stood tall and erect, as he had always carried himself since he was taught to do so by his mother, though she, too, was now nothing more than a soft voice faintly heard in the wind at night. How many friends had he lost along the way as well? How many loved ones had passed across the black veil into the unknown who had once come to visit him by boat, not unlike the one quickly approaching now, across the dead calm of the bay? How many times had he stood where he stood now, anxiously awaiting a friend's familiar handshake, a relative's warm embrace, or a lover's pulse-quickening smile? He bowed his head down, and forcibly turned his thoughts away from the past. It did no good to dwell for too long in such places.

His sharp and well-trained mind, quickly recovering, returned to the present day, and to the task at hand. He looked up again, and the boat was larger now, clearly a shrimper, like so many who docked in the harbor, but one that he knew rarely went out to work these days. Squinting his eyes, he could just make out the old captain steering from the back, and alongside him was a young man who was standing with his right hand over his eyes, shading himself from the low rising sun and the glare that reflected off the still water. The old captain behind the wheel seemed to not notice the harsh brightness, and the man on the dock knew the captain was probably singing some awful sea shanty, loudly and off-key, above the noise of the engine.

As the old boat approached the dock, he saw the captain point to the fenders, yell something, and then laugh to himself, his head briefly tilted backwards in mirth as he slowly guided the vessel in. The young man first threw the stern fender, and then the subsequent fenders, over the side, and walked toward the bow before he then returned again to grab the stern spring line from where he'd coiled it on the deck earlier at the start of their short voyage out to Wellspring Island. The captain returned to singing poorly, and the man on the dock smiled a little as he heard wisps of a hoary, familiar song he knew Mr. Delacroix enjoyed well beyond his ability to chant.

"Cheer'ly, man!" he distinctly heard, just before Mr. Delacroix cut the engine, quitted his rough serenade, and glided, almost effortlessly, along the smooth water toward the side of the dock. Continuing to hum to himself quietly, he adjusted the wheel slightly, and eased the fenders against the wooden beams.

"Well, throw him the line, already, ya damned dingbatter!" the captain yelled out at the young man perched mid-ship, the spring line in his hand. The young man looked back irritably, and then looked over to the man on the dock to intimate he would throw the line. The tall man on the dock got a good look at the young man's face, and his heart trembled, just for a moment, and he did something he rarely did these days—he hesitated. Quickly recovering his composure, he held his hand out, as if to signal it'd be okay to do so, and the young man tossed the rope with excellent precision, as though long practiced, into his waiting hands.

"Welcome, young man! Welcome to Wellspring Island! Please, go ahead and disembark. I'm sure the estimable Captain Delacroix has many important things to do today, and must be on his way. Is that not so, my old friend?" He smiled at the old shrimper who appeared to scowl a little at what he assumed was probably highbrow mockery.

"I've all the time in the world, sir, as you are aware, but I could always stand to do a little work on the 'ol *Flyin' Horse.*" He patted the wheel a few times, and muttered something under his breath, something the tall man had seen him do a thousand times before.

Ambrose continued to stand on the deck, witnessing this conversation, uncertain if he should truly jump on to the dock or not. Questioningly, he glanced quickly back toward Captain Delacroix, and then toward the man standing on the dock.

"What are ya waitin' for, man? The second comin'?!" he heard the salty captain holler at him.

"Yes," the man on the dock said. He smiled. "Please make yourself at home."

Ambrose stepped off the boat, and the older man quickly threw the spring line back into the stern of the *Flying Horse*. Charlie Delacroix turned the engine back over, put it in reverse, and started to back away from the dock almost immediately, as if he were eager to not have to stay any longer than he was required to.

"I suppose we shall have the honor of your presence again this evening, my good captain?" the tall man called out. His deep, baritone voice easily sailed over the sound of the running engine.

"Yeah, yeah...," Delacroix muttered as he turned the wheel to pull the boat away in reverse. "Here's hopin' the water's still slickcam, but I doubt it. I'm sure we'll get a terrific afternoon thunderburst to throw a wrench in your beautiful plans, old man."

"Five o'clock then, Captain Delacroix, as we agreed upon," the tall man replied.

Captain Delacroix didn't reply, but waved dismissingly toward the dock in general, as if disdainful of the whole enterprise. He deftly steered the boat away from the dock, threw it in forward, and drove off without another word of conversation. A mournful, old sea chant started up again as he headed back toward the mainland, and it lifted indistinctly above the fading noise of the engine.

"He's a good man, but he's set in his downeast ways, I suppose. Drinks a little more than he should, and he's not of a personable nature. Yet, he's generally reliable, and more importantly, discrete."

Ambrose Wells stood at the end of the dock, and put out his hand, having intended to introduce himself to the mysterious man before this moment. However, he suddenly felt as if he should reply with a comment on Captain Delacroix's rather unique personality. Before he could do either, the older man suddenly spoke again.

"Ah, of course! But where are my manners?" he exclaimed. Laughing to himself, he extended his right hand, and grasped Ambrose's manfully. His grip almost hurt, but the warmth in his smile and the twinkle in his light, watery-gray eyes gave Ambrose an almost palpable reassurance. The older gentleman seemed to radiate a warm glow that filled Ambrose with a sense of restrained happiness, though he could not fathom why he felt that way.

"My name—as I'm sure you are aware—is Peyton Grimball, owner and sole resident of Wellspring Island, and the last of a long line of Grimballs who have had the honor of living in this veritable paradise, as I do hope you will find it during your visit here. It is my distinct pleasure to meet your acquaintance, Mr. Wells. Is that correct? Mr. Wells? I'm afraid I cannot fully trust my poor captain's memory on such specific details, but he conveyed to me that your name was a Mr. Ambrose Wells."

Ambrose smiled despite himself. The old man's natural gregariousness and easy manner, combined with his radiant smile, was infectious. He felt as if they had something in common, or as if they were old friends long removed from each other's company, yet ready to pick right up where they had left off. He was immediately comfortable.

"Yes, sir," he replied. Now shaking his still-clasped hand firmly, he said, "Ambrose Wells. It's a pleasure to meet you. I'm sorry to bother you out here, sir. I work for the state of South Carolina, as I hope Captain Delacroix made you aware of, and I need to assess the property's value. For tax purposes, of course. I've been told its assessment is many years overdue. I hope I'm not a burden to you."

"It's not a problem, my good man," Mr. Grimball replied with an almost excessive level of enthusiasm. "I fully understand the demands of the state, and desire to be of assistance to help you in any way that I can. There are no secrets here at Wellspring, despite what the folks in town may whisper amongst themselves breathlessly! There are only queries you have yet to inquire about, and answers I have yet to divulge."

He paused for a moment, as if to let his words sink in, and then glanced up the short dock as it continued through the taller reeds and became a small, dirt trail that disappeared under the branches of a beautiful live oak hugging the water, with half of its extensive root system threatening to collapse into the sound.

"Come and join me in the main house. It would be my pleasure to show you around the island, including the land and docks, and to have you do any assessments that you may be required to do of the house. I've arranged for Mr. Delacroix to return at five o'clock. I hope that's not too long or too short a visit for you. I have no phone, and you may find that your cellular telephone is of little value to you out here in the bay. Those ugly towers on the mainland do not appear to have made much of an impact on the airspace over Wellspring." He smiled again, and then began to walk up the dock. Ambrose took his phone out of his pocket, saw that he indeed had no service, and followed along a step behind.

As they walked, he took note of Mr. Grimball as he walked just a little in front of Ambrose, though the older man often glanced back as he spoke to make sure that Ambrose was close behind. The man was tall, perhaps an inch or two taller than Ambrose, and seemed strong and hale. His beard, it was true, was graying, especially around the chin, but it was well-trimmed, and it graced an almost-chiseled jaw line, which gave him the look of a hearty outdoorsman rather than a lonely, cloistered hermit—how Ambrose had pictured him on the ride out to Wellspring. Ambrose had already taken note of the man's light eyes, with just a faint wisp of crow-lines at their corners. They lit up, almost shone, with some type of inner luminosity that initially had caused Ambrose to be taken aback. In fact, it had been his eyes, and the brief momentary look of profound sadness on the man's face, that had given Ambrose pause when he'd stepped off the boat. The man's eyes lent his slightly creased forehead and graying beard a touch of spontaneous youth, and the contrast between the two was striking. His teeth were perfectly aligned with his jaw it seemed, and were white, almost shiny. He had a full head of jet-black hair, with just enough gray in it to provide a salt and pepper look. It lent him a studious mien of wisdom, and it, too, contrasted with his sparkling, arresting eyes. He walked with youthful, large steps, and with purpose, and he stood tall and erect. He wore an old pair of jeans, worn, leather boots, and a white, sea-island cotton shirt. His entire bearing was a sublime amalgamation of youth and old age, of the possibility of fledgling spontaneity tempered with measured wisdom, of restrained strength and emotion. Ambrose had never met anyone so immediately captivating and mysterious, yet as soon as he had shaken the man's hand, he had felt at ease. He was, he thought as they walked under the shade of the large oak by the dock, at once both foreign and familiar, seemingly strange but somehow known.

It had been an unusual day already for Ambrose Wells. After another night of somewhat fitful sleep, made worse by memories of his unpleasant interaction with Auntie Dawes the day prior, he'd awoken feeling less than refreshed. Once his alarm had gone off, he'd suddenly found himself exhausted, nearly incapable of activity, and he wanted to do nothing more than sleep the day away in his room at the Anhinga. However, he'd made a tentative plan with Mr. Delacroix, and not wanting to miss perhaps his one chance at getting out to Wellspring, he'd taken a piping hot shower, made some awful coffee, and slugged it down as he changed for the day.

On his way out the door, he noticed the smelly little burlap charm Auntie Dawes had given him lying on the counter next to his keys and wallet, just where he'd left it the previous evening. He paused for a moment, and after he slipped the set of keys and his old, leather wallet into his pocket, he sighed. Did he really need that superstitious little amulet? The rational part of him thought it'd be ridiculous to even consider putting it in his pocket, and he almost walked out without it, but at the last minute, a little voice had popped into his head. *Just put it in your pocket if you're headed out that way.* He had smiled as he thought of good old—somewhat crazy—Willie Dawes, perhaps the last good friend of his father's Ambrose would ever meet. He'd grabbed the stinking gris-gris bag, and pushed it into his back pocket before he ran out the door, and then drove to the dock to meet Charlie Delacroix at their arranged hour.

The old captain looked as radiant as ever, despite smelling of old whiskey and body odor. He'd been waiting on the boat with the engine on when Ambrose had arrived, and he cheerfully declared that if Ambrose had arrived one minute later, he'd have called the whole affair off. It turned out the man on Wellspring Island would deign to see him after all, even if Ambrose was just a damned college boy from the big city. Mr. Delacroix took great pains to explain to Ambrose how he'd done everything in his power to convince the man on Wellspring that it wasn't worth his time, and that he was just passing the message along and would be happy to let Ambrose know that he wasn't wanted or needed. However, Mr. Grimball had insisted the captain bring Ambrose out after all, and so Mr. Delacroix, a sailor of his word as he'd mentioned several times, would be certain to bring Ambrose out as they'd agreed upon the day prior. He made no mention of a fee, and Ambrose failed to remind him. Afterwards, he'd begun singing an awful song, and from then on it was as if Ambrose was no longer on the vessel at all.

Not until they'd nearly arrived at the lonely little dock jutting out into the bay, did Mr. Delacroix stop singing, and he'd yelled at him above the noise of the engine to throw out the fenders, and be ready to cast the line—unless, of course, he "wanted to swim the last fifty yards." Ambrose had dutifully obeyed, but afterwards he'd returned his gaze to the man who had been standing on the dock, erect as a soldier, waiting for their arrival. Ambrose had noticed him standing there in the morning sunshine as the boat slowly made its way toward the island, and the man hadn't moved a step their whole way in. After the fenders were out, Ambrose had stood there, the spring line in his hand, noticing the man's eyes that were youthful and penetrating, and Ambrose had felt a brief moment of trepidation. His left hand had reflexively moved toward the amulet in his back pocket, but the captain had then yelled some nonsense about throwing the line, and the man on the dock moved—seemingly for the first time—and indicated that he should throw the rope. Ambrose had felt surprised, as if a statue had just sadly beckoned to him. As he threw it, Ambrose had the awful feeling, for a brief moment in time, that coming out here had been a horrible mistake, and that the man on the dock was irreparably broken—that he should stay on the boat, and instead meet with the man's lawyer in Charleston, and flee from Edisto. Then he caught the man's eye, and heard him say, "Welcome to Wellspring Island." Ambrose then found himself settled again, as if his momentary caution, and the man's fleeting look of abject sadness, had never occurred at all. The very idea of some insidious threat, so plausible just a moment previous, suddenly seemed the height of foolishness—an absurdity that didn't even seem possible. And so it was that Ambrose Wells found himself walking down the dock, and under the large, leaning oak tree along the dirt path while Peyton F. Grimball continued to welcome him to his island home.

"The island is an aberration of geology in this otherwise beautiful, flat paradise of barrier islands, salt water, oysters, and Spartina grass," Mr. Grimball said, and looked behind him again to check on Ambrose as they walked under the shade of the huge oak falling, eternally and slowly, into the sound. Ambrose quickened his step, and walked behind the man's firm, purposeful stride, trying to keep a half-step behind, but he was unable to fully walk beside him due to the narrow path that headed surprisingly upwards, higher and higher above the water.

"You'll note the distinct change in elevation, roughly fifty feet above sea level at its height where the main house is located. It's a unique feature of the island that also gives it several advantages. For one, it's allowed my family to keep this place for several centuries, despite the occasional devastating hurricanes that make their presence felt from time to time—Hugo, the storms of 1910, 1911, 1822, and of course the 1890s in general."

Ambrose noticed the man shaking his head wistfully as he talked about storms Ambrose had never heard of, with the exception of Hugo.

"Of course," Ambrose replied. He was fascinated by this man who spoke as if he was reading a book aloud. Ambrose found his legs tiring as they struggled to propel him uphill and away from the water. Small beads of perspiration began to accumulate along his brow, but his host continued along, talking all the way, dodging small roots or areas of loose dirt, as if he were long-practiced in negotiating the subtle difficulties of the track. Ambrose assumed he probably was. He stepped back so he could walk more directly behind him, and follow along in his foot tracks, after he nearly stumbled on an exposed root, and tumbled back a few steps toward the pier.

"Wellspring is made up of primarily oolitic limestone, unlike the rest of the surrounding countryside, which gives it its firm foundation and slightly higher elevation, along with subsequent protection out here in the sound. It's the same stuff some of the Florida Keys are made up of, but for some reason the elevation here is noticeably higher." The man stopped walking, and turned around, smiling at Ambrose.

"You know, I consider myself a learned man, but I've never been able to explain where this limestone came from, or the remarkable elevation of this place. Ironically, though, it may be my favorite aspect of the island."

Mr. Grimball extended his right hand, pointing behind Ambrose, and laughed suddenly as if he was breathing joy in from the air, and exhaling it in a giant whoop of exuberance.

"The views! Such wonderful views! And though I've been here for years, it simply never grows tiresome."

Ambrose had stopped climbing, and, turning around, his gaze followed the direction of Mr. Grimball's outstretched hand. Through a small break in the thick foliage, he could peer out over St. Helena Sound and back toward the mainland. The South Edisto River could be seen dumping tons of silt from her dark effluvium out into the big water, and to his right he could make out the southern end of the beach with all the Charlestonian beach homes dotting the coastline in evenly spaced intervals. Each one stared back at Wellspring Island, and each one was a sort of figurative island in and of itself. Taking stock of his surroundings, he looked left and right, and noticed that they were close to the top of the limestone escarpment. A small breeze reached through, and rustled the palmetto, the larger pines, and the smaller oaks that dotted the plateau. A few fat, golden orb spiders could be seen sitting in their large, ornate webs several feet off the trail between the branches of the larger trees. Despite the heat of the mid-morning, Ambrose shuddered. He'd found those spiders unsettling ever since he was a child, despite, or perhaps because of, their brilliance.

"We're almost there now, Mr. Wells," Peyton Grimball declared suddenly. He turned to take the last few steps upward that led to a flat area, at the center of which was a large, age-worn and weather-battered stone fountain. To the right, and behind the fountain, Ambrose could make out a large house through the foliage, and to the fountain's left, the trail continued, appearing to head back down toward the ocean's side of the island. The fountain itself was impressive, and looked to be ancient, like it was the embodiment of time itself, as dark water weakly gurgled out from its center. There were three statues—so worn with age that Ambrose had trouble making out their specific features—that seemed to be holding hands in unison around the center of the fountain. The water bubbling in the center, seemingly from out of nowhere, provided the always pleasant sound of moving water. Bathing in the center of the fountain, in between the mysterious stone sentinels holding hands, were three large, green, beautiful, noisy, and—to Ambrose—familiar birds.

Chapter Six

AMBROSE STOPPED IN HIS TRACKS, dumbfounded. The only other bird like that he'd ever seen in his life, he'd killed with his windshield just two days ago. He'd received a text message reply from his friend Pete the previous night in regard to the unusual creature he'd struck down, though it hadn't been all that helpful. It had read, *Hey, Ambrose! Good to hear from you, man! Hope you're well down in SC. Thought you fell off the planet. Imagine my surprise when I finally get a message, and you want me to look in to a parrot! You know I'm a damned herpetologist, right? Don't know shit about birds! I passed the message along to a buddy of mine who's an ornithologist here. Haven't heard back yet, but you know how those twitchers can be. May take a minute, but I'll let you know. Personally, it looks like some type of African deal. Probably someone's pet you smoked out there on the highway. Glad to hear you're okay, though. Talk soon, and call for Christ's sake!*

Ambrose had shrugged when he'd received it. He practically considered the issue to be dead by now. He had become much more interested in whether or not he'd make it out to Wellspring, and if he did, what he might find there. He never thought he'd find more large green parrots bathing in a fountain.

Mr. Grimball noticed that Ambrose had stopped walking, and he turned around, smiling benevolently.

"It is an impressive old fountain, is it not? It's actually a natural spring, hence the name of the island. My forebears found it here, and later generations commissioned the statues around it. Do you know who they are?"

Ambrose, feeling perplexed, looked first at Mr. Grimball, then back at the fountain, then back at Mr. Grimball, and then finally at the birds again, who were ruffling their brilliant plumage in the dappled light that shone through the swaying leaves above them. They washed, and sang raucously in the dark, cool water.

"I'm sorry," he finally managed to mutter. "Do I know who what is?"

"The statues!" Mr. Grimball gesticulated toward the spring. "Do you know what they represent?" He laughed, and indicated to Ambrose that he should approach so he could take a closer look.

Ambrose, still stunned about the birds, hadn't given much thought to the statuary. He cautiously approached, and two of the three birds squawked angrily at him before flying off into the trees. There, to Ambrose's great surprise, perched several more of them, preening, gregariously cooing, and loudly chirping and screeching at each other. The third large bird cocked his head at Ambrose as if he was evaluating him, and, finding nothing of acute interest, returned to the important business of bathing in the mid-morning heat.

"What are they?" Ambrose asked, forgetting all about the statues.

Mr. Grimball laughed again, a deep, sonorous and baritone expression of mirth, and looked up at the flock above him with obvious joy.

"Those are the resident Wellspring parrots! It is the other grand mystery of the island. I've been told a great, great ancestor of mine brought them from Africa. And I've also been told they are the descendants of an old family pet that escaped from the gilded cage many years ago, only to find itself on a windswept island. I've never bothered to look into it further. It took a long time for me to realize this, but it is good to have a little mystery in one's life."

Ambrose smiled, and looked back at the sole remaining bather.

"It's just, you see, I…." He paused again. "Well, you see, Mr. Grimball, it's the craziest thing, but I hit a bird on the way to Edisto two days ago, just over on the main road, and I caused an accident. Everyone was fine, but the bird was killed instantly."

Mr. Grimball frowned.

"Well then, I would contend that most assuredly everyone was not fine."

Feeling embarrassed, like he'd made a faux pas, Ambrose backtracked.

"Well, of course the bird was most unfortunately killed. However, I found it after the accident, and buried it on my family's old property, out along the river." He decided against describing its unusual rate of decomposition, not wanting to sound crazy to a host whom he was afraid he may have already offended. Mr. Grimball paused as he seemed to consider Ambrose's words.

Mr. Grimball smiled a little once again, though not as widely as before, and Ambrose felt himself sighing in relief. He didn't want to anger the man. After all, he barely knew him, and Ambrose was seemingly alone here with him on his property. Mr. Grimball looked like the kind of man who could row back to the mainland without breaking a sweat.

"It was kind of you to do so, Mr. Wells. Not a lot of people these days would have. I suspect you are kind, which is important. But are you well read? Do you thirst for knowledge? I noted that you graduated summa cum laude from USC, just up the road, with a degree in history and a double minor in philosophy and western literature. You wrote your thesis on the ancient Greeks, more specifically the Trojan War and its influence on the modern era. I enjoyed it."

Mr. Grimball paused, and then walked slowly toward Ambrose until they were both standing in front of the spring. He smiled kindly, and Ambrose tried to process how it was possible for this mysterious stranger to know so much about him.

"Forgive me, but I took the liberty of looking into your qualifications before allowing you out here to perform your charge—state-sanctioned though it may be. I simply can't allow just anyone to pleasure-cruise out to Wellspring. I'm a man of intense privacy. I enjoy the quiet nights, the waves striking the shore over and over again, ceaselessly and unwaveringly, the stars and the wind, and the slow rhythm of the seasons. I'm happy to show you a sliver of my world in order to maintain all compliance with the powers-that-be, but I would ask that, should you find something that does not pertain to your prescribed duties and commitments of employment, you will keep it to yourself. I understand that concepts of privacy and trust are old-fashioned, and almost looked at as quaint in today's busy, interconnected world, and yet—for me, anyway—they are sacrosanct."

He turned and focused his gaze on Ambrose.

"Can I trust you, Mr. Wells?"

Ambrose wavered for a second.

"Yes, yes, of course, sir. Your business is your business. I only need access to the grounds and main house, some documents—the deed or a copy of it at least—the overall specifications of the island and the buildings upon it, and any geographic specs. I hope I'm not a nuisance for you. I can probably be in and out in a day. I'll need access to your estate manager. I believe his name is Mr. Benjamin Legare in Charleston? But I can do that later. I hope this is as painless as possible for you. It's just that, according to our records, it's been over seventy-five years since the house was assessed, and, well, the state of South Carolina isn't exactly sure how you've slipped through the cracks for so long, but they do feel that the property should be assessed to tax you accurately." Ambrose blushed, fully aware that the presence of a tax assessor would be nothing short of the worst type of visitor to someone like this man who wanted nothing but quiet seclusion.

"Of course. Of course. I understand, Mr. Wells. You shall have access to anything you require, within reason. But you never answered the question. Do you know what the statues represent?"

Ambrose tore his eyes away from the large, green bird happily cooing now in the shallow water. He looked up at the first statue that stood silently across from him by the far wall of the fountain, knee-deep in water, with more water bubbling up from the center of the spring situated several feet in front of it. An old, decomposing, moss-covered stone wall was in the foreground, roughly two-and-a-half feet tall, encircling all three marble sculptures. Each statue seemed to be holding hands with the other as they faced inward forming a ring around the center of the spring.

Ambrose treaded around the circular wall that enclosed the spring, and carefully looked at each statue. Knowing now that his host seemed to have researched him, he felt like this was some type of test—and he wanted to pass it. The first statue, the one he had originally stood next to, was so worn with age that its facial features had almost weathered away completely. This proved to be true for all three of the statues, though it was nevertheless obvious they all three represented women, with breasts and what appeared to be longer hair. All three were dressed in what looked like a toga or some sort of dress, but the details of their clothing had long since been lost to the inexhaustible decay of time and weather.

In her left hand, the first statue held a long, cylindrical object with a circular disc-shaped base. The object tapered down to a narrow point, and there appeared to be a bas-relief string emanating from it, stretching along her chest and right forearm toward her other hand. She held this line in her hand, and seemed to be in the process of passing it to the second statue, who then held the string aloft in her left hand, also passing it along her chest, down her arm, and through to her right hand. This second statue had her head cocked downward a little, as if studying the string, but her features were no longer recognizable. The string ran from the second statue's right hand, down along the left arm of the third statue—and then, just like the others, across her chest and into her right hand. In her left hand, next to the second statue, she held what appeared to be a rather dainty, scissors-shaped object, and the string lay within it—a marble representation of a string, about to be clipped. The third statue's right hand touched the first statue's left hand, which held what Ambrose now assumed was a spindle, thus closing the circle. He smiled. It was obvious.

"These are the three Fates, doling out lives for humanity just as the ancient Greeks believed."

Mr. Grimball laughed aloud again, as if just watching another human being solve a riddle gave him joy. Ambrose smiled a little self-consciously. Perhaps Mr. Grimball was truly and deeply quite lonely, he thought to himself.

"You've got it, son! I don't often have visitors these days, and I doubt many your age would have figured it out, but you chose a magnificent course of higher learning. The classics represent the foundation of civilization. I pray that you and I are not a dying breed, though I fear it greatly."

He circled the fountain, excitedly talking and looking up at the statues.

"Indeed, indeed! This one here, with the spindle, is Clotho—the spinner, creating and distributing each man's life, which is represented by the thread of course. And here," he continued, as he circled around to the second statue. He put both arms up toward the statue as if he was a proud father showing off his newborn to a stranger. "Here is beautiful and fickle Lachesis—the allotter, determining the duration of each man's worldly, terrestrial time. And finally," he said, as he approached the third statue, "here we have the arbiter of our souls according to the Ancients. She who would determine the manner of our deaths with her awful cutting shears! Her name—"

"Atropos," Ambrose said, quietly cutting him off. "Greek for 'inevitable.' We will all die, and she represents this most basic truth."

Mr. Grimball stopped short and, surprisingly, had a slightly bemused look on his face.

"Well done, Mr. Wells. You were taught well, I see." He paused. "Please, come and see the house. There is a feature of it that I think you may appreciate."

"Wait," Ambrose replied. "The birds. Are they only here? On Wellspring? You see, I grew up on Edisto, and spent all my time tramping through the marsh and in the woods and I never saw a bird like that before—at least not until two nights ago. Now I'm looking at a whole flock of them." He looked up to make the point and several birds flew off into a nearby tree, and continued their loud, incessant chatter.

Mr. Grimball looked up, and followed them with his eyes.

"Yes, well, I believe they may only live here. It's quite a distance across the sound to the nearest mainland, and though they are good fliers, they seem to prefer the Island. They've all they require here; clean water," he said, motioning toward the spring, "food— mostly nuts from the trees that grow surprisingly large up here on the Island's plateau—and plenty of company." He smiled as he finished his sentence. "I mean to say the company of the other birds of their kind, of course. I am out of practice as a conversationalist, and it has been decades since I've been to a salon or a coffeehouse; however, what I mean to say is that the other birds are here, and they seem to prefer the fellowship of their own species. I suspect a dearth of natural predators contributes to their cause as well; although, every now and again, I hear reports of one escaping. I cannot prove it, but I've always thought the most intrepid individuals of their kind were simply too curious to live out their lives solely on Wellspring."

He gazed off toward the mainland again, almost wistfully, Ambrose thought.

"Yes, the most audacious and keen of them will venture off into the unknown; however, they rarely return to share their adventures with the rest of the flock, and, sadly, I suspect they may quickly become the victims of vehicles, coyotes, insecticides, or God knows what else."

He paused again, as if he were thinking of an old problem he'd never solved that he'd forgotten had existed until just now.

"Sometimes, though, I wonder if any one of them, after having escaped from their island home, has ever simply died of loneliness. Perhaps they missed their old friends out in the sound. Twilight, and evening bell, and after that, the dark! And may there be no sadness of farewell, when I embark."

"For tho' from out our bourne of Time and Place, the flood may bear me far, I hope to see my Pilot face to face, when I have crossed the bar," Ambrose finished for him. It had always been a favorite poem of his, so much so that he'd read it at his father's funeral. It had been the only eulogy he could come up with, and yet he knew his father had disapproved of his interest in literature in general and poetry specifically.

"Tennyson is never a bad choice," Ambrose said. The older gentleman turned and looked at him now with less bemusement, and more genuine respect. Ambrose, feeling a little proud at winning the man's esteem—at least temporarily—walked forward and away from the fountain, and, not knowing what else to say, he inquired if the house in front of him now was the main estate.

"Indeed," Mr. Grimball replied. There was a hint of restrained pride in his voice. "It is. The original foundation is from the mid-seventeenth century, or so I have been told. It's pre-Revolutionary, though the house has had more than a few makeovers. Wind, heat, humidity—nature spares no one."

The two men passed by the fountain, went around a small bend in the trail, and then suddenly the entirety of the house was visible. Ambrose immediately thought it handsome. The dirt track they were upon became an oyster-shell trail that led up to an old brick staircase that opened broadly on to the track, and then narrowed at the top, which leant the house an inviting air. The front porch had an old hurricane light hanging from the ceiling, and two more were mounted on each side of the large front door. There was a second-floor porch directly above that, with another lantern hanging from that ceiling as well. Two windows perched on either side of the ancient wooden door—which was adorned with a heavy silver knocker in the unusual shape of a tortoise—on the porch, all of them facing Ambrose and Mr. Grimball, and all bordered with dark green shutters. The second floor had an identical architectural scheme, giving the structure an overall aesthetic presence of symmetry that was pleasing to the eye. The external structure was clearly old tabby, as Mr. Grimball was happily pointing out in a running stream of fascinating commentary. But it was the inside, as Ambrose discovered, that made the house splendid.

Walking in through the front door, the two men entered the beautiful old, wooden hallway that was lined with hand-painted murals of pastoral Lowcountry scenes. The floor planks were old but solidly made, and were wide, and clearly built to stand the test of time. Despite their age, Ambrose noted there were few significantly squeaky boards, or depressions in the floor, like the kind he had learned to avoid at his father's old house. The lower level was composed of four main rooms, two on each side of the central corridor. The upper level was similar in structure, but the rooms on the left side of the upper level were combined into one large library—the crown jewel of the old Grimball island home. The downstairs rooms included a snug and tidy little study just to Ambrose's left, with the dining room located behind it, and on his right was a small sitting room, with the kitchen then located on the other side of the sitting room's small swinging door. Directly in front of him, there was a stairwell that sloped gently upwards, and then, hitting the back wall, split in both directions, which gave one a choice as to which direction to finish the ascent. Above him, the stairwells both emptied into a wide hallway. There was a main bedroom, and a guest bedroom on the right that was connected by a bath, and on the left was the grand teak library. There were fireplaces in every room, and as Ambrose saw, each room commanded an expansive view of either the ocean, or the sound and the mainland, depending upon which direction the room faced.

The entirety of the house had a cozy warmth that emanated from it, and within its thick and sturdy walls, Ambrose immediately felt at ease. As they passed through each room, Mr. Grimball went through great pains to explain a painting or an artifact that was positioned just so in order to highlight its own best attributes yet also complimented the overall theme of the room. In the kitchen, there was an old set of silver Russian cutlery with beautiful and ornate engravings of images of stags and bears set into the handles that, as Mr. Grimball explained, had once belonged to Tsar Alexander I, but which were "not loved by his poor wife Louise". In the sitting room was a spyglass that had been used by Wellington, who, during the peninsular campaign of the Napoleonic Wars, was apparently a "good man to have in a tight spot, but no Marlborough." There were two vases in the parlor from the early Han dynasty, that Mr. Grimball described as a marvelous depiction of Xiang Yu at the banks of the Wu River. In the upstairs guestroom there was an actual painting by Monet, and in the main bedroom, a Remington landscape, about which Mr. Grimball noted "It is the raw animal power of the horses that I love." In the upstairs bath there was an ancient Persian mirror, allegedly from the Abbasid Dynasty that had been owned by Al-Musta'sim himself—or so Mr. Grimball had been told, concluding with, "Hulagu had liked the mirror more than the man, as he'd preserved the one while the other he'd had trampled to death."

Ambrose walked about the home for the better part of an hour, and felt enchanted, as if he'd walked into a world of which he'd once dreamed. The house was sumptuous yet never ostentatious, classy yet comfortable, and at times was like a museum yet strangely familiar and warm. In the main bedroom, there was a beautiful wrought-iron circular staircase that seemed to disappear into the roof. Ambrose climbed dutifully behind his happy host until they eventually popped above the crawlspace in the ceiling to find themselves inside a beautiful glassed-in cupola that sat on the roof. How Ambrose had missed seeing it from the front when they walked in was almost beyond comprehension, but he assumed that it was his admiration of the front veranda that had garnered his attention at the time instead. The cupola itself was large enough to easily fit two people, along with two rocking chairs that faced south toward the front of the house to best catch the prevailing breeze when the windows were opened.

"It is here that I love to sit and listen to the ocean, and the sounds of the evening." Mr. Grimball peered out over the ocean as he stood next to a large brass telescope that pointed upwards, and Ambrose could imagine him doing just as he'd said. In fact, Ambrose could imagine himself doing the same thing, enjoying the night sky immensely, unhindered by the bright city lights.

"It is an incredible house," Ambrose responded weakly after an hour of the grandest tour he'd ever been on. From the very first time he'd stepped on to the elegant island home's front porch, thousands of compliments and questions had coursed through his fertile mind. He felt ashamed that the first thing he was able to mutter was that it was merely an "incredible house."

However, Mr. Grimball simply looked at him, and stated, "It is indeed, sir. It is indeed. However, you have yet to see the acme of my adoration, the crowning achievement of the estate—perhaps of my life! Let me show you to the library, where I hope you will also be able to find the majority of the documents you require, and where you may work in peace."

Descending the circular iron staircase, they seemed to float down through the ceiling until they emerged in the main bedroom. They then crossed the hall where there were two large, impressive wooden doors that were closed with an old skeleton key stuck in the lock. Mr. Grimball paused in front of the doors with his right hand on the key, and turned to look at Ambrose, a sparkle in his spry, blue eyes.

"In this room lies the wealth of ages. It is my personal library, yes, but it is far more than that. It is a fount of knowledge, the summation of the human experience—as miserably far as we have been able to proceed, anyway. It is what I am most proud of, and I think young man, that you will appreciate the collection as much as I do." He winked, and turned the key with his right hand, simultaneously pushing the doors open with his left. Ambrose gasped as he followed Mr. Grimball into the library, before quickly and reflexively smiling with joy like an innocent child.

The library was vast. Bookshelves covered the walls from floor to high ceiling, with occasional step-ladders mounted on rollers spaced between each window. There were two large, deep, well-used fireplaces, one on each side of the room. The fireplace that faced the east had wooden winged dragon statues carved in to both ends of the mantel, their mouths agape toward the hearth. The other fireplace, facing west, was flanked by two tigers that exhibited a similar posture to the dragons across the room. There were two deep, leather sofas in the middle of the room that faced each other, with a large, dark, wooden table between them. The fireplace furthest from Ambrose hosted two large, high-backed leather chairs with side tables, and across from the other fireplace, near where he stood, there was a large mahogany desk with a chair, both facing the hearth. Several candles, letter openers, and other literary instruments sat atop the desk. At the far end of the room, in the back corner, there was a small bar with several bottles of liquor, a decanter, and three pristine crystal glasses sitting atop it.

And the books! From floor to ceiling, there were books, and many of them appeared to be very old, with dusty, leather spines—all of them itching to be read, interpreted, and pondered. Ambrose felt mildly lightheaded from the internal, warm glow of the deep-seated contentment he felt. The glow seemed to slowly animate his core as he walked into the room. He sweetly and pleasingly exhaled.

Walking to the closest bookshelf to his left, he glanced upward, and felt his heart skip a beat—Austin, Goethe, Euripides, Cervantes, Tennyson, Frost, Twain, Chaucer, Shakespeare, Moliere, Dostoevski, Bulgakov, and Voltaire. He continued to ecstatically read aloud the authors—Bronte, Bierce, Dickens, Dickinson, Tolstoy, Wilde, Orwell, Ellison, Faulkner, and the list went on and on and on. Moving rapidly beyond literature, he was suddenly surrounded by philosophy. Fifteen feet away, Mr. Grimball watched Ambrose with a broad smile on his face. He no longer had to give a tour.

"Hegel, Aristotle, Plato, Heidegger, St. Augustine, Sartre, de Beauvoir, Aquinas, Spinoza, Descartes!" Ambrose almost yelled. "Is that an original Nietzche? Jesus Christ!"

He swiftly moved down the aisle.

"Politics! Montesquieu, Machiavelli, Paine, the Federalist Papers, Burke, Marx. Unbelievable! Even von Mises, Friedman, Hayek, Adam Smith, Keynes. Shit, I've moved on to economics!"

He'd gotten halfway down the room now, while Mr. Grimball had followed him past the ancient bookshelves.

"History. My God"—Ambrose stopped in his tracks—"Is this an original Macaulay next to an original Gibbon? Cicero, Polybius, Livy, Herodotus, Churchill, Foote, McCullough."

Another ten feet away, as he approached the other fireplace, he came upon the science and mathematics section, and his eyes lit up seeing the various authors' names: Archimedes, Newton, Einstein, Pythagoras, Maxwell, and Darwin. Across the hall, to which he nearly ran, were the Eastern thinkers, like Confucius and Lao Tzu, along with a beautiful old Bhagavad Gita. There was an ornate copy of the Vedas, the Mahabharata, and the Tao Chi, not to mention the Bible, the Talmud and the Torah, and the Koran, along with other various religious texts.

Moving back up the opposite wall, Ambrose found actual textbooks, mostly about science, but also art, sculpture, music, etiquette, and even dancing. There were ancient texts that Ambrose did not recognize, in languages he could not read. This room was truly a fount of knowledge, and Ambrose felt dizzy and absolutely stupefied, surrounded by the wisdom of the ages.

"To sit in this library! To read and to learn! There are no words."

Dumbfounded, he stood in the middle of the room looking up at the volumes of wisdom and literature that towered above him on all sides, and he sighed contentedly. He wanted nothing more than to sit down, and dive into the closest book. He'd forgotten all about the task at hand.

Mr. Grimball smiled broadly, and he gave a brief yet booming laugh that rang out, echoing across the room, that had such vitality to it that it startled Ambrose from his state of near ecstasy and wonder.

"It is a joy—especially in the winter with the fires roaring and a cool northwestern breeze blowing—to sit in here and read the finest and most erudite thinkers civilization has ever produced. I freely admit to spending years in this room—happily, I might add."

Mr. Grimball walked over to the fireplace that was guarded by tigers, and motioned for Ambrose to join him.

"Here you will see I have collected everything I could find in regard to the house. There is an original deed, as well as statements from the last tax assessment, and copies of recent tax receipts, though I suspect you have seen those yourself. Some of the material may be difficult to interpret due to their very age; however, I should think you will have most of what you require, including geologic surveys, and an appraisal that was done some one hundred and twenty years ago by an unfortunate, and very small, man who was appointed by the state for that very purpose." He looked over at Ambrose now. "I suspect, however, that you are of far greater character and constitution than that poor, diminutive philistine." Despite the character attack on Ambrose's long-dead vocational predecessor, Mr. Grimball smiled kindly.

"I suppose your grandfather or great-grandfather wasn't too impressed with the tax assessors of their time?" Ambrose asked, blushing just a touch.

"Ha! Indeed they were not!"

Mr. Grimball laughed that booming laugh of his, accentuated now by its echo off the walls.

"Nor were their grandfathers, for that matter. But I suppose we Grimballs have lived on an island for generations. Even when we had significant holdings on the mainland for rice, indigo, and eventually sea cotton, we spent most of our time here on Wellspring."

He pulled out the ornate wooden chair that was in front of the desk for Ambrose, and motioned for him to sit down. After Ambrose had done so, he looked at the grand stack of dusty paperwork amassed on the desk in front of him that blocked his view of the tigers, and sighed. He thought it might take a while to sift through the clutter of historical records—perhaps a long while—but it could also mean more time in this wonderful repository of knowledge, he happily thought. Perhaps he might need to return here after today to continue his work. The thought excited him, and his pulse quickened as he looked up at Mr. Grimball who was still standing next to the desk.

"Well, I'll go ahead and get started then," Ambrose said. He removed the first paper from the large, dusty pile, and looked down at it. It had an unusual feel to it, and Ambrose was surprised when he saw the sprawling calligraphy that read,

"Charles II, on our year of the Lord 1671, the King of England, Scotland, and Ireland..."

"Wow," Ambrose nearly whispered. "It feels different from paper, like—"

"Vellum, my young friend," said Mr. Grimball. "Yes, it's the original charter from Charles II. 'We have a pretty witty king, whose word no man relies on. He never said a foolish thing, and never did a wise one.'" He quoted, and chuckled to himself quietly. Ambrose smiled along with this amazing man. He felt charmed, and he wanted to get to know Mr. Grimball more. There was a certain camaraderie Ambrose sensed, an early friendship that he wanted to foster.

"This is the original royal charter?"

"It is indeed, young tenderfoot! My family's roots run deep, and they were influential once upon a time. They were able to secure the royal charter for lands in these areas once the British had a foothold. After all, possession is nine-tenths of the law, even back in those dark ages."

"Do you mean to say your family preceded the British presence here?" Ambrose asked, incredulous.

"I imply nothing other than what's based on family lore, and the evidence you have in front of you," Mr. Grimball replied. "But there are many things that the learned historians forget to write about, and once forgotten, they're rarely remembered—for better or for ill." He sighed a little, and walked to the open library doors.

"I will leave you in peace to acquire whatever information you need. If there is anything that you want for still, I have my attorney in Charleston, Mr. Legare—who also retains many important documents—and I will be happy to direct you there going forward. In the meantime, please make yourself at home here, and if you'd like I can bring some tea at four o'clock."

"Thank you, sir. That would be nice."

The older man turned to walk out the door.

"Oh, and Mr. Grimball!" Ambrose said, to which the older man turned expectantly in the doorway.

"Yes, Mr. Wells?"

"Thank you for allowing me to come out here, and for showing me around. I know you don't have, or want, a lot of guests. I appreciate it." Ambrose blushed again, and felt a little silly at having thanked him for simply allowing Ambrose to do his job efficiently.

"Of course, Mr. Wells. I've enjoyed making your acquaintance, and I always wish to remain in the good graces of the state."

Mr. Grimball smiled obsequiously, and then quietly shut the magnificent wooden doors, leaving Ambrose alone with his thoughts in the most wonderful room he had ever sat in, and with a seventeenth-century royal charter in his hand, apparently granted after the Grimballs had already been living in South Carolina.

Chapter Seven

AMBROSE SAT AT THE DESK, staring at the hearth with its two silently roaring tigers, then down at the ancient royal charter, then moving on to the pile of important-looking historical documents in front of him, and then back down at the seventeenth-century original charter he held in his hands. He felt like a modern-day Howard Carter exploring a tomb, or a present-day Indiana Jones who declared, "It belongs in a museum!" Yet it was all so very real. Standing up, he wandered over to the closest bookshelf, and pulled out an incredibly ancient book. He looked at the title: *Description de l'Egypt:, ou, Recueil des observations et des recherches qui ont été faites en Egypte pendant l'expédition de l'Armée Française, publie par les ordres de Sa Majesté l'Empereur Napoleon le Grand.* Remarkably, it was hand written.

As Ambrose delicately flipped through the book, time inexorably passed by, but the intensity of his interest made it seem like a brief interlude. He cursed his inability to soak up seventh-grade French, but, remembering his history of western civilization, he believed he held in his hand a hand-written copy of Napoleon's famous account of Egypt during his African campaign. It felt like a crime to place it back on the bookshelf. Nearby sat a copy of Moliere's *L'Avare*. Harpagon never looked so good than with his current audience to bookend him. On one end, there was Livy's account of the early Roman monarchy, and on the other, Polybius' account of the Romans' defeat of Phillip V at Cynoscephalae.

Ambrose felt intoxicated. How could he ever pay attention to the job at hand with such a library at his disposal? Each bookshelf and book therein brought him to the next book. A history of Vienna lent itself to the Ottoman Empire, which lent itself to Richard the Lionheart, which then lent itself to his brother John at the fields of Runnymede, and from there this went on and on with no distinct end in sight. Lost in his own thoughts, he was suddenly interrupted by his host who held a large tray of tea, and had an apologetic, yet sincere, smile on his face.

"It has been several hours, and I'm afraid you haven't been able to walk away from the first bookshelf you stumbled upon," he said. "Don't worry, though. Knowledge of any import is lost on those who gloss over the source material. I can see you would give yourself a day for your colleagues' hour. A week for a day, and a month for a week. Yet"—he paused, thinking aloud—"is it not fascinating how rapidly time moves when one is deeply immersed in excogitation?"

"I'm sorry," Ambrose replied. He was surprised the heavy oak doors had opened so quietly. He quickly placed Livy back in its prescribed place on the bookshelf. "Is that an original copy from the Napoleonic campaign?" he said, referring to the first book he'd pulled out. "I mean, I heard the only other original was burned in Cairo with the rest of l'Institut during the Arab Spring." He paused. "That was a tragedy of ignorance."

"It did not burn, but many other important manuscripts did during the riot. A tragedy of ignorance you think? Is there any other type?"

"Of tragedy?" Ambrose asked.

"Of ignorance." Mr. Grimball set the tray down on the beautiful table between the sofas in the center of the grand room.

"I suspect not," said Ambrose as he walked over to the sofas. He then sat down across from his host. "You're right, though. It is funny how fast time flies when I'm deeply interested in something, like this magnificent library of yours, for instance. I mean, really, Mr. Grimball, this is the most wonderful room I've ever set foot in."

Ambrose couldn't help but smile as he gestured with his right hand at the incredible library that surrounded him. Mr. Grimball grinned brilliantly in acknowledgement, and his light eyes flashed as he poured hot, black tea into the cups in front of him.

"Sugar, my young friend?"

"No, thank you," Ambrose replied. "Black is fine."

"It is an irony of life that the perception of time is so rapid when concentrating on something of interest, and yet, when bored, time seems to grind along as slow as a swamp turtle." He laughed gently, and placed a cube of sugar in his own tea. "Of course, that colorful expression reminds me of old Adwaita of Calcutta."

Ambrose took a small sip from his hot tea.

"I'm sorry, who is Adwaita?"

"You don't know of Adwaita? Perhaps I can teach you something today after all! You knew the secret of the statues, and were so well-versed in the various artifacts and curiosities that I have lovingly placed throughout the house; however, it appears that my educated catechumen has not heard of old Adwaita!" Mr. Grimball took a slow, prolonged sip from his tea, as if trying to intentionally build psychic tension.

Ambrose felt like laughing. Indeed, he hadn't a clue who "old Adwaita" was. He'd never heard of him.

"Adwaita," Mr. Grimball continued after a brief moment of silence, "sadly passed away some years ago in a zoo in Calcutta. He was a 256-year-old tortoise, purported to have been originally owned by Clive himself. I have often wondered if he felt bored with his existence after so long upon this mortal plain—that is, of course, if a tortoise is capable of boredom."

He took another long sip of his tea, and Ambrose wondered if that was simply how he preferred to drink it—slowly, as if to build conversational tension. Yet how many visitors did he really receive out here in the sound? Probably not too many, Ambrose thought.

"I hadn't heard of him. I doubt he was so old as to have been Clive's. It seems improbable, even for a tortoise. And I doubt they are capable of boredom," said Ambrose. "Does the mayfly, maturing to adulthood—for what, a brief day or two? Feel gipped about its brief existence? I doubt that, too! It's all they know. Their day, if they could conceive of the concept, is probably comparable to our three score and ten. If they can perceive time, I suspect their minute is your week, their day your seven decades."

"Well, you are speaking of mayflies. I agree it's not likely they are capable of that level of cognition." He laughed his deep, booming laugh as his eyes continued to sparkle with inner light. "And yet what about your pet dog? He lives, say eight or nine years, and any dog owner will tell you that their beloved pet has feelings and that it thinks—perhaps not at our level, but it can certainly perceive time. He misses you when you are away for a few hours, and is all ecstatic tail wags and yips of adoration upon your return. Is your two hours at the store his two weeks? Is it a perceptual form of relativity? Is time truly different for Fido, or is it all a trick of the mind, a perceptual illusion of consciousness?"

Ambrose set his tea saucer down, briefly wondering how in the world he ever got wrapped up in such a conversation.

"Do you mean is time truly slower for them? Like Einstein's hypothetical space-traveling twin? A fast clock runs slow, and so on and so forth. Or is it just perceptually slow? Like when I was a kid, and summer vacation lasted for an eternity, and today a summer season flies by in the blink of an eye. I suspect the latter. I can't imagine how fast my life will pass by when I'm the ripe old age of fifty."

This caused Mr. Grimball to erupt into a fit of ecstatic laughter that actually surprised Ambrose quite a bit. Mr. Grimball's entire body shook with mirth, and he had to set his teacup down to avoid spilling hot tea into his lap.

"Oh, what a statement, sir!" He gently wiped tears from his eyes. "Only a man in the springtime of his life could make it.

Oh, but please don't be offended, Mr. Wells. It is a joy to have a conversation about a deep and probing question with a supple intellect. Forgive my behavior. I am unaccustomed to visitors, and this has been more fulfilling for me than you can imagine."

He frowned a little, noticing Ambrose's displeasure at having been laughed at. Ambrose had felt embarrassed, but was reassured by Mr. Grimball's sincere apology.

"It's nothing, sir. Not a problem. I didn't mean to be comical is all," he said.

"No, no. Of course not! Of course not, Mr. Wells. It is I who should apologize for my lack of tact. It is an honorable inquiry. Time moves perceptually faster as we age. It is a fact, I can assure you of this, though I have no stronger proof than my own age and my honorable word. When one is twenty, this concept is hardly noticeable. At thirty, it starts to become a concern, and at forty or fifty, it is a problem of the greatest import! As a child we want nothing more than to speed up our lives, and as an adult we scream at any sentient being who will listen to please slow down. The older you are, the less time you have, of course, but what is worse, is that the time you do have seems to move along much quicker. It is a cruel phenomenon. We are all, of course, spinning and rotating around the sun at the same speed. We are not hopping on to theoretical spaceships and moving at velocities that approach the speed of light. Time is not changing because of anything we are doing here on Earth; it is rather we here on Earth who are changing our perceptions of time unwittingly—and quite probably unwillingly! As such, actual time—space-time, if I am to be accurate—does not change for us down here on terra firma. It is all an illusion. A nasty trick of consciousness. If I may offer a small bit of advice: Do not let it get to you. Until we have interstellar travel figured out, we all move through space-time more or less in the same way. It may be a mean trick, but nature is an equal-opportunity illusionist."

"It must be true, because a child hasn't lived long—compared to an adult, anyway—and a month or an hour or any segment of time, really, is an amount of time greater in proportion to his entire life, and thus time must seem to progress slower." Ambrose was thinking aloud now, lost in his thoughts, and staring into his teacup. "For an adult, that same amount of time would be a much smaller proportion, percentage-wise, to his entire life, and time would therefore seem to slip by with greater speed."

"Exactly! I couldn't agree more. But a question for you: if you could be one of Einstein's famous twins who you mentioned, and hop on that space shuttle that's traveling at the speed of light, zooming around the cosmos for decades before returning home to Earth, would you be tempted to?"

"Do you mean would I want to live for decades on the space shuttle, and then come home to a world in which everyone I know is dead and gone? I think not," Ambrose replied pensively.

"Ah," replied the older man. "But what if you had, at your disposal, a library such as this one, but better even? And a laboratory on board in which to perform experiments while you saw places and planets that no other man had ever laid eyes upon. Would you then reconsider?"

"Well, you sweeten the deal nicely," Ambrose said. He laughed, looking up from his dark, swirling tea. "That would be a harder choice. I'd have to think about—"

"No, no! You've no time to think, my boy," Mr. Grimball said, cutting him off. "The shuttle is leaving with or without you! Will you fly into the mysteries of the universe, or will you stay here on Earth to be with your family? With your wife and children? Quickly now; the doors are closing! In or out!"

"Okay, okay!" Ambrose replied. "I guess it would depend on what I had going for me here. A wife and kids would be hard to abandon, but single, childless, without even a loyal dog…I think I'm on that ship!"

The older man smiled, and took another long and purposeful sip of tea.

"I thought you might be bold with the proper motivation," he said. A sly, strange little grin ticked upward from the left side of his mouth.

Ambrose smiled, feeling comfortable again. They both sipped their tea, and Ambrose leaned back to take in the grandeur of the room. To spend days here, weeks, or months even, reading and soaking in the history and knowledge of the world, would be like a beautiful dream. He suddenly remembered that he would indeed have to return. He'd done absolutely no work of consequence today other than admire the ancient charter signed by Charles II. But would Mr. P.F. Grimball want him back? He was an established hermit after all, no doubt set in his ways despite his warmth and apparent desire to converse with Ambrose about nothing that had anything to do with Ambrose's state-sanctioned task.

Ambrose sat forward again, and awkwardly cleared his throat.

"I'm sorry, Mr. Grimball, to have to ask you this; however, you see, I…"

"Yes, of course you will need to return. I highly doubt that your curious mind was even remotely satiated by your perusal of the library today! And of course, given the dust that remains on the pile of documents on the desk to my right, I suspect your work will require another visit or two. And no," he continued, before Ambrose could speak, "it is not a problem. I've enjoyed your company immensely. I have almost forgotten just how much I have truly missed intellectual discussion, the company of another perspicacious and clever human being. I feel invigorated, Mr. Wells. I would be honored if you would return. The library is always here, and these documents have not gone anywhere in quite some time. They can wait a little while longer for your attention." He smiled generously, and Ambrose thanked him.

Ambrose then looked at his watch, and noticed it was ten minutes to five. Captain Delacroix would be making his way across the sound to pick him up at the dock. His heart was heavy at the sad prospect of leaving Wellspring, but he felt simultaneously elated at the prospect of returning soon.

"Thank you, sir. And I'm sorry I didn't get much done today. This library is just truly magnificent," he repeated. He sighed audibly. "It's almost five, and I should probably head back to the main dock."

"It's not a problem, Mr. Wells. If you are able, why don't you return two days from now? Same time, and I will make the necessary arrangements with Captain Delacroix."

Ambrose smiled.

"That sounds good. I'll look forward to it, and I promise to be more productive the next go around."

"I have no doubt," Mr. Grimball said as he stood up, and began walking to the door. Ambrose followed him, and the two men exited the library, pausing to gently close the heavy wooden doors. They walked back downstairs, and outside, then past the gurgling fountain and riotous green birds, and then back down the twisting, steep path to the dock. As they approached, Captain Delacroix and the beaten up *Flying Horse* closed in, and gently glided up along the edge, right on time.

"Thank you, Mr. Grimball," Ambrose said. He turned to shake Mr. Grimball's hand. "Thank you for allowing me to come out here and intrude on your peace. I know you love the solitude."

"The pleasure has been all mine, Mr. Wells. Trust me when I say that I look forward to seeing you in two days' time. Safe travels, and until then!"

Ambrose hopped on to the shrimp boat as Mr. Grimball approached the stern to speak with Captain Delacroix, who was scowling, no doubt at the prospect of having to continue to ferry Ambrose back and forth. The captain waved his hands in the air as if to suggest it was all a waste of time, and he then turned back to the wheel.

Mr. Grimball waved goodbye, and before Ambrose could even return the farewell, Captain Delacroix was pulling away in reverse, and yelling at Ambrose to pull in the fenders. Ambrose felt sad to be leaving as they pulled back into the sound, and he gazed silently at a gradually smaller Wellspring Island. Mr. Grimball, once again, stood like a sentinel on the dock until his faint form was indistinguishable from the pier he stood upon. The sun was beginning to get a little lower, and soft light flickered off the small waves of the sound as they returned to the mainland. Captain Delacroix ignored his passenger completely, and struck up another nearly unrecognizable sea shanty. Despite the off-pitch singing, it was a pleasing trip back to the mainland with the cool evening air blowing Ambrose's hair back, and the smell of the sea reminding him of the normalcy of life there.

Arriving back at the Anhinga, Ambrose discovered a small notecard taped unceremoniously to his door, the contents of which briefly requested his presence in the main lobby. Shrugging his shoulders, he sauntered down to the reception area where the proprietor, upon being summoned by the cheerful ring of the front desk bell, slowly approached the desk in a manner that suggested the mere request of his presence was a completely absurd and unnecessary waste of his God-given time. Ambrose thought this ironic, given that it was the motel owner who had requested Ambrose's presence in the first place.

"Yeah?" the proprietor said to Ambrose. He rested his hands on the counter, casting an irritated glance in Ambrose's direction.

"I'm sorry to have bothered you, sir, but you left this message on my door."

The motel owner looked down at the piece of paper as Ambrose held it out to him. A look of recognition slowly passed over his face, as if thinking for him was especially difficult.

"Oh, yeah. Sorry, that happened right when you left early this mornin'. Forgot all about it. Ms. Hampton from over on Belleview Plantation swung by, asking to see you. Said something about Wellspring Island, and wanting to chat with you I hope you don't mind, but I told her you were indeed staying here, and that I'd let you know she swung by. Didn't think you'd mind a pretty, rich girl like that paying you a visit."

Ambrose smiled, and blushed a little, thinking that the motel owner was right on that score, and that he didn't mind it at all. He was upset to have missed her.

"Well, did she leave a number or a way to get a hold of her?" Ambrose asked, a little more eagerness to his voice than he had meant to let on.

The old motel owner winked at him, and smiled for the first time.

"She told me to tell you to swing by Belleview tomorrow. Any time after nine would be fine. Do you know how to get out there? Over off the main road, just past the little red shrimp shack. It's your first left, and then a long, pretty driveway to the big house."

"Thanks. I know of the place."

Ambrose turned to leave, suddenly feeling very optimistic about the day tomorrow, but he was also curious about what might have brought her out to the Anhinga in the first place. If anything, he figured she'd be pretty mad at him, given the state of her wrist, not to mention her car. Maybe she was angry?

"You think you'll be staying a couple of nights longer then?" the motel owner called out to Ambrose, who was walking through the lobby door and back out to the parking lot.

"Yes, I have a lot of work to do still. At least through Wednesday. I'll keep you posted."

"I'm sure I'd stay through Wednesday, too, with women like that checking in to see me!"

The motel owner laughed before he turned his back to Ambrose to return to the television program he'd left on in the private room behind the counter.

Ambrose rolled his eyes, and walked back to his room, feeling curious about what Ms. Cora Hampton might want to see him for. His initial feelings of excitement quickly soured when he thought she might simply want to get some more information for the insurance companies. He did feel awfully bad about the whole affair, and he resolved to pick up some flowers beforehand tomorrow. Retiring for the night, he lay down on the less- than-comfortable motel linens, and thought about the amazing library on Wellspring and the mysterious but affable man who owned it. As he drifted off into a deep slumber, he imagined the beautiful, liquid-blue eyes of Ms. Cora Hampton, sparkling in the fading light of summer's dusk.

Chapter Eight

THE NEXT MORNING, AMBROSE AWOKE with the alarm on his cell phone jarring him into semi-consciousness. He'd slept deeply for the first time in weeks, maybe months, and it surprised him for a moment or two. He had to look around the strange motel room, blinking confusedly, searching for something familiar. Spotting his duffel bag in a dark corner of the room by the bathroom, he suddenly remembered where he was, and smiled. It was starting to feel nice being back on Edisto, albeit in room eight at the Anhinga, and he was as surprised about that feeling as he was appeased by it. Despite the sultry and uneasy homecoming at his family's old house, and the somewhat alarming and unexpected introduction to Auntie Dawes in her dark, cramped trailer, the events of the preceding day had set him at ease. The incredible trip to Wellspring, with its unbelievable literary repository, combined with Mr. Grimball's unexpected graciousness and welcoming demeanor, had been topped off with a note from the prettiest woman he'd run into—almost literally in years—and these things had all melded together into an overall sense of peace that Ambrose had almost forgotten was possible.

Thinking of Cora Hampton, a small whisper of doubt crept into his mind, disturbing his brief moment of psychic tranquility. What if she was angry with him? What could she really want that couldn't be done via email? He was intrigued, but a little worried. He quickly showered, got dressed, and then checked the clock on his phone—twelve minutes after nine. He'd decided the previous evening to pick up some flowers, so he made his way to where the local florist was when he was a kid—two blocks down from the lighthouse over by the slightly busier "beach" part of town. It was where tourists, looking to escape the pell-mell of Folly Beach closer to the city, might come if they were willing to stretch their drive out a bit more. The florist was no longer in existence, and in its place squatted a cell phone repair store. It looked foreign to Ambrose. Foreign and ugly, like trash in the marsh. Sighing, he got back in the Bronco, and drove a half mile back the way he had come to the local Piggly Wiggly.

Their flower selection proved to be limited. They did have roses and tulips, and a smattering of sad-looking bouquets that Ambrose wouldn't put in a coffin. The few roses they had were elegant and pretty, but roses seemed to send the wrong message—or at least a rather strong message, one that could be seen as an inappropriate consolation for being sorry he caused her to crash her car and break her wrist. Tulips, it would have to be. Red seemed, again, a little presumptuous, or so he suspected. White seemed sterile and benign. Yellow roared, "Let's be friends!"—which wouldn't necessarily be a bad thing, except there was a small part of Ambrose, if he was being honest with himself, that wanted more than a platonic relationship to develop. He would have liked to get indigo tulips, but the Piggly Wiggly wasn't exactly a Dutch market for tulips, so necessity pushed him toward pink—not as boring as white, but certainly not expressing the ardor of crimson.

Having wasted twenty minutes deliberating at the store, he got back on the road to head out toward Belleview. He remembered where the place was from when he was a boy, as his father had often done menial jobs at the estate alongside Willie Dawes, among others. Once or twice he'd ridden out there with them, but had always been instructed to stay in the car while business was quickly taken care of between his father and, usually, the groundskeeper or butler. Thinking about those times in his life, with his father who had so often seemed so cold, brought back a sullen feeling of angst, and he quickly pushed those thoughts out of his mind as he sailed past the red shrimp shack, and slowed down to search for the turn to Belleview.

Spotting the big metal gate, he noticed the two large stone egrets perched on each end of it, the one on the left with a large amount of Spanish moss dripping off its beak. The gates were open invitingly, and Ambrose cautiously turned in the dirt driveway that immediately required him to veer left. He then went over an old wooden bridge that crossed a small creek bed, and angled right again. Turning the corner, he came across a beautiful avenue of ancient oaks that went straight on for about a quarter mile. The now-warm sun shone down through the oak trees, and their large beautiful limbs, hanging over the road above him, cast a speckled pattern of swaying light on to the dark red, earthen track of Belleview's driveway.

He drove slowly down it, enjoying the view immensely, before the track angled right again. He then passed through a low and wild thicket, and went around a small pond that lay in front of the beautiful and ancient home. The back of the home faced the main deep-water creek that timelessly ran another five hundred feet behind the house. Ambrose whistled to himself quietly, admiring the quiet grandeur of the place, as he threw the Bronco in park and killed the engine. He'd seen the place as a kid once or twice, but its beauty had never struck him as it did in the morning light right then.

Slowly, as if he feared his presence might grossly disturb the pastoral tranquility of the property, he stepped out of the car, and then quietly shut the door. He walked around the vehicle as it gave off residual heat like a caged bull, and the warm engine clicked away as it cooled off under the shade of one of the largest oaks he'd ever seen. He grabbed the tulips, and noticed they now looked quite unimpressive after being moved from the store to the grand, front entrance of Belleview. Ambrose quietly padded up the moss-covered brick steps, and rang the bell.

After a moment of silence, he heard quick footsteps as they approached the door, which was then opened rapidly to reveal a rather obsequious yet suspicious-looking man dressed in brown slacks, with a brown vest, and a stiff, white button-down shirt that looked as if it had been overly starched for years. He had a light-blue bow tie on, and a look of consternation on his face. He was immaculately groomed and clean-shaven, which made his peevish grimace all the more unsettling, as if to imply that Ambrose should apologize immediately for disturbing his peace in this beautiful place.

"Yes?" asked the small, irritable man. He had a rather high-pitched voice that did nothing to take away from his agitated persona. He was easily four inches and forty pounds smaller than Ambrose was, and he reminded Ambrose of a second-place jockey after losing by a nose at the big race—but without the splattered mud.

"Um, yes. I'm sorry to bother you, sir. I'm here to see Ms. Cora Hampton?" Ambrose unsuccessfully hid the tulips behind his back, fearing that he must look like an unexpected suitor.

The little man gave a look of grave perturbance.

"Was she expecting you?" the man inquired slowly yet somehow impatiently as he stared down quizzically at the tulips peeking from behind Ambrose's back.

"Yes, sir. She swung by the Anhinga yesterday, where I'm currently staying, and asked me to come by today." He suddenly realized what that sounded like, and blushed a little.

The man at the door arched his left eyebrow.

"Ms. Hampton swung by the Anhinga?"

"Yes, sir," Ambrose replied. "I'm visiting from out of town. The name is Ambrose Wells." Ambrose shrugged his shoulders as if to say, "What are ya gonna do?"

"I see," the man replied, adjusting his bow tie. "Wait here, and I'll see if she's expecting you."

Before Ambrose could reply, the door was perfunctorily shut again, and he briefly thought about running back to his car and throwing the tulips in the back seat. Before he could come down one way or the other about the tulips, the door quickly swung open again, and the irritable doorman stepped backward, indicating that Ambrose could now enter unmolested.

"Yes, she thought you might be coming by," he said half begrudgingly, as if he'd been anticipating—and looking forward to—rejecting Ambrose, and also half-surprised, as if his first instincts were rarely incorrect.

"Thank you, sir," he answered as he stepped across the threshold. He entered into a magnificent hallway, which belied greater wealth than even Wellspring's grandeur had hinted at—yet wasn't necessarily as steeped in history. The diminutive doorman shut the door quietly, and passed by Ambrose. He then quietly walked along a soft Persian carpet that ran down the wide mahogany hallway that was lined with beautiful paintings of Lowcountry scenes.

Ambrose treaded softly behind him before the two men turned right, and passed through ancient pocket doors into a large parlor that held a beautiful, jet-black grand piano sitting gracefully in the corner. They crossed the room toward French doors that were wide-open, their linen curtains blowing in the soft southerly breeze. Beyond the curtains, there was a large veranda that looked out toward the nearby creek that flowed along another fifty yards past the porch. In between the creek and the back porch was an immaculately landscaped yard, and a large oak that seemed even larger than the one Ambrose had parked under.

The small doorman grabbed the undulating curtains, and held them aside so Ambrose could pass by to get to the beautiful porch, painted white with a light-blue ceiling to help keep the insects off. The view of the creek, which moved out now in the ebb-tide, seemed like an impressionist painting set into motion. The creek made its way under the low-hanging branches of the trees on the shore, and past a dock with a large sailing yacht tied to it that seemed to sparkle in the bright sunlight.

"Thank you, Tristan. If you wouldn't mind checking in on the horses, I'm afraid they're rather bored without their customary morning activity."

Ambrose heard her before he saw her, and quickly looked to his right in the direction of her lovely melodic voice. Cora Hampton was reclined on a wicker chaise, and she seemed to bathe in the sunshine that snuck down through the trees and under the side of the porch roof. A cold and sweating glass of sweet tea sat on the small table to her right. As she got up, the sun reflected off her long, golden-brown hair, and, Ambrose thought guiltily, off the splint around her right forearm.

"I'm happy to see that you received my message, Mr. Wells. The innkeeper at the Anhinga isn't exactly known for his work ethic. How he keeps that ship afloat at all is something of a mystery to me, and yet every summer I see cars parked outside of the place. I guess it pays to be a big fish in a small pond."

She smiled graciously, stood up, and walked toward Ambrose, unconsciously holding her splinted right forearm with her left hand. Ambrose smiled, and went to shake her left hand with his, exposing the pink tulips. He blushed a little after he'd realized she had seen them. Her kind countenance radiated warmth as she released her injured forearm to shake his left hand with hers. Ambrose felt immediate relief; perhaps she wasn't too upset after all.

She shook his hand with a strong, steady grip that took Ambrose a little by surprise. He felt compelled to speak.

"I'm so sorry about your wrist, Ms. Hampton, and I appreciate the opportunity to come and tell you that in person." He held out the flowers in his right hand. He had practiced that line in his head on the drive in, and thought that he had delivered it pretty well.

She smiled kindly once again. Ambrose felt his pulse quicken. He immediately noticed her soft blue eyes, and was entranced for a second. She released his hand, and took the flowers.

"Tulips. How very thoughtful of you, Mr. Wells. It is appreciated, but I want you to know that I understand that accidents happen. I'm happy that this is the only injury of any significance that anyone sustained." She nodded toward her injured forearm. "My x-rays were negative, but the doc at the ER told me that sometimes a wrist can be fractured even though the x-rays look good, and so they put me in this here splint as a precaution more than anything. I have an appointment with a hand surgeon later in the week, and this accursed impediment will hopefully be removed at that time. It's keepin' me from my horses."

"I'm glad to hear it. You can't imagine how badly I've felt all weekend, and how happy I was to receive your note last night. I was away from the motel on business when you swung by, and I was sorry to have missed you."

"Well, that's sort of why I did swing by," she said. "I was hoping to chat with you about that a little bit." She intimated that Ambrose should follow her back toward the chaise at the corner of the veranda. Walking behind her, he watched as she gently placed his tulips on the table by her glass of sweet tea, and then knelt down to pull out a second glass from a small cupboard built in the lower half of the table. She picked up an ice bucket Ambrose hadn't noticed that was sitting nearby, and placed three cubes in the glass before she picked up a large pitcher of sweet tea that was next to the ice bucket. As she poured him a glass, she nodded toward the wicker chair on the opposite end of the table, and Ambrose sat down across from her chaise.

"I'm a straight-forward kind of girl, Mr. Wells," she began.

"Please, call me Ambrose," he said, gently interrupting her.

Cora smiled before taking a sip of her iced tea.

"Of course, Ambrose. Yes, well, unlike many ladies that grow up around here, I believe in calling a spade a spade, and not beating around the bush, so to speak. I've heard you have business on Wellspring Island with our resident hermit, Mr. Grimball? Or so I was told by Mr. Dawes. He's a little upset about the whole thing, but he's a kindly, superstitious man, and a lot of unpleasant things are said about Wellspring."

She paused for a minute to take another sip of tea. "The vast majority of which, I suspect are nothing more than tall tales and local lore—the type of nonsense any small town has I suppose."

"Well, I don't mind telling you that I work for the state," Ambrose said. "I assess property, for tax purposes, you see. It's rare that I have to actually go see the properties in question, but Wellspring sort of fell through the cracks over the last, well, over the last several decades at least. My boss was afraid it was being taxed at 1940s prices, so he wanted me to try to get some more information on the place. To be honest, we were wondering if Mr. Grimball was still alive, or if it had passed to a descendant unbeknownst to us. We just didn't know anything about the place other than the property taxes are paid on time by the estate every year, always on the first of April, sent from a lawyer's office in the city. I suspect I'll make a swing through Charleston on the way home as well," he added as an afterthought.

Cora arched one eyebrow upward, suspicious.

"Forgive me, Ambrose. But of all the minions they have up in Columbia, they sent a Wells back home to Edisto? Seems a little more than a coincidence, if I may be so direct."

He blushed, and awkwardly took a sip of his iced tea. Did the entire island know he grew up here? He felt a brief moment of irritation that everyone should seem to know his business, but the feeling passed as quickly as it came. Small-town gossip was still the same small-town gossip. He hadn't missed it.

"No. I know it's not a coincidence. My boss knew I spent time here growing up. Thought I'd be a good candidate for the gig."

"Spent time here? Ambrose, you spent every blessed minute of your life here until you packed up for college." She smiled kindly.

He paused, searching for the words.

"Yes, I did. My world was salt marsh and pluff mud and shrimp nets. But I wanted to see what else was out there. I had to get away for a while."

"Well, you certainly were gone for a good long time, but it's nice to see a local come home." She sounded like she meant it. "Did you check on your pop's old place? I'm afraid I heard that it had fallen on hard times, over there off Raccoon Creek."

Ambrose wasn't sure where the conversation was headed, but it seemed easy to chat with Cora about things he would normally never talk about with what few friends he still had back home.

"Yeah, I swung by there a couple of days ago, right after I got here. It's a disaster. I'm not sure it's salvageable, or that I'm the guy to salvage it. I might sell the whole lot, as is. It's a pretty piece of the creek." He shrugged, and placed his half-empty glass of tea back on the table.

"Well, please don't sell it to any more damned developers. This place is startin' to look like Kiawah, what with all the gated communities, and even a golf course. I can't think of anything more hideous than a golf course."

Ambrose laughed out loud. He'd been taken by surprise by the spirit of her invective. She did not laugh with him, and he quickly stopped.

"I'm sorry, Cora. I didn't mean to laugh. I agree with you. The marsh here on Edisto is truly the most beautiful place on Earth, and that's not just lip-service. It's got a rhythm and a pulse. It's magnificent. Being back here has reminded me of that. Sometimes I guess you gotta leave a place to realize just how special it really is."

"Well, I couldn't agree with you more. I was sorry to hear about your father," she said. "I heard he passed suddenly, and is buried out at the First Baptist Church. He was a good man, you know, though a little misunderstood."

Ambrose felt a little piqued once again. Everybody seemed to want to tell him about his father, as if they knew more about the man than Ambrose had. He took a deep breath.

"Thank you, Cora. He was a tough guy to get along with growing up. It was as if we had nothing in common. His death was unexpected, and despite everything, I regret the way things ended up between us."

"Well, my condolences regardless," she said. "He did odd jobs out here, often with Willie, and was by all accounts a quiet, honest, and decent man."

Not knowing what else to say, Ambrose chose to remain quiet, and there was an odd pause in the conversation as the birds continued to chatter. A small, red-and-green hummingbird buzzed by a bright red nectar bowl that hung from a peg screwed into one of the posts nearby. It reminded him of other birds he'd seen recently.

"Did you know there are a bunch of beautiful, squawking parrots out on Wellspring?" he asked, abruptly changing the subject. "It's the damndest thing. In fact, I hit one of them, and that's what caused our accident. I guess it had flown to the mainland, and gotten lost."

"I didn't know that. It's been a long time since there were any parrots on Edisto. Are you sure that's what they were?"

"Well, I'm no ornithologist, but that's what they look like. Mr. Grimball told me they'd been out there for as long as he could remember."

Cora finished her tea, and gracefully placed her empty cup back on the table.

"So you met him then? Mr. Grimball? And what did you think of him? Is he the bogeyman that Willie Dawes says he is, or just a tired, old hermit?"

Ambrose thought it about for a second.

"You know, I really enjoyed meeting him. He was really a very accommodating and welcoming host. He seemed—" He paused as he tried to think of the right word. "Erudite… erudite and lonely. Like he'd forgotten what another person's company was like."

"Well, I can imagine, living out on that rock."

"Yes. He's isolated himself out there, but you know, despite this hidden melancholy that I sense, he seems rather content. As if he's settled his affairs, and arguments with God or whomever, and he's okay with the straw he drew. You know, that place out there in the sound; it's incredible, really. The history there, and the library. Well, it's the most amazing collection of books I've ever seen. It's a stunning little microcosm he's created for himself. I got so lost in that library that I hardly got any work done. I'm going to have to return tomorrow morning, and try to be more productive."

He smiled at the thought. Cora did not return the sentiment. She stood up suddenly, and began to walk to the back steps.

"I'd like to show you something," she said. "Follow me."

Ambrose stood up, a little confused, and trailed behind Cora down the back steps, and out on to the grass. Cora waited for him there, and they walked together toward the massive oak that was the centerpiece of the back lawn. It would take at least five men holding hands to encircle the tree, and its vastness became clearer to him as they approached. Some of the older branches dipped down to the ground, while parts of certain branches—themselves as thick as normal trees—were partially buried under the ground, and then reemerged and shot upward once again.

"As I'm sure you are aware, the Grimballs are an old name here on Edisto, Ambrose. Their family stretches back to the first British colonists, some say to even before that time, to the Spanish explorers who came up the coast searching for cities of gold. While some of that is no doubt hyperbole, they've been around for as long as anyone out here can remember, for even longer than my father's family."

She smiled coyly, almost hesitantly it seemed to Ambrose, like she was embarrassed of the fact.

"Yes, I vaguely knew they'd been around for a while, longer than the Wells certainly, though I would've thought you Hamptons had been around for just as long," Ambrose said as they were passing under the shade of the outermost limbs of the grand tree.

"Yes, well, the facts are certainly lost in the mists of time, but it is popular wisdom among those who know these types of things that the Grimballs are somewhat cursed. Legends abound about the origin of said curse: a voodoo ex-slave hex, a dying pirate's final words, a Union soldier's death rattle—or as I like to think of it, bad luck and poor decisions. What is also known, though now mostly forgotten, is that Mr. Grimball's great-great-grandfather, also named Peyton Grimball, and my great-great-great-grandmother, Ms. Elizabeth Hampton—Elizabeth Welch at the time—were once deeply in love with each other. Peyton wanted to propose, but Elizabeth Welch's father was a staunch supporter of maintaining the Union, and the Grimballs were known secessionists through and through. The war was coming up fast, and he wouldn't allow his daughter to marry a Grimball, despite their wealth and status. It was,

I am told, a heart-breaking affair. They met one night at the house here, and promised themselves to each other, right in front of this tree."

She stopped as they approached the large oak, and pointed to the ancient bark. Inscribed deeply in the wood were the initials P.G. and E.W., circumscribed by a heart. Underneath that, Ambrose noticed a Latin phrase.

"*Damnatio memoriae*," Ambrose read aloud. "What does it mean?"

"It means 'damnation of memory,'" Cora said softly, as if it were an unlucky and probably unwise thing to say.

"Well, that's a hell of a thing to put under your girl's initials," Ambrose said. "What do you suppose they were up to?"

"Actually, as the story is told in my family, it was originally just the heart and the lover's initials. Shortly after they were etched into the tree, Fort Sumter was bombarded, and Peyton, the consummate good son, went off to fight. Taking advantage of the situation, and using the war in the South as a very good excuse for doing so, Mr. Welch sent Elizabeth to finishing school in safe and chilly Newport, Rhode Island. While she was there, she slowly forgot about poor Mr. Grimball, off fightin' Yankees in faraway battlefields, and she fell head-over-heels for a New Hampshire man named William Hampton."

"I guess it wasn't true love after all," Ambrose said.

"Indeed, apparently that was not the case," Cora said. She smiled wanly. "Well anyway, Peyton came home on a small leave to take care of family matters and to check in on Elizabeth, only to find her gone to Rhode Island and to have her father tell him to not bother coming back. He made mention of William Hampton, and Peyton apparently ran off into the humid mist. The next day he was due to head back with his troops, and Mr. Welch found this lovely, hastily-scratched, Latin post-script carved underneath the proclamation of love that had previously been so painstakingly inscribed."

"Oh, so it was added afterwards," said Ambrose.

"Yes, the work of a terribly broken heart."

"So what happened?" Ambrose asked. He found himself genuinely interested in the story.

"Well, that's about it, really. Peyton Grimball returned to his troops, and died gloriously at the Battle of Sharpsburg. I am told he was waving the Stars and Bars to urge his men on, and was killed by a ball through his forehead, like Desaix at Marengo. He died before he hit the ground. Lucky for me, Elizabeth married Mr. Hampton, and had three boys, the oldest of which was my great grandfather. She got her man at the end of the day, and Mr. Hampton married into one of the finest little estates in the South, if I may say so myself."

"Still, it's a sad story from Peyton Grimball's perspective," Ambrose said as he touched the carved letters of the Latin inscription, almost lovingly and unconsciously. He stopped, and looked up at Cora, who was now watching him with keen interest. It gave Ambrose a moment's pause.

"But why are you telling me this?" he asked. "I mean, don't get me wrong, it's a fascinating story. And this ancient graffiti, or etching or whatever, is really interesting to see, but I'm not sure what it has to do with my current job, or with the car accident."

"I thought you'd like to know a little history about Wellspring since it seems you had never heard more than the local gossip about the place while you were growing up here." She approached the tree, and lightly touched the carved letters, just inches from Ambrose's outstretched hand. "This place, this island home of ours—I say 'ours,' because it's your home, too, Ambrose. You can't just move away, and think that it forgot about you, even if you want to forget about it. Everything about this spot is special, including the people born here. There is an interconnectedness between us, and between every ripple on the marsh and every grain of sand on the beach; between the crabs that scuttle into their holes in the pluff mud and the gators that wallow nearby; between the sun's rays reflecting off the tide pools at low tide and the moonlight that on a clear night makes the swaying oaks look like they're cast in silver."

She had been staring off over the creek as she spoke, but suddenly turned toward Ambrose. He found himself staring into her watery eyes, and trapped this time, he thought he might drown in them if he didn't look away. Yet he couldn't stop looking at her. She was the loveliest thing he'd ever laid eyes on.

"Blood runs thick here, Ambrose," she practically whispered now. He had to lean in to hear her. He could smell a saccharine, musty odor of sweat and jessamine that was intoxicating and pleasing. "Every little piece of land has a story to tell, and if you listen to the wind rustling through the leaves or the tide crashing on to the shore, I swear you can almost hear those ancient words. And you and me and Willie Dawes and Peyton Grimball and everyone else are all playing our part, and writing our own chapters into that grand tale. If you wanna read it, you just gotta remember where you came from. And you gotta know where to look."

She suddenly smiled again, and looked away, breaking the spell she'd cast on Ambrose. She pointed down toward the old inscription on the oak tree.

"You just gotta know where to look, Ambrose."

He felt his cheeks flush, and became suddenly very self-conscious, unsure how to respond. He felt embarrassed, as if he'd gotten too close to her just then.

"Yes, well, of course. I'll keep that in mind." It was an idiotic response, he knew. "I shouldn't take up any more of your time, though. Please let me know what the damages are to your car, and what your medical bills are. I'll make sure my insurance covers it."

"Oh, don't worry about all that now. I'm sure it'll all sort itself out."

They walked back to the porch in awkward silence, and then through the blowing linen curtains into the parlor. After they had passed down the hallway, Cora opened the front door for him.

"Ambrose, it's been nice seeing you. Would you like to come back later this week? Say, Friday morning? Same time would be good for me. I'm hopin' to have this accursed splint off by then. Maybe we could go for a ride? Are you comfortable with horses?" She positively beamed as she spoke, and even though Ambrose had very little familiarity with riding horses, he wasn't about to turn down that invitation.

"A little," he said. "I'd love to try it with you, though. Friday would be great for me."

"Friday it is. I'll count on seeing you then."

"Goodbye, Cora."

She quietly shut the door, and Ambrose felt light as air as he skimmed down the porch steps, and over to his waiting Bronco. He'd be sure to thank Big John when he called him later to let him know he'd need a few more days on Edisto. This was the best assignment he'd ever been given, and to think he'd been dreading it!

Chapter Nine

THE BRISK SOUTHERLY WIND THAT BLEW across the sound kicked up a decent chop in the water, making the ride out to Wellspring a little bumpier than it had been during Ambrose's first trip. Captain Delacroix, however, paid it no more mind than he had the empty bottle of Navy rum into which he constantly ashed his wooden pipe. That remarkable little pipe was probably the most used, and ironically, the most well-taken care of piece of equipment that the *Flying Horse* carried on board. The shrimp boat's helm was thrashed and littered with liquor bottles, the seats of the cockpit lockers had long been divested of their cushions, and there was no hope of any life vests to be found on board. Ambrose highly doubted that any of the running lights were functional, though he hadn't seen the boat run at night—nevertheless a journey he would be sure to forego if given the opportunity to join the dipsomaniacal captain. Charles Delacroix seemed more interested and less critical of Ambrose on the second trip, and even permitted him to peer into the cabin just before they set off. (The charting table was covered in ashtrays, and there were seven or eight small hammocks hanging from every available nook, most of which were filled with rum and rotting fruit.) The stench alone had convinced him the trip would be more amiable, and far less odiferous above deck, despite having to put up with a constant barrage of seemingly made-up sea shanties.

As Ambrose peered off toward the island, whitecaps spontaneously sprung to life at the end of the sound, and then died. The rare seagull that had missed the dawn shrimp boat exodus struggled to find purchase in the constantly shifting gusts of warm gulfstream air blowing in from the tropics. The chop was noticeable, and he hung on to a life line, one leg in the cockpit, while Captain Delacroix mumbled and grumbled from the corner of his mouth, first the refrain from an old tune, and later a quick insult about the sea not sparing "boys with fancy degrees and brains full of vapor and library dust."

Ignoring the old salt, Ambrose thought back to his unusual meeting with Cora the previous day. Everything after leaving Belleview had been a bit of a blur, and yet the forty-five minutes or so he had spent with her seemed so crisp and sparkling. The taste of the iced tea, the feeling of the rough bark on his fingers, the light touch of the linen curtain on his cheek, all seemed permanently scarred into his psyche. The rest of the day, spent mostly in between his room, where he'd unsuccessfully tried to nap, and the main restaurant at the Anhinga, was hazy, and it had seemed like a brief interlude between when he'd left Cora and when he'd woken up this morning. He remembered, rather awkwardly, that he had promised Cora a certain practical knowledge of riding horses, and despite the fact that this knowledge consisted historically of an hour or two, at the tender age of twelve, riding mules at a neighbor's house, it didn't seem to be prohibitive for his next meeting with her. He figured he'd cross that bridge when he came to it. How hard could it be? The thrill he felt at the opportunity of spending time with her again quickly pushed such nagging doubts aside.

After he had left her estate, he'd headed home, and vaguely remembered contacting Big John up in Columbia to let him know he'd need a few more days to really "get to the bottom of this mess," as he'd succinctly put it. Big John, even more apathetic than most of his colleagues, expressed his usual insipid mix of languor and disdain, made a few consensual grunts, and hung up the phone. This, as far as Ambrose was concerned, was the perfect response—implicit consent with little unnecessary conversation.

He'd then called his friend Pete up in D.C. to see if he'd made any headway into the identity of Wellspring's unique winged fauna, but received a canned voicemail response, and hung up in frustration. Voicemails weren't worth the time it took to leave them these days. Pete would get in touch with him when he had more information, and, Ambrose figured, on Pete's own time. Ambrose, however, could be patient. This particular problem was not in any way terrifically frustrating, and he had to admit he was rapidly losing interest with everything else going on. He'd talk to Pete when he talked to Pete.

Now, as the *Flying Horse* puttered slowly through the waves, the forlorn dock on Wellspring reached out into the sound to greet them yet again. Just as before, Ambrose could make out the stoic figure of Peyton Grimball, standing on the end of the dock watching their approach. Ambrose's excitement on this occasion was in sharp contrast to the apprehension he'd felt on his first trip out, and he smiled to himself as a large wave broke over the bow, casting salty spray across the deck. The captain slowed the engine, and yelled at him to throw the fenders in again.

"Mr. Wells! I welcome you back with great joy!" Peyton yelled over the engines. Captain Delacroix put the old boat in neutral, and it swung gently into the dock, bouncing lightly off the grimy fenders Ambrose had tossed overboard.

Ambrose stepped off the boat on to the swaying dock, his hand outstretched to grasp Peyton Grimball's.

"It's a pleasure, sir. I assure you I've been looking forward to it as well."

Ambrose heard the old captain slip the boat back into reverse to take off immediately.

"Mr. Delacroix, I trust we will see you here again at five o'clock as per usual?"

"I might could," Ambrose heard the captain yell over the engine. Mr. Grimball laughed heartily at his noncommittal response.

"Mights—as you yourself once told me, Captain—grow on chickens!"

Ambrose watched as Captain Delacroix broke into a smile, the first he could ever remember seeing from the salty old man.

"Aye, that they do!" The captain roared a laugh that seemed like it could have only come from the most ancient of souls, the laughter of Methuselah. "And you know as well as I do that I have never been late. Why do you think I'd be today, eh?"

Mr. Grimball nodded his head in agreement.

"It's true, good sir. I am glad that I didn't abandon you in an open boat, like Hudson and his boy!"

Captain Delacroix reverted to his usual scowl, and said, "Hudson deserved what he got, and he still had the damned bay named after him...better than most..."

Ambrose lost the rest of what he said to the roar of the engine, as Delacroix slipped the boat back into forward, and started to pull away from the dock again.

"Five o'clock then, my good man!" Peyton yelled.

The *Flying Horse* pulled away, and Captain Delacroix, ignoring Peyton outright now, broke into another discordant tune. The boat pulled away from the dock as Delacroix ambled nimbly up along the decks to pull the fenders in, before he returned to the cockpit. As the boat's speed increased, Delacroix would soon get back to his regular mooring, and Ambrose imagined he would have a boozy day full of lounging around, and probably harassing the waitress at the Anhinga.

"He's a good man, you know, but a down-easter man is first and foremost a down-easter man. I am of old Lowcountry stock, and so we clash on specifics, but we agree on the larger, more important issues of the day." Peyton Grimball gave a winning smile, and Ambrose immediately felt at ease again, as if he'd been coming out to Wellspring for years.

"It's good to see you again, sir. I'm hoping I can get through the documents you showed me last time a little more efficiently than I did during my last visit," Ambrose said, shaking Peyton's hand a second time.

"Ah, yes. You'll find them to be just where we left them in the library. I can take you there forthwith."

With that said, the two strode up the steep incline toward the venerable dwelling atop the hill. They passed the beautiful fountain at the zenith of Wellspring, and Ambrose again reflected on the brilliantly green, screeching birds that were bathing, and making a cacophony of noise. The hoary, ancient trees gave the spring a little shade from the hot, rising, South Carolina sun.

"So I went out to Belleview yesterday, and met Ms. Cora Hampton." Ambrose casually mentioned as they walked up the gorgeous, flying staircase. Peyton appeared to not have heard Ambrose as they alighted on to the upstairs hallway and proceeded in the direction of the library.

Mr. Grimball arched his left eyebrow, glancing over at Ambrose, and reaching into his pocket to pull out the old key for the library doors. He inserted it into the lock, and twisted it to the left, then turned the handle, and swung the doors open to that most magnificent of rooms. As they entered, Ambrose noticed the large pile of paperwork on the desk that he had neglected to go through his last visit.

"Was Ms. Hampton as gracious a hostess as I have heard her to be?" Peyton asked. "Her reputation does precede her."

Ambrose looked away.

"Yes, she was lovely." He paused for a moment. "Do you know she showed me this remarkable etching that was set into the oak tree in her backyard? Her great-great-great grandmother and—so she tells me—your great-great grandfather are the ones who inscribed it."

Mr. Grimball stopped walking as Ambrose approached the desk in front of him.

"Is that so?" he asked.

"Yes. It also had an unusual Latin inscription underneath it. *Damnatio*—"

"*Memoriae,*" Peyton interrupted.

"You do know of it then?"

"Of course I do," Peyton replied—almost snappily, Ambrose thought. "It is the remaining vestige of an unlucky love story," he said, finishing with his usual polish.

"I heard it wasn't meant to be—between the two families, I mean. Star-crossed lovers, and what have you." He began to sense the impropriety of his line of questioning, and did not want to offend his host, whom Ambrose felt was warming to him.

"Yes, well the Hamptons have their version of events, and the Grimballs, well, our memories are our own. But that was many years ago, and the cast of actors have long since departed from the scene. Buried in that pile of documents, you just might find vestiges of their time spent here on this rotating blue sphere. I hope it should satisfy you; however, if there is anything you are missing that is required of your superiors, then I am certain Mr. Legare in Charleston will prove to be an invaluable final resource. If what you are seeking is not here, and also not with Mr. Legare, then I assure you it does not exist, and never has."

"Thank you," Ambrose replied softly. He felt a little embarrassed that he had brought up what might have been a sore subject. It had been a long while, but Ambrose knew that blood ran deep in South Carolina, and ancestral pride ran strong throughout the generations, like water through the old rice sluices. "I hope I didn't bring up anything uncomfortable."

"No, it is nothing," Peyton said. He turned at the doorway, and smiled graciously again. "It is an old family quarrel that is water under the bridge. If you need anything, feel free to roam around the house or the island. It is not a big place, and I will be around, tending to my cabbages." He winked, and chuckled to himself.

"Oh, okay. Thank you, Mr. Grimball. I'll be sure to do that."

Ambrose felt at ease again, and reassured. He hadn't angered the man.

"I leave you to your labor then," Peyton said. He then silently closed the doors, but left them a few inches apart so as to not give Ambrose the impression he was locking him in.

Ambrose glanced around the room, and fought every natural inclination to explore the spectacular collection of literature he again found himself surrounded by. He turned toward the large oaken desk, and the pile of dusty paperwork that sat atop it. Sitting down in the leather chair in front of it, he pulled the first document from the top. It was the vellum charter from 1671. *Could it be real?* he thought to himself. He hesitated to touch it without gloves on.

Gingerly, he picked it up. It certainly felt real, but it all seemed so unbelievable. He thought that it ought to be in a glassed-in exhibit somewhere, under soft light in a temperature-controlled room. He realized he was holding his breath as he gently held it, and exhaled slowly. Smiling at his own uneasiness at handling the ancient document, he delicately laid it down to his right, and took out his cell phone so he could take a picture of it. He then removed a small notepad from his back pocket, a pen from his breast pocket, and wrote "Wellspring

Island Estate Assessment," followed by the date. Pulling the next document from the pile, he noted that it was an early-twentieth-century title issued by the state of South Carolina. He quickly took another picture, and made some notes. The third sheet was an older deed, yellowed and dry, issued, Ambrose noted, by the Confederate States of America. Amazed, he gave out a low whistle, took another photo, and made some more notes. He continued this routine and quickly became absorbed in his work, losing track of the day.

Three hours flew by faster than any three hours of work Ambrose could ever remember having done. Usually he dreaded anything he did for Big John and the boys in Columbia, and an hour at his desk would tick by interminably slowly. In truth, he hated his job, but somehow his unhappiness toward it helped create an alibi for his depressed state in general. His aloofness toward his coworkers—most of whom he couldn't stand anyway—his lack of any close family or nearby old friends, his dead-end employment—it all contributed to his loneliness and melancholy. However, he nevertheless clung to the idea that if it weren't for his current vocation he might be happy and loved again. In his heart, though, he knew that his vocation was a symptom of his emotional lassitude, and not the cause of it. Coming home again, being on Wellspring, that intoxicating visit with Cora Hampton, felt like a shot of psychic adrenaline. He'd forgotten what it was like to wake up in the morning and be excited about the prospects of the day.

He beamed as he took another sheet of ancient paper from the pile, and bent over to examine it. It felt so damn good! He couldn't remember the last time he was this truly happy.

The only specter of uneasiness that disturbed his currently tranquil and content soul, was the nagging thought that it would all end soon, when the job was over and complete. Like all inchoate angst, it was difficult to fully grasp in any concrete way. Yet a frustratingly persistent whisper continued to speak to Ambrose, and he thought he kept hearing the words, "This, too, shall end soon, and then what?"

"And then what?" he said aloud to himself. The grandfather clock in the corner of the room ticktocked as if it were making an attempt to respond, and Ambrose sighed. He hated to admit he didn't know what was next, but driving back to Columbia, throwing this report on Big John's desk, and quitting on the spot seemed like a good start. A new beginning. Maybe move back here, sell the old land, and buy a new place. Start again. Maybe convince Cora he was a good man. Sitting in that remarkable room, filled with optimism and removed from the real world, this seemed like an excellent place to begin.

He stopped working, and glanced at his watch: 12:30 p.m. His notepad had several pages that were now covered in his poor cursive. They showcased his detailed descriptions of the legal history of the property—as best as Ambrose could make out, given the disjointed, and somewhat randomly organized, documents he'd just sifted through. The last document on the desk turned out to be a receipt for a sailing yacht that had been built.

"*The Bucentaur*," he read aloud. "Well, that's an unusual name."

His stomach growled, and he realized how hungry he was after skipping out on breakfast that morning. Wondering if Mr. Grimball was around, he made his way to the door, opened it, and stepped out into the empty hallway. The only sound that could be heard was the constant, unceasing noise of distant waves breaking against Wellspring Island, as they had for centuries, and the sound of the breeze passing through the trees outside. These dulcet and natural sounds echoed through the open windows, and were amplified within the narrow chamber of the hallway. Ambrose felt alone yet comfortable, the way a traveler becomes accustomed to being in foreign places, learning to feel at home among the exotic and the strange.

"Mr. Grimball?" he asked. He cautiously ventured onward, not wanting to disturb the older man if he was perhaps napping. The wind and the waves were his only reply. Peering into the bedroom across the hall, he saw that it was also empty.

"Mr. Grimball? Are you up there?" he called out. He glanced up the wrought iron circular stairwell leading to the cupola above. But all was silent. He passed through the upstairs bathroom and the guest bedroom, before he exited on the opposite end of the hallway near the staircase. He shrugged his shoulders, walked down the steps, and then around the downstairs rooms, calling out Mr. Grimball's name to no effect.

Feeling a little perplexed, Ambrose stepped outside into the hot sun, tempered only by the cooling, vigorous breeze, and crossed the yard toward the fountain. He paused there to remark upon the ancient beauty of the three Fates, ironically aged themselves by wind and time, and he thought of Shelley's "Ozymandias," one of his favorite poems from college.

"'My name is Ozymandias, king of kings: Look on my works, ye Mighty, and despair!'" Ambrose said out loud to himself, and he chuckled a little under his breath. It was a funny thing what a man might remember from his college education: The smell of the grass in the quads; the enormity of the place as a freshman; the claustrophobic feeling as a senior due to its small size; a heartbreak—maybe two or three; and maybe a professor, or a class or two. For Ambrose, it had always been the poetry, history, and literature classes. Before coming out to Wellspring, he'd forgotten how much he loved those subjects. Now, having come out here a second time, it was like a forgotten gate in his memory had reopened, and verse and prose came leaping out like caged animals. It gave him great joy to see his old friends again, and he felt a little remiss for having forgotten them for so long.

Smiling wistfully, he glanced around the fountain, and called out Peyton Grimball's name again—still no reply. He wandered around the fountain, and saw the path leading down to the main dock. He continued around, and then spotted the other path coming up that he'd noticed on his first visit. Glancing left and right to see if anyone was watching—then immediately feeling foolish for having done so—he decided to see where the path led. The small, dirt track was even steeper than the other one, and on a wet day, in slick conditions, it would be downright treacherous. The foliage was thicker as well, and he felt a little nervous. Remembering that Mr. Grimball had said it was okay for him to wander around, Ambrose tried to reassure himself.

He descended the path, which suddenly became deep, stone steps that plunged through a narrow gap in the sharp, grey limestone, and wrapped around to the right. The sound of the waves became much louder, and Ambrose realized he was on the ocean side of the island, the rock walls slick with spray from the ocean. The path became darker and narrower as the sharp, rocky walls loomed above him, and Ambrose realized that the steps descended into a cave. He stopped short, and wondered if he should proceed. The darkness of the entranceway was a little daunting, especially after coming from the bright, sunlit hilltop. He reached into his pocket, and pulled out his cell-phone to turn on its flashlight.

"Mr. Grimball?!" he cried out into the darkness of the cave. He heard it echo off the walls, and then disappear into the inky gloom.

He hesitated for a moment, but he couldn't contain his curiosity, and decided to proceed as far as he could. Stepping down into the shadowy, almost cabalistic, darkness, his cell phone light illuminated the way forward, and cast an insultingly harsh glare off the narrow walls. Ambrose shivered in the cool, murky corridor, and tried not to brush his arms against the wet rock closing in on him from both sides. The path seemed to wend further around to the right, and leveled off so that Ambrose no longer thought he was walking at a decline. Initially, the noise of the waves crashing somewhere against the rocks nearby was loud, but as he proceeded another twenty or thirty yards, the sound seemed to gradually dissipate, and he could hear drops of water trickling through the porous rock onto the ground, and upon his head, each one chilling him a little more.

He felt his nerve starting to give way as he realized that even turning around would be a little difficult, given the confines of the passageway, but just as he thought he'd had enough, he felt a breeze against his forehead. It smelled of the ocean, refreshed him instantly, and lifted the sense of dread that the dark, cramped passageway had set upon him. He walked a few steps further, and noticed that the walls were beginning to open up, and as the path widened a bit further on, he saw a light. It was not his own, and it made him simultaneously relieved, but a little frightened. He slowly approached, and saw that it was an old lightbulb hanging from a hook on a rusty ring that had been drilled into the rock many years ago. Peering forward, he saw another lightbulb about twenty yards ahead, and it reminded him of movies he'd seen about miners who worked deep in the earth.

He continued forward, and saw a third and fourth light. He suddenly realized he was no longer in the narrow, dank corridor, but was instead inside a grand room, the center of which was made not of stone at all, but was part of the ocean that had snuck in, giving the cavern the appearance of some type of vast, subterranean lake. The path continued along the far left side of the massive chamber, with lights that appeared every twenty feet or so. Perched on the far left wall—docked as it turned out—was a beautiful, two-masted sailing yawl that sat against the stone path cut into the very wall itself. Daylight from above shone through two, relatively-large holes in the high cathedral-like natural ceiling, and cast eerie spotlights on to the grotto's lagoon, which helped illuminate the space. At the far end of the cavern, daylight could also be seen coming from behind a curve in the lagoon, which seemingly led to the ocean outside, and to the big, noisy world beyond.

Ambrose stopped walking to drink it all in. Just when he thought Wellspring could not get any more fascinating or amazing, he'd stumbled across this unbelievable scene, as if it had been waiting all his life for him to discover it. He'd nearly dropped his phone, so he quickly turned off its flashlight, no longer needing illumination, and placed it back in his pocket. Breaking the mystical cavern's spell, he carefully treaded along the stone path, taking care with its the slippery floors so as to avoid falling into the lagoon to his right. He then noticed an almost antediluvian, iron handrail that had somehow been drilled into the rock to his left, and grasped it. He slowly walked along the narrow ledge that hugged the rock wall toward the ship, and saw its name inscribed on the massive stern: *Bucentaur*, it read.

He continued to approach the stern of the ship, and then curved around along her port side, where he could hear a strange yet familiar old tune that whistled up from below deck. It had a haunting character to it, and though Ambrose was certain he'd never heard the tune in his life, something deep within him seemed to recognize it. It simultaneously felt strange and familiar, like a word on the tip of one's tongue, or a smell that takes one back to his or her youth—forgotten but never gone, and ready to come back at a moment's notice. He listened as the sound became louder and louder, and then suddenly, almost painfully, stopped.

"Why hello, my young scholar!" Grimball's voice boomed down at Ambrose from the deck above. "I see you've managed to pull yourself away from your worldly tasks. This is the *Bucentaur*! My pride and joy!"

Ambrose wasn't sure what to say. He stood tongue-tied for a moment, gazing at the boat and Peyton Grimball standing on the stern deck.

"What is this place?" he asked. It was all he could manage. Peyton grinned from ear to ear.

"This is where I keep my most prized possession. I've been spending more time with her recently. It's been a while since we've been out on the open ocean together, but the signs are imminent that I may be due for another trip. The augury is never wrong, just unfortunately misinterpreted at times." He laughed, and made a grandiloquent flourish of his arms as if to wave off invisible birds in the air above him.

"Are you planning a trip?" Ambrose asked.

"Yes, a trip of sorts, you might say," Peyton responded as he walked down the port side of the boat. He nimbly climbed over the safety line, and made a well-practiced leap onto the slick, stone causeway that lined the wall of the cave. "I've been considering a trip for some time now; however, I wasn't certain. Two fates bear me on, or so I have read. I'm still not completely sure, however, as I said, recent signs have been pulling me in that direction. One mustn't mess with fate, you know. There are some things in life that we do not control, despite our modern notions of human ability."

He winked, laughed again, and slapped Ambrose firmly on the back, nearly knocking him into the water. Peyton's vitality and strength were incredible, Ambrose thought as he quickly recovered his footing, trying not to show he'd almost slipped into the water.

"I'd have you aboard, my boy, and show you around a bit, but she's a right mess at the moment. Not quite ready for the sea yet, I'm afraid. A little love here, and some attention there, though, and I think I can have her ready to go for a good, long run up the coast. Perhaps in about a fortnight, if all goes well."

He started walking along the wall, away from the *Bucentaur*, and Ambrose followed along, absentmindedly looking backwards at the incredible wooden vessel anchored there in the huge, underground, watery cave.

"This place," Peyton continued, as if there was nothing at all unusual about their surroundings, "is the natural product of water and limestone—as I mentioned the other day, an unusual geographic anomaly for this particular area of the world. I'm not sure most folks back on shore even know it exists, simply because nobody would ever think to look for a place like this here. And yet"—he paused, looking back furtively at Ambrose—"it exists."

"It is strange, and sublime, really," Ambrose said. "I would never have imagined this would be here in the Lowcountry." He stared at the huge, natural holes in the ceiling that let in the brilliant sunlight, illuminating the water below.

"Yes, it must have been a breathtaking find by my ancestors. You see, the water comes around a curve in the rock there, behind a natural breakwater and shoal. From the ocean, it looks impassable, as if it is simply a rocky shore of the island. There is a small, deep-water channel that sneaks around the back, curves into this massive cave, and ends at the tight, narrow passageway you just walked down."

"How did they ever find it? Your ancestors, I mean," Ambrose asked as they made their way to where the path narrowed again. The two men began to climb back up through the tight, claustrophobic crack in the limestone.

"Legend has it that it was pure luck. There was a bad summer squall, and my great- great—and many more greats before him—grandfather was out in a dinghy, collecting fresh water for the main ship that was anchored nearby in the safety of the sound. It was by a complete stroke of luck that his small skiff was pushed by the tides into the deep channel. It was fate, one might say, if one were so inclined, and as the winds died down, he rowed right into this cave."

They passed further up the passage where the rocky walls opened up, and the sunlight started to make its way down to the bottom of the crevice again.

"Did he explore the island at all? Or tell the captain of his ship about it?" asked Ambrose.

Peyton roared with laughter at this, and his response echoed off the closed-in walls, amplifying the volume of his mirth.

"An honest man might have, but my forebears knew a good spot when they found one! Peyton—that was his name, and my namesake—climbed up through this very passageway, and found the island and the natural spring at the top of the hill. The squall had happened at sundown, as they often do, and he'd been forced to spend a beautiful night under a full moon. When he returned to his ship the next morning, they'd all thought he was dead, and were preparing to leave without him. He reported that he'd found nothing of note, and somehow neglected to make mention of the spring, or the breathtaking, secretive natural wonder behind us. 'Vipers and rude natives,' the official report read. Nobody else bothered to go and check on the veracity of his somewhat-mendacious description, such was his honest reputation and good moral standing."

"So how did he claim it at all?" Ambrose asked. The hot sun beat down on them both once again as they climbed back up the steep path that led toward the main house and the fountain.

"He returned, two years later, as part of one of Charleston's first waves of immigrants. He made his way back to the area, and rowed back out after treating with the locals, who, interestingly enough, had avoided the island for fear of evil spirits that allegedly roamed around on moonlit evenings. They claimed it was haunted by the spirits of their vanquished enemies, looking for revenge in the world beyond this one. He surveyed the island, claimed it for the Lord, the Crown, and, most importantly, for himself—not to mention sizeable holdings on the mainland of Edisto that helped lay the foundation for the Grimball fortune, such as it was before the Revolution and the war between the states."

They stopped walking, now at the top of the hill, and rested by the fountain under the shade of one of the large oaks that graced the plateau.

"You saw the charter upstairs yourself. It was a valuable document to have in those heady times, I can assure you, son. Valuable indeed!"

"I'd say the charter itself is valuable now." Ambrose grinned.

"I have no doubt of it, Mr. Wells, no doubt at all. The library may be the second-best secret on the island."

They both rested on the fountain, though Ambrose had the sneaking sensation it was only he who was resting, while Peyton merely pretended to rest, and was simply thinking.

"Why don't you come inside, and we'll have some lunch? Are you finished with your labor in the library?" Peyton asked.

"Yeah, I've gone through all the documents there. All I really need is a more up-to-date schematic of the island, and the most recent tax documents, preferably last year's with your name on it, but I have a very good sense of the property now. I certainly think there is enough here to adequately value and tax the island appropriately."

"I believe my attorney, Mr. Legare, can provide you with copies of that information." Peyton stood up and began to head toward the main house. "His office is downtown, on Latitude Lane, South of Broad Street, on the peninsula. He's a quirky old man who runs his own hours, but he is usually in his office in the afternoons."

"I was thinking of running out there on Monday. I have plans with Ms. Hampton again tomorrow. She's invited me to go riding." Ambrose couldn't help but sound a bit proud of himself. He was looking forward to it, despite his lack of any significant equestrian skill.

Peyton stopped on the landing of the front porch, and turned to look at him.

"Is that so, my son? Remember your French literature: When a woman strikes the heart, she rarely misses, and often the wound is mortal—or at least permanently etched within the soul."

Ambrose wasn't sure how to respond. He felt he was being warned, and yet Peyton smiled that mysterious Cheshire grin of his. Peyton turned to enter the house, leaving Ambrose with the peculiar sensation that the old man was able to somehow peer into Ambrose's mind, reading it like one of his library books. It would have been unnerving except for the man's easy grace, and his reassuring, calm demeanor.

They entered the house, and walked into the kitchen, where there was a small, oak ice box. Peyton reached in, and pulled out a roasted hen, some mayo, lettuce, and a fresh tomato. The inside of the chest was lined in zinc, and filled with mostly local produce and cuts of game. Curious, Ambrose opened the top drawer, and saw several large hunks of ice sitting within it. He'd read about Victorian ice chests before, but had never seen one, let alone one that was operational.

"This is amazing. I've never seen one in use before. But who brings you the ice?"

"Ah, yes, that is an older piece of furniture. Beautiful and useful. There is nothing so aesthetically pleasing as form and function working in natural tandem together."

He cut the chicken, and the tomato, as he spoke, and then began to slice some French bread, which had been covered in a towel and had sat in a hanging basket above him.

"Captain Delacroix is retained in my employ. He brings supplies once a week or so, sometimes more often if I have need of him."

"How do you call him to let him know he's needed? I mean, there isn't any telephone or Internet connection out here."

"I simply hang a light at the end of the pier; white to let him know to come the next morning, and red if there is any emergency that requires immediate assistance. However, that is a very rare occurrence. With his help, I am very self-sufficient here. We've been working together for decades, and he understands the needs of Wellspring almost as well as I do. He brings firewood in the late Fall and winter, food supplies year round—mostly fresh produce from the local area—ice during the warmer months, and specific needs, such as candles, lamps, tools for general wear and tear, batteries, generators, paint, etc. I do all my own repairs. Despite my age, I feel as fit as a man of thirty. Time has been kind to me, though I attribute my longevity to the cool breezes, clean water, and constant mental and physical exertions of which the island demands of me."

He turned around just as Ambrose finished inspecting the beautiful ice box. In his hand were two plates of chicken sandwiches. He placed his on the table, and walked over to the kitchen sink. He pumped water out of the tap with the hand pump perched next to it, and cleaned off the carving knife before drying it and placing it back in the knife block.

"The drinking water is pumped directly from the natural spring with the hand pumps; however, for bathing I use the cisterns that collect rain water. There are several around the house. There is a compost toilet on the far side of the island by the cliffs, and far from the spring, though Captain Delacroix kindly also takes some waste away with him." He paused to take a bite from his sandwich, as if he was reflecting on his situation. "It is a very pleasant life out here, and in fact, for the right type of person, it is perfect."

Ambrose nodded his head in agreement as he chewed the first bite of his sandwich. It was delicious. The chicken was tender, and the produce fresh and crispy. The tomato was especially tangy and flavorful, while the bread was only a little harder than he would have preferred. *Not bad for all the way out here*, he thought to himself.

"How much do you pay the captain for services rendered?" he finally asked, happily swallowing his first bite.

"We have a gentleman's agreement," Peyton replied, now almost completely finished with his sandwich. Ambrose was almost shocked at how rapidly Peyton had devoured it. Reaching back into the ice chest, Peyton pulled out a glass bottle almost running over with iced tea. He poured two glasses, and handed one to Ambrose.

"It is an almost unbelievable story, but many years ago I saved his life, and the good captain has felt duty-bound to repay the favor in such a manner ever since. I do not pay him in any hard currency, having preserved his life once so many years ago now."

Ambrose stopped eating, and studied the older man. He had spoken with such simplicity, such equipoise and casual quietude, yet the story itself was remarkable, almost unheard of. Was he putting him on? Ambrose couldn't be certain. There was a pause before Ambrose spoke, as Peyton finished his sandwich, and took a long draught of his iced tea.

"You saved his life?" Ambrose inquired.

"Yes, my boy. I pulled him from the roiling sea in a tremendous hurricane. I was thinking up in the cupola"—he pointed above him toward the ceiling with his right hand—"and I saw a little forlorn vessel trying to make it to the mainland. Knowing he wouldn't make it there, and seeing the difficulty of his situation, I hurried down to the *Bucentaur*, shoved off, as it were, and sailed out toward his much smaller, very-poorly-built skiff.

By then the sound was roaring, and the lightning display was phenomenal. The good captain was taking in a considerable and fatal amount of water over the gunwales. He was yelling at God, and bailing water as I approached. As he saw me, he stood up—a very unfortunate decision given the local conditions at that very moment—and a large wave sprung over his stern, knocking him clear into the water just on my port side."

Peyton took another long, final swig of his drink, and placed the sweating glass on the counter before he went on to finish his tale.

"His head popped up right next to the port bow. I hate to admit it, but I almost ran him down. I quickly locked the wheel, ran down the side of the vessel, and snagged his shirt with the boat hook. I pulled him to the side, and with a mighty heave, I hauled his dead weight on to the deck. Dragging the sopping man down the tossing deck, I threw him in the transom, grabbed the wheel, made a tough tack through the gale, and steered my trusty *Bucentaur* back into her natural, safe harbor."

"Was he all right?" Ambrose asked, genuinely interested.

"Well, I got him up to the house with Herculean effort, but he remained unconscious for several days. He briefly woke up to tell me his name and rank, but then slipped into a coma. I thought he'd die on several occasions. There was nothing I could do for the drowned man, as the gale continued on and on. He must have drank some seawater, as he developed a fever and more labored breathing. However, after some nursing and Wellspring hospitality, he started to improve, and ultimately made a full recovery. By the time the hurricane was over, he was up on his feet again, the poor wretch, and I explained to him what happened. He then, in a generous act of thanks, promised to help me in whatever way he could. It turned out he was something of a forlorn and lost soul. His family up in North Carolina had all passed recently, and I often wonder if that was why he was out in the ocean in the middle of such a storm in such a small boat. He told me he'd like to help me, and our little arrangement was thus worked out. He's been in his current capacity ever since, and I must admit, it has been very helpful for me, and I think it has given him motivation he would have otherwise lost. A good job, manfully applied to, can do wonders for a lost sense of purpose."

He smiled wanly at the end of his story as Ambrose finished his tea, and took the final bite of his sandwich.

"I suspect," Peyton concluded, "that he is not as disagreeable as he first appears. Having peeked behind the black curtain of death, he is one of those rare entities who can tell you the value of his life."

"Captain Delacroix? But all he does is drink, and ferry back and forth between here and the mainland. I'm not so sure he values life too highly."

Peyton raised an eyebrow.

"And yet he has never chosen to seek another watery grave, or any other sort of untimely end. Who can judge the value of a man's life other than himself? After all, young man, if I am honest—and I always am—I look at you, and I see melancholy, first and foremost. You have a job you cannot stand, and—excuse my forthrightness and assumptions—not a lot of family or friends to speak of. I knew of your father, and he is passed on. You have never spoken of a woman you miss, or friends whose company you enjoy—not that I have asked—but these are things that often come up in conversation spontaneously, like the weather or the current state of affairs of the local sports team."

Ambrose started to protest, but Peyton cut him off.

"And yet it is clear to me that you have found the sweetness that exists in life. You were so entranced within the library, that your work was not only neglected but blissfully ignored! I believe, if you don't mind me saying, that you love the richness of humanity far more than the average individual of your generation. Perhaps it is simply that you had not, until recently, found an outlet for your passion."

Ambrose smiled in spite of himself. He wanted to walk right out of the kitchen in a show of anger, but he knew the old hermit was right. He had loved the library. He was falling hard and dangerously fast for Cora. He felt reawakened to the mystery of life, the beauty of existence, and the passions that had laid dormant underneath the rote boredom of his recent, everyday existence.

"I take, by your silence, implicit agreement," Peyton continued. "In truth, I must admit to you that I've enjoyed your company immensely as well. Someone to converse with, an old soul, one similar to my own, I confess, to debate ideas and history, philosophy and literature with. This has been a somewhat unexpected pleasure. I wanted to offer you an open invitation to return. I understand your work is mostly concluded, but you know how to reach me now. This library should be studied and loved by a kindred spirit to my own, and I suspect I will not be around forever. If you want to return, Ambrose, anytime, really, I would be happy to receive you out here."

Ambrose was stunned. He would love to return, even just to sit in the upstairs library for hours at a time, and read. Hadn't he been thinking about starting life anew anyway? Perhaps he could quit his job, and return to Edisto full time after all? His heart leapt at the thought.

"It would be incredible to spend more time out here, sir." It was all he could muster in response.

Peyton laughed, and clapped his hands together.

"Well, it's settled then! I am happy that we see eye to eye! Let's repair to the library to celebrate. We have several hours before we can expect the old captain back at the jetty. Tell me, I've been reading Heidegger recently. What are your thoughts on *Being and Time*?"

With that, the two men walked upstairs to the library, happily chatting away as the sun arced across them overhead, and time slipped quickly by without either of them hardly noticing.

Chapter Ten

RETURNING TO THE MAINLAND THAT EVENING, the *Flying Horse* ran into a summer squall that bounced them around a bit, and thoroughly soaked both men on board. Captain Delacroix had yelled at Ambrose to take cover below deck, but he ignored the order. Between the motion of the boat on the waves and the putrid smell of the cabin, Ambrose was afraid he'd vomit, which was the last thing he wanted to do in front of the old salt. It had been hard enough to earn this much respect, and he didn't want to lose whatever credit to his reputation he'd built so far by throwing up at the first sign of foul weather. As such, he got drenched in the sudden downpour above deck, and the two pulled into the dock looking like soaked rats. However, Ambrose couldn't help but notice that the captain had seemed a little proud of him for not ducking in, and he held his usual verbal disdain to a minimum, merely commenting that it was good to know college lads didn't melt when exposed to precipitation. Ambrose had laughed at the man's ingenuity in disparagement, and to his surprise, the captain guffawed right along with him.

"I'd like to return the day after tomorrow, same time, if that's okay with you, Captain," he'd said, after he'd jumped back on to the mainland.

"Yeah, yeah. I suppose if that's what the old man wants, then that's what the old man gets," he'd replied, before ducking back below deck without so much as a goodbye.

Ambrose had taken that as a vague form of agreement, and left it at that. He'd returned to the Anhinga, extended his stay for a few more nights, and grabbed some dinner before heading back to his room to turn in. He'd wanted some rest before seeing Cora again, and he wanted to research horse riding on the Internet so he didn't look completely foolish the next day.

Unfortunately, foolish was exactly how he felt as he walked out to the stables with her the following morning. The doorman, Tristan, had met Ambrose at the door again, but other than his recognition of Ambrose as a human being he'd once met before, his overall tone and posture continued to exude general disdain. Begrudgingly, he allowed him across the threshold, and Ambrose had waited in the foyer for a minute or two until Cora came through the parlor pocket doors at the far end of the luxurious hallway, dressed in riding boots and white pants. She had riding gloves pushed into her back pocket, with a smart, light-blue, button-down shirt tucked in. Noticeably, her splint was gone, and she extended her right hand for Ambrose to shake. She gave him a smile, which Ambrose returned as he fervently shook her hand and wished her good morning. She was beautiful in the soft morning light; however, her riding gear had also intimidated Ambrose, and he realized he really had no idea what he was about to embark upon.

They'd taken their leave of Tristan, and walked back across the front driveway to the right of the pond toward a large stable on the north side of the main manor house. She thanked him for returning, and told him how excited she was to ride this morning, it being the first opportunity she'd had since the accident. She'd been cleared by the hand surgeon at her appointment the day prior.

"I'm glad to hear your wrist is ok after all," Ambrose said.

"It was probably just contused, or so said Dr. Laroia. Anyway, better safe than sorry, and I'm just happy to be done with the whole affair. My horses have missed me, of that I am certain," she said as she slid the large stable doors open, and entered the large structure. There were three stalls on each side of the main walkway through the barn, with five large horses in them.

"This big fella' here, is Samson. Don't need to guess why, looking at his stature," she said. She laughed a little, and patted the big black horse over his muzzle where there was a white, diamond-shaped marking in between his nostrils. He snorted, and kicked his head back in response, and Ambrose was a little afraid by the obvious strength Samson exhibited in that one small movement. He did not want to ride Samson.

"Over here," Cora continued, pointing toward the stall on the left, "is Lily. She's an old timer around here. A more sedate ride. She's calm and cool; just don't expect to be galloping across the countryside on her."

She looked back at Ambrose as she said this, and scratched Lily behind her right ear. Ambrose took a long look at the older horse, and decided that if he had to ride a horse, Lily might be the horse to ride.

"I wasn't planning on it." He laughed awkwardly as she smiled in response, and pointed to the next stall on the left.

"This here is Zorro, because of a marking on his right thigh that looks a little like the famous mark of Zorro. He's a good ride. Fast, when he wants to be, but a little lazy if the grass is looking nice. Personally, I find him a bit stubborn for my liking, but we can usually figure it out, can't we, Zorro?" Zorro snorted in response, and took a couple of steps back, away from the gate to the stall. *Also not for me*, thought Ambrose warily.

"Across from him is my favorite ride, good old, reliable Lucy." She smiled at the smaller, calmer horse. "Hey darlin'," she said, ignoring Ambrose for a moment. "I've missed you, girl. Let's get out on the property today."

"And finally," she continued, "this young colt is three years old, and admittedly hard to handle. Unless you've got some serious skills and more than a little nerve, Mr. Wells, I'd pass on young Marcel here. Needs a little bit more breaking in!"

Marcel snorted and kicked his head back while taking a few steps in place, as if to confirm the reputation attributed to him.

"Which one will you be riding?" Ambrose asked as he warily glanced at Marcel, who seemed to narrow his eyes, scrutinizing Ambrose.

"Which would you like, cowboy?" Cora laughed.

"Well, if I'm honest," Ambrose muttered, looking down, "I don't have as much experience as you. Perhaps Lily?"

Cora smiled knowingly.

"I'll be takin' Lucy out today, and Lily is a safe bet for you. She knows the land better than I do, and won't throw you to the moon like Marcel here. And it's no worry, Ambrose. I didn't take you for some expert equestrian. I'd be happy to show you the ropes. Just glad you wanted to come along, really. I don't get a lot of riding companions out here on Edisto."

Feeling instantly better about the situation, Ambrose grinned and nodded. Walking back toward Lily, he reached into the pen and scratched her behind the ears. She seemed to reciprocate the affection by butting her head against his hand, and Ambrose felt like he'd found his Rocinante.

After a good half hour of Cora teaching him how to put the appropriate clothing on and saddling up the horses, it was quite clear that Ambrose was a total novice. Cora graciously didn't remind him of that, but instead patiently explained to him every step of the process as Lily stood there waiting expectantly while he fumbled with the basic horse tack. Placing the helmet on Ambrose, Cora then showed him how to mount, using Lucy as an example. She then dismounted as if it was the most natural thing in the world, and gracefully sprung back to Earth.

"Now you try," she said encouragingly.

Ambrose took a deep breath.

"Well here goes nothing, Lily!" he managed to say, despite his racing heart and sweaty palms.

"Just put your left foot in the stirrups there, and when you feel you're stable and ready, then swing your right leg back over her, and you'll be sitting in the saddle where you oughta be…facing forward!" Cora explained, and laughed. Ambrose couldn't be certain if she was laughing with him or at him.

He took another deep breath.

"Stay right there, Lily!" he whispered to the old mare. He secured his left foot in the stirrup, bending forward a little, boosted himself forward and upward, and swung his right leg over the saddle. Barely clearing it, he suddenly found himself at a much higher, and somewhat novel, perspective. He grinned at the thrill of it all.

"That's great, Ambrose! Now get your right foot secure, and take the reins with both hands!"

He looked down, and slid his right foot into place before appropriately taking the reins. Lily didn't move an inch.

"You did it!" Cora called up to him. "I think you might be a natural."

"Well, I don't think it would have gone so well on Marcel," he said as Marcel snorted loudly, and paced in his stall, as if in annoyance that he'd been left behind.

"Most certainly not," she said before she effortlessly mounted Lucy. "Now just gently shake the reins, and I'll show you some of the land."

She clicked supportively to Lucy, and the horse automatically walked out of the main barn door toward the back pasture. Before he could do anything at all, Lily followed along, seemingly without a need for any direction from Ambrose. Seeing as they were headed in the same direction, he decided not to make any sudden movements, and wait to receive further instructions outside the barn.

The sun had risen higher in the sky, and was already bearing down on them as Cora patiently taught him the basic commands with the reins. They eased out onto the property at a slow walk, and she pointed out various interesting historical features of the land. She spoke of the old Indian clamshell mounds, and of the early settlers, of when the island was still in possession of the Crown and then an early-American experiment in Republican government, of the ante-bellum period, and the difficult post-war years tainted with Jim Crow, and of the slumbering decades that passed before the South began to slowly recover from what had been years of devastation wrought by slavery and subjugation. Her knowledge of the area, and of her land specifically, kept Ambrose spellbound, and he almost forgot that he was riding a horse for the first significant time in his life.

Crossing a long field, the two riders approached a dense line of trees on the far side that Cora led them to the edge of, and then parallel along, before ducking down a barely noticeable trail between two large bushes. Lily seemed to follow, as if her equine mind knew the path well, and it took virtually no effort for Ambrose to keep up behind them, so long as he didn't fall off the gentle old mare. Once in the forest, Cora called back to make sure he was okay.

"I'm fine!" Ambrose called out. He was enjoying the cool shade cast by the larger trees.

"I don't usually bring my students over here," Cora said. "It's a bit too far for the younger kids, and honestly, I kind of like coming here alone."

"Kids?" Ambrose asked.

"Oh yeah," Cora replied. "I teach dressage and basic riding skills to kids of all ages. It was a passion of mine, growing up out here, and I love to encourage it in the next generation."

"That's great, Cora. I didn't know you taught."

"What'd you think I did out here all year, Ambrose? Sip tea on the porch?"

Cora laughed at herself, and Ambrose grinned sheepishly.

"Of course not," he answered. "I just didn't know, is all."

The woods were darker than expected, as the upper canopy blocked the hot sun, which provided relief for all four living beings passing beneath the old oaks and pines. There were large banana spiders here and there that had created grand, thick webs between trees and bushes. Ambrose had an innate fear of the harmless spiders, but he watched with admiration as Cora simply knocked the few that blocked the trail out of the way with her riding crop. This sent the brilliant web artists scurrying up the remains of their silky supports toward the trees and bushes that offered protection from blue jays and other birds that enjoyed swooping down to devour them this time of year.

Suddenly, the dark, cool shade of the woods opened up along a small clearing that abutted the creek, well upstream from Belleview. The area had a small, sandy embankment that rose above the waterline, and was still shaded by overhanging branches from the larger trees behind them. Small crabs scattered and darted into their dark holes as they approached. Water gurgled by, as a smaller creek emptied into the larger river that eventually flowed past the Hampton's estate, and into the estuary and the sound. Large fish could be seen occasionally breaking the water's surface, and the cool breeze provided sweet relief after the hot trip from the big house. Cora stopped Lucy at the edge, and turned toward Ambrose.

"This is one of my favorite spots on the land. Found it one day when I was a little girl, maybe ten or eleven or so. It's always a little cooler in the summer, and a little warmer in the winter. And the fishing's not so bad either."

"It's beautiful. And that breeze is to die for."

Lily walked up next to Lucy, so that Ambrose's leg was almost touching Cora's. She turned away, and pointed upstream.

"Do you recognize the creek at all?" she asked, facing away from him.

"No," Ambrose replied. He'd never seen this part of the property as far as he could recall. "Should I, though?"

Cora turned back toward him, and laughed a little again.

"Well, it's Raccoon Creek. The same as what passes by your pop's property just about a half mile up in that direction."

"Really?" Ambrose hadn't realized that the two plots of land abutted each other. "You know, as a kid I was up and down this creek, but I guess I didn't make it this far."

"There's an old fence line where the land gets real marshy up there. That may have put a stop to your explorations."

Ambrose pondered that information for a while.

"You know, I vaguely remember something like that. It's been a long time since I thought about it. Had I only known you were hanging out down here as a boy, I might have tried a little harder to get downstream some."

She laughed, and Ambrose felt relieved that he hadn't overstepped propriety with that comment.

"Well, I probably wouldn't have been great company, if I'm being honest with you, Ambrose. I found this place right after my mom died of breast cancer. It was a place where I could come, and be left alone. I don't think I could have told you then, but this was a place where I grieved and threw rocks in anger and finally came to a reconciliation with God." She paused and looked out over the passing water. "It took a while, though."

Ambrose looked down, and listened to the water and the birds singing happily in the woods behind him. He didn't know what to say, but words suddenly spilled out of his mouth like they'd been pulled out of him by some invisible force.

"I know what you mean, I think. A little, anyway. I never even got to meet my mom. She died just trying to get me into the world."

He stopped, and looked up at Cora. He suddenly realized, in some unknowable way, that she had known that already, and before he could stop himself he spoke words that he had never dared utter to any other living soul in his life.

"My pops wouldn't talk about it. He might have mentioned her two or three times the whole time I knew the man. I found a picture of the two of them once in his sock drawer when I was looking for ammo for the little twenty-two I used to go shoot cans with. When I brought it to him, he grabbed it from me, almost ripped it, and demanded to know where I got it from. I had never seen him so mad, and I thought I had pissed him off pretty good prior to that. He put it back in his pocket, like he was hiding it from the world. He kept his left hand right in there with it, turned, and walked out of the room. We didn't speak again for four days. I must have been about thirteen."

"I'm sorry, Ambrose," Cora began to say, but Ambrose just kept on speaking; now that he'd begun, he found he had to finish.

"When we did speak again, he was a few beers in, and told me never to go through his shit again, that the ammo for the twenty-two was in the kitchen drawer where it always was. He had tears in his eyes, and he told me that every time he looked at me, all he saw was her. I thought he might get violent then, though he never hit me, I should tell you. He'd just get a little loud, curse a little, and storm off into his bedroom. Well, on that day, he stood up, and walked over to the front door. He turned, took a long look at me, then just shook his head, and walked out into the yard down the driveway. Took him three hours to get the mail that day. He came back, made dinner, and went to bed, and that was the end of that. I guess I do have my momma's eyes."

He paused, and they both looked upstream again, toward where his old house still sat, half demolished, half grand, looking out over the same black-water creek that flowed unceasingly.

"It must have been tough not knowing her, Ambrose. It was tough when my momma passed away, but I did get eleven great years with her that I would never trade for anything."

"The tough part was growing up and thinking I'd killed her; that somehow my very existence took her from me and pops; that I was at fault for his failings, and my own loneliness. Eventually, I just had to accept that, logically, I couldn't control any of that. The world is what it is, and that's it. It was only after I saw that picture of the two of them, laughing on the pier together, so unbelievably happy—my father happier than I'd ever seen him—that I realized every time he saw me he was reminded of what had been taken from him. That realization was like a salve to me when we would often fight as I grew older. It was what let me forgive the old man for so much, but it also wracked me with innate guilt. I do wish she had lived. Everything would have been different. The lives we might have lived..." He looked away. His cheeks were flushed, and he felt hot and ready to leave to head back to the barn. He'd said too much.

"Ambrose, I have something for you. I've been debating about giving this to you because it's one of my favorite shots of my own mother. I didn't know that you didn't even have a picture of her, but I have to say, you really do look like her. I think it's your eyes, too."

Ambrose looked up, surprised, and wiped his cheeks with the back of his hand. Cora held out an old Polaroid picture she'd taken out of an envelope that had been in her breast pocket. He slowly reached out, and took it from her.

Looking down at it, he saw a picture of two young women, perhaps in their late teens or early twenties, laughing riotously in each other's arms on a city street underneath a gas light. One of the women had chestnut-colored hair and watery blue eyes, and looked much like Cora. The other was a few inches shorter, with black hair and green eyes like Ambrose, and she had an impish grin that belied a quick intelligence and an easy, graceful temperament. Both women were laughing, and it looked to Ambrose like they were practically dancing in the dim light of dusk over a cobblestone street. Ambrose caught his breath, and stared at the picture for at least thirty more seconds before he looked up at Cora again.

"Is that her? With your mom, too? When was this taken? Is that Charleston?"

He completely dropped the reins, and looked back down at the old, somewhat crumpled, Polaroid. Cora let him look at it for another fifteen seconds or so, until he looked up at her again.

"Where did you get this?" he asked. "It's amazing!"

"It's an old shot, probably from sometime in the early eighties. They were best friends back then. Went to school together downtown at Ashley Hall. Mom once told me that they were inseparable. When she died, it broke my momma's heart, I think. I didn't know your mother, Ambrose, but seeing how close she was with my own momma makes me think she must have been one hell of a woman."

Ambrose kept looking down at the picture, as if he couldn't believe he was holding it, and then back at Cora, who was now smiling.

"Can I…?" he started to ask.

"Keep it, Ambrose. It's yours. I brought it out here to give to you, though I do hate to part with it." She paused. "I think it would be better kept in your possession, though."

Ambrose felt like jumping off his horse and hugging her, but instead he carefully put the picture in his own breast pocket after he had given it one final, long look.

"Thank you, Cora. You have no idea what this means to me. Thank you for this."

She continued to smile, and then made a clicking noise with her tongue, and shook the reins a little. Lucy looked up, and started walking around Lily and Ambrose.

"Let's head back in. It's only gonna get hotter out here, and the other horses will get jealous if we dawdle for too long without 'em!"

Lily started to follow automatically, and Ambrose, after checking to make sure the photograph was secure, leaned down to grab the reins that were hanging uselessly. His trip to Edisto had become far more fascinating than he would have ever guessed when he'd originally set out. He ducked to avoid a low-hanging tree branch, and smiled to himself. He felt genuinely happy for the first time in years. The crabs emerged from their sandy dens as the wind picked up along the creek. The banana spiders scurried back into the trees and the forest birds chirped as Lily wended her way along the path. He closed his eyes as they passed back out into the fields, and headed back to the stables. He listened to the wind through the tall field grass, and leaned back in the saddle a bit, trusting Lily to get them back to the barn. He was happy to be home. He was content.

Chapter Eleven

SEVERAL WEEKS FLEW BY in a pleasant blur of sweet and mellow tranquility, as Ambrose spent his days either reading and discussing literature and philosophy with Peyton Grimball out on Wellspring, or learning to ride comfortably throughout the expansive and beautiful grounds of Belleview with Cora. He found himself alternating between the two, often spending his days on Wellspring, and his evenings at dinner with the most engaging woman he'd ever had the pleasure of dining with. He could not think of a happier time in his life, as his only interruptions were the occasional angry and impatient phone calls from Columbia, where Big John had threatened to fire him on more than one occasion. Finally, after about a week of irritating intrusions into his otherwise idyllic new life, he'd gone ahead and made good on Big John's threats, and quit. Both Cora and Peyton had been advising that particular course of action; Cora, because life was too short to be unhappy and he belonged on Edisto, and Peyton, because that monotonous existence wasn't the life of the mind that a man like Ambrose yearned for and needed.

It was the first time he'd ever heard Big John go speechless, and for about five seconds he'd wondered if they'd lost the spotty connection. Taking it surprisingly well, Big John asked about the Wellspring job, and Ambrose promised to bring the report up next week, when he would also clear his desk, pay his last month's rent, and take care of other sundry tasks that inevitably occur when one moves. He hadn't told Big John, but he still needed one final document to complete the report, which was last year's tax information that inexplicably was kept at Peyton's accountant's office in downtown Charleston. When Ambrose had informed Peyton of this last week, the recluse had somehow gotten ahold of the man, and arranged for Ambrose to swing by that Sunday, which is what he was planning to do that afternoon. The date had arrived suddenly it seemed, and Ambrose felt surprised that another engaging week had slipped by so quickly. Cora had only reminded him that it was Sunday when he'd arrived at Belleview at nine o'clock that morning for their now-customary jaunt down toward Raccoon Creek.

"Your riding gets better every day, Ambrose!" Cora yelled at him as they cantered along one of the longer fields on the property. He had graduated from Lily to Zorro, and had taken a real liking to the older gelding. Marcel, who Cora was bravely riding today, was still the rambunctious colt he'd met several weeks prior, and he had no desire to try his luck with him. Zorro, however, proved to be calm, generally responsive as long as the grass didn't look too delicious, and had seemed to take a shine to Ambrose. He, too, felt they had developed a comfortable rapport after two weeks of getting to know each other.

"Thanks!" Ambrose yelled back at her. She smiled brilliantly, and the morning sun on her face, as she sat so naturally in the saddle, made Ambrose think of Annie Oakley, or maybe Joan of Arc. Her beauty and their natural camaraderie had taken Ambrose somewhere he'd never been before. He was in love with her, and he was pretty damned sure of it, too. It was not a childish infatuation, or some lustful desire, but rather a solid, deep foundation, which he knew innately could grow into something complex and beautiful with the right amount of tenderness, patience, and time. It was a large reason why he'd allowed himself to be so quickly talked into staying on Edisto for a bit while he figured out his next career move. It seemed, in his heart, to not only be his best option, but also the most consequential and important decision he'd made in many years. He smiled at her as she reached the far end of the field where the land dropped a little bit and the ground was constantly wet and marshy.

Several egrets flew off, croaking angrily, upset at having been disturbed during their normal morning hunt for frogs and other dietary staples that lived in the murky water. Ambrose quickly caught up, and then reined Zorro in as they approached the wetter lowlands.

"Do you think you're ready to try to gallop?" she asked as he approached.

"I'm not sure about that. Do you trust old Zorro here to not trip into a hole or something?" he asked nervously.

"Zorro knows the land better than I do," she replied. "I'll tell you what, though, if we're gonna gallop, lets hook around this marshy area here. There's a nice, flat little field that you can see on the other side where we could give it a try, but…" She trailed off, and Ambrose noticed a mischievous twinkle in her eyes.

"But what?" he asked, curious.

"Well, it's not Hampton land over there. We're at the edge of it way out here. We'd be on someone else's property."

"Who's?" Ambrose inquired.

She laughed, simultaneously spurring Marcel into the marshy water that headed toward the other side.

"It belongs to you, Ambrose! How many times have I gotta' tell you? We're neighbors! A man really oughta know his own property better!"

Zorro followed Cora and Marcel across the small marshy area, and over to the edge of the field. This particular field had tall, unkempt grass, but was flat for a good fifty yards, all the way across to a line of trees that Ambrose seemed to vaguely recognize.

"If you enter the trees over there, and go about a quarter mile, you'll hit an old, dirt track that should be fairly recognizable to you. It leads off and to the left, toward your pop's old place."

Ambrose studied the tree line, and as he did, he thought he could make out certain landmarks: a large oak tree over toward the left, the remains of an old fence line on the opposite side toward his right seemed remotely familiar to him, like listening to an old song from childhood and thinking you might know the chorus.

"Well, now that you mention it," he said quietly, almost under his breath.

"Let's get a closer look! In order to gallop, all you really gotta do is get into a nice canter, then give 'em a little encouragement, lean low, and hang on! It's a lot smoother than you think. Nothing like trotting was for you." She smiled knowingly at Ambrose. He laughed to himself, but was glad for the reassurance. Trotting had been hell on his balls, and getting the rhythm right with his legs, and the up and down movement of the horse, had been difficult for him early on.

"I'll take your word for it," he said, but Cora had already turned, whipped the reins, and given Marcel a little kick of encouragement, which he hardly needed. Off they went, kicking up a cloud of red dust behind them.

"Here goes nothing, Zorro," he whispered anxiously into the horse's left ear. He leaned forward onto Zorro's neck. The horse stomped the Earth down with one large, right hoof, and it was clear he was eager to give chase. Ambrose could feel his heart pounding as he sat up a little, and shook the reins. As soon as he did, and before he could even give a little kick, Zorro took off. He seemingly skipped right over walking, trotting, and cantering, and went from zero to gallop before Ambrose had become aware of the transition. Suddenly terrified at what he had encouraged his large steed to do, he thought of Cora's advice to lean low and hang on, and he pressed forward and clutched the reins as tightly as he was holding Zorro's thick, muscular neck. Initially closing his eyes, he then opened them at the realization of the smoothness of the ride. The ground beneath him was racing by in a blur of melded, mute colors. Determined to look up, he saw the field racing by him as if he was gliding across it without a care in the world. He could feel the impressive power of the animal underneath him, coursing through Ambrose's legs, and into his heart, almost dictating its tenuous rhythm, as it sprinted across the field, chasing after Marcel who was now just a puff of dust about forty feet ahead of them. Ambrose suddenly laughed with reckless abandon. His entire spirit convulsed in fits of riotous glee as the powerful beast beneath him raced across the open field. Decades of pent-up emotion wrenched themselves free of whatever mental chains they had been enslaved within prior to that moment. Surprising himself in that exhilarating moment, the sound he released from his open soul, as Zorro flew across that South Carolina field, was like a Greek chorus of auditory catharsis. It was the ancient battle cry of the worn-down Celts under Boadicea. It was the sound of the death of soldiers at Ypres. It was the howl of a newborn. It was buried under the cacophony of hoof beats.

Tears streamed down his cheeks, but they were whipped away as fast as he could produce them, disappearing into the atmosphere and adding to the August humidity. In the twenty seconds it took Zorro to cross that desolate field, a fragile man of letters grabbed the reins, felt the wind on his face, and remembered why it all mattered.

At the far end of the field, Marcel slowed down, and behind them by just a few seconds came Ambrose, who was still riding with his mouth open, yet no sound emanated from it. He'd exhausted himself of any remaining expiratory breath to continue his primeval yowl. Cora, who was waiting for him with a grand and handsome grin, seated on a haughty, unapologetic Marcel, suddenly frowned as Ambrose approached. The pounding of equestrian hooves into the loamy soil still pounded through her ears, and she was only vaguely cognizant of the sound her riding partner had released as he had galloped from one universe into another.

"Are you okay, Ambrose? Was it all right?" she asked, genuinely concerned.

Ambrose took a moment to collect himself. *Those are the reins, still in your hands as they ought to be*, he thought. *Still alive! What a trip!*

"Yes, I'm…I'm fine. It's just I've never done that before. It was breathtaking to move that fast. Zorro is amazing." He was unable to continue, keenly aware that a tear had found its way down his right cheek before it had gotten hung up in the red dust that coated his face.

"Yes. It's amazing what these boys can do when they put their minds to it," she said. "Are you really okay?"

Ambrose wiped the errant tear from his cheek, and wiped the dirt and salt water on his shirt absentmindedly.

"Yeah. I'm sorry. I'm fine. Just quite a ride, is all." He gave her an unconvincing smile. "So we're back on the old farm, huh?"

"Yes, Ambrose. This is your land. More than most, I suppose. I hope you'll reclaim it."

He peered into the dark forest in front of him. It seemed as menacing as it had been when he'd driven home to bury the bird he'd hit earlier in the month. The woods here were the same deep Carolina woods they had always been, but for some reason they seemed murky and foreboding, as if it were a place that didn't recognize his authority, and certainly didn't give a damn for his welfare.

"It seems so malicious over here, though," he shuddered, peering into the tenebrous shadows in front of him. "As if I'm not just some stranger who stumbled into the wrong neck of the woods, but rather an enemy invader who should have known better in the first place."

Cora peered into the forest, and then looked up at him, expressionless.

"It seems like all forests seem to me, Ambrose. I hear the morning birds, and Marcel is ready to run home. I don't sense anything unusual. I'm sorry."

"It's nothing," Ambrose said, feeling a little embarrassed for casting aspersions on his own land. "I'd like to gallop again. I never knew how thrilling it could be."

Her bright eyes perked him up enormously.

"Are you done with Wellspring after you head out to Charleston this afternoon?" she asked, as if it was the most natural question in the world.

A little taken aback, Ambrose was unsure how to respond, and spent a few more seconds staring into the woods before he turned back to her.

"Well, technically, yes. But I've enjoyed getting to know Peyton. I love his knowledge and his library. His company is really…enthralling. I've never met anyone like him. I plan on still heading out there when I can. His library alone—"

"Stop it, Ambrose," she said, curtly cutting him off. "There is nothing good that can come from that island."

As Ambrose sat on Zorro, who was now munching weeds nonchalantly underneath him, he was shocked. He was reminded of Auntie Dawes, but couldn't reconcile her words with Cora's.

"I don't think I understand, Cora. Everyone seems to say that, but what could be bad out there? He's an old man with a library, a philosopher who has maybe spurned the world a little—yes, I'll admit it—but what could be bad from—"

"From a man who spurns the world?" she asked. It seemed like she was almost mocking him, Ambrose thought. "Quite a bit, Ambrose. The world must be embraced, not ignored."

"His library alone is a testament to his love of ideas, of the world, of humanity, and perhaps all that's ever been born of it. He may not feel the need to get beers at the Anhinga, but he's certainly not ignorant of the world," Ambrose protested. He hated to argue with Cora.

"To fall in love with ideas is inconsequential if one falls out of love with those who thought of them. If they're just ideas, and nobody benefits from their genius, then I have to ask you, what's the point of living on an island anyway? He's all theory and no practice, Ambrose; all brain and no heart. I've only known you for three weeks, Ambrose, but you've got a heart."

After a confused second or two, Ambrose finally responded.

"He's not heartless, Cora. Just heartbroken, maybe."

"One may lead to the other," she said.

"Not for Mr. Grimball. He's too full of life to not care for it. Really, he's a good guy, Cora," Ambrose said, and smiled. "I'd love for you to meet him. I'm actually headed out there tonight. He's meeting me at eleven thirty. Captain Delacroix is gonna take me out for a late excursion. Peyton says he wants to show me something, but won't tell me what. I can only imagine."

He was genuinely happy, and he was excited to see what Peyton Grimball might have in mind. He figured it was probably something to do with his incredible telescope, and his unhindered view of the constellations from the cupola. There was an awkward moment of icy stillness as Cora looked at her own fingernails, and Marcel kicked the earth, eager to run again.

"Don't go, Ambrose," she said quietly. "Don't go out there ever again. Whatever Mr. Grimball has to show you, whatever it is he's got under his sleeves, it's unnatural. It's best left to Wellspring. Stay here tonight, with me. I have a guest bedroom. You can drive to Charleston, conclude this Wellspring business, return to Belleview, and then get your feet back on the ground here on Edisto." She looked up at him with such tenderness and sweetness, he felt like he might slide off his saddle. "Stay here on Belleview with me. It is a nice place to stay, and I am very good company."

Ambrose felt his pulse speed up, and his cheeks flush.

"Are you sure?"

"Yes, I'm sure, Ambrose. Do I look like the kind of woman who wastes her breath on fools? I won't ask twice."

"Of course. I'd love to Cora. It's just that—"

"Good!" She laughed again. "It's settled then! See you back on the other side of the old Wells field!" She suddenly turned Marcel, and kicked him soundly. "C'mon Marcel! Let's see what you got, old boy!" Marcel whinnied happily, and kicked off across the field. Zorro, noticing that Marcel had taken off, looked up suddenly, as if inquiring whether it was decent for him to take chase. Laughing happily at the unexpected invitation, Ambrose gingerly flicked the reins in Marcel's general direction, and Zorro knew what to do.

Zorro turned sharply to his right to gallop after Marcel, quickly kicked up some dust, and started off rapidly. This time Ambrose didn't close his eyes, or hug Zorro's neck as much. Anticipating the thrill of sprinting across the field, Ambrose felt delighted as Zorro took off after his younger stable companion, determined to catch him. As they flew into a steady rhythm, Ambrose watched with amazement at their incredible speed, and he felt the raw, incredible power of the horse beneath him as it carried him pell-mell across the open field at breakneck speed, faster and faster it seemed, until all of a sudden the horse stopped.

Ambrose, in the span of perhaps two or three seconds at the most, felt an almost unbearable amount of time pass. There was a jarring, sickening lurch to the right. The reins were immediately out of his hands, which he thought to be very disconcerting, as his legs lifted off the back of the horse. He was distinctly aware of missing those reins, as if their presence made the fact that he was barreling along on the back of another animal completely humdrum, but they were suddenly gone, flying in the same general direction as the horse. Ambrose's right foot had slipped out of the stirrup, and his left initially locked in before freeing itself from such a dubious fix on gravity. This, of course, sent Ambrose careening over the head of a rapidly-decelerating Zorro, but now with a violent, rapid torque to add to his nauseating head-over-heals rotation.

Ambrose felt the initial shocking decrease in speed in his gut first. He'd been staring at the horizon, when all of a sudden it snapped away from him, and all he saw was the brown of Zorro's neck, the brilliant green-and-yellow grass, the horizon again, the clear blue of the sky, the green of the grass, a flash of brown as Zorro pulled hard to the right to avoid him, and then more green, followed by a brutal, final blackness. This rapid succession of brilliant color that finished with the terminal finality of black nothingness seemed to pass over the course of eons. Every distinct color, blurry as it was, seemed like an epoch, and he loved them all. His heart, still overflowing with the excitement of galloping across a field, and with new love on the horizon, didn't seem to care that all of a sudden everything had gone terribly wrong.

His ears first heard the wild roar of wind rushing by, and then the noise of a distressed animal whinnying in the morning air before he finally took in the sudden, never-ending buzz of eternity; the same eternity that hides in basements and other quiet places when one turns off the lights, closes one's eyes, and really listens. The low cosmic hum of the metaphysical rang in his ears, and his final thought was that it was all really quite beautiful.

Chapter Twelve

Weak sunlight oozed in through an open window somewhere to his right, and dimly lit the otherwise dark room Ambrose found himself in. He'd woken up sweating, with a constant buzz reverberating through his skull. It was throbbing in rhythm with his heartbeat, which seemed distinctly present as blood pushed painfully through his carotid arteries, and into his brain where every pulsatile movement seemed to echo between his ears. The pain he noticed first; the nausea, second. After lying there confused, with his eyes shut tight, he moaned a little. Surprised at the sound that escaped from his lips, he quickly stopped, and gingerly opened his eyes. He briefly wondered who had kicked his ass so efficiently.

The window was open, and a refreshing southerly breeze blew through it, sending the airy linen curtains billowing into the room. He closed his eyes again for several seconds, and tried to remember what had happened to him, and where he was. It was all very confusing, and the buzz in his ears, and the nausea and the headache, made concentrating on anything other than his heartbeat difficult. He opened his eyes again, brought his hands to his face, and wiped the cold perspiration away from his clammy forehead and cheeks. A gust of wind blew the curtains high, and exposed more light into the room. Ambrose saw that he was in a small, square, little chamber with two windows to his right, the closest of which was open, allowing fresh air and sunlight to come in, while the other was closed, and appeared to be shuttered. He lay in a small single bed with a soft, comfortable sheet upon him. He noticed that his boots had been removed, but he still had socks on. His pants, too, were still on, though he realized he was missing his button-down shirt, and was now wearing the nondescript white t-shirt he vaguely remembered he'd put on that morning.

Something stirred to his left, and he was briefly startled. He jerked suddenly, which only aggravated his searing headache, and he looked into the wan light to see Cora, who was seated in a petite wooden chair next to the bed, looking at him with deep furrows of concern riven across her forehead.

"What happened—" he started to gasp, but she cut him off.

"Hush now, Ambrose," she said gently. There was a quiet authority to her voice, and she took a cool washcloth from her lap, and placed it on to his throbbing forehead. He felt immediately improved, as if the cool rag had just soaked the pain right up. He lay there for a moment with his eyes closed again, his hands now holding the miraculous washcloth to his head. The incessant hum in his ears and the throbbing pain became muted and tolerable, and his nausea dissipated. He took a few deep breaths, and tried to collect himself. He remembered riding Zorro now, and being on the far side of his family's land.

He remembered the thrill of galloping at a terrific speed, and that was it. Everything else was black as midnight.

"Thank you, Cora," he finally managed to say, sounding much stronger. "This helps."

"That's the least I could do, Ambrose. I should have called the ambulance, if I'm honest with myself, but you wouldn't have it. Do you remember any of that?"

Ambrose thought about it again for a moment, but had to admit he was drawing a large blank on whatever it was she was referring to. He shrugged a little, and flipped the rag over.

"I'm sorry, Cora. I don't know what you're talking about."

She smiled sweetly, and Ambrose tried to sit up in bed, suddenly quite conscious that something bad must have happened, and afraid he might have jeopardized things with Cora. She leaned over, and put her hand on his chest. This had the immediate effect of calming him down, and he lay back on the pillow, his head hurting a good bit again from the effort.

"What happened to me? How did I get here? And where are we?"

"You were thrown from the horse, Ambrose. Thank the good Lord you had that helmet on. I do believe it saved your life. The helmet is cracked almost in half! Gave me one hell of a scare."

"Shit. Really?" It was all he could muster in response. He didn't remember any of that.

"Really. I turned around to watch you gallop toward me, and suddenly Zorro pulled up real short, without any warning. I've never seen him do anything like that before. You went up over his head, and spun around ass-over-elbows. Must have gone ten or fifteen feet before you landed—right on your head and shoulder. I screamed, and went right to you, and you were knocked out. Oh, Ambrose, I thought you were dead. I really did!" Her voice cracked a little, and Ambrose felt touched that someone could care for him as much as she appeared to.

"It's okay, Cora. I'm all right." He reached out with his left hand, and felt an aching, deep pain in his shoulder, and winced. He reached with his right hand to rub it, and felt pain over the top of it.

"Careful now," Cora said. "That's the injured shoulder. I think you may have separated it, but I'm no doctor. You can still move it pretty well, which I figure has got to be a good sign." She smiled weakly, and Ambrose felt immensely better. "I jumped off Marcel, and there you were, knocked out, just sprawled along the grass. I checked your pulse, and I cannot tell you how good it felt to know you weren't dead. I was fishing for my phone, when you groaned and vomited right there in the field, so I rolled you over, and you said..." She trailed off.

"What did I say?" Ambrose asked, curious, and a little afraid.

Cora blushed, something he'd never seen her do, and the added color in her cheeks made her appear even more beautiful than he could remember ever having seen her.

"You told me not to worry. That you were fine."

Ambrose sensed that he might have said more than she was letting on, but Cora continued the story before he could pursue it further.

"Yes, and then you very shakily took your busted helmet off, and I told you I was calling the ambulance, but you became very adamant that you were fine, and there was no need. I told you to sit and rest, and not to stand up, and I went to collect Zorro—who was standing a good twenty feet off, looking very ashamed of himself, I might add. I could have killed that old horse if I didn't love him so much. As I walked over to bring him toward us, I saw something slither away in the tall grass, and damned if it wasn't one of the biggest copperheads I've ever seen. I've cut the heads off quite a few with my daddy's old spade. Smelled just like cucumber. I'd have ended its life, too, if I'd had the right tools for the task, but he sneaked off, apparently quite satisfied with having almost killed you. I think Zorro was spooked by that nasty creature, and that's what caused him to stop so suddenly—not that I'm trying to make excuses for the old boy, but it was quite a snake."

"Jesus, I don't recall any of that!" Ambrose was amazed, and felt thankful to be alive.

"Yeah, we walked all the way home, and you just kept telling me the same things over and over again. 'Thank you for the picture of my mother, Cora. It's the finest gift I ever got.' I'd say it was no problem, and you'd smile sheepishly, and then stop to hug me—very sweet, really—and then a minute later, it was, 'Thank you for the picture of my mother, Cora.' I was pretty worried about you, but we made it back, and you felt sick again, so I took you upstairs to one of our old guest bedrooms, and put you in bed. You've been out of it for several hours. I was honestly about to wake you up, and take you to the ER, Ambrose. I think you should get checked out, and just make sure you're okay."

"I'll be all right, Cora. Thank you, though, really. I think I just got my bell rung. I have a bit of a headache, but that's probably to be expected. I'm sure I'll be right as rain for my appointment with Mr. Legare in Charleston later." He stopped suddenly. "Shoot, how long did you say I've been asleep for? I'm supposed to meet him downtown at four thirty!"

"You're okay. It's just a few minutes after two. You were out of it for quite a while. Talking in your sleep, Ambrose. Please tell me you'll swing by the hospital if you're heading downtown this afternoon. It couldn't hurt to have a doctor look at you. You really took quite a bump to the head."

Ambrose looked over at her, and could see she was concerned. He slowly swung his feet over the bed, and sat in front of her. He took her hands in his, and smiled despite the throbbing pain in his temples.

"Thank you, Cora, for being so wonderful to me. I don't know how I'll ever repay you for your kindness. I'll swing by the ER maybe, after I see Mr. Legare, but I don't want to miss that appointment. Mr. Grimball set it up for me with the express purpose of finishing this report. I can take it up to Big John tomorrow, and then be done with the whole business. Then I can move back down here, figure out what to do with Dad's land, and see you and Mr. Grimball on a regular basis. I feel like I've been drifting for so long, and now that I have a plan I want to get started on it immediately." He paused. "I'd like to see a lot more of you, too, Cora. If you'd like, of course."

She smiled, but seemed a little sad.

"What is it?" Ambrose asked, suddenly terrified he may have somehow said something wrong.

"Ambrose, I'm really happy for you, and of course I want to see you—lots of you—and I intend to as well. It's just that I was hoping you'd get away from Wellspring. I know you love it out there, but there's more to it than you think. Willie Dawes and his auntie are on to something. It's just not a"—she paused, searching for a word—"natural place."

She leaned over to her right, and picked up Ambrose's wallet, car keys, and a nasty-smelling little bag of spices and weeds. She handed the objects to Ambrose.

"You took these out of your pants pockets before you laid down. It looks like Auntie Dawes was trying to protect you too, in her own sort of way."

She spoke quietly, as if she was afraid to talk about it, and Ambrose felt a little frustrated. He could not understand her aversion to Wellspring. She hadn't been out there, and although he'd tried on several occasions to convince her that Peyton Grimball was a decent guy who just enjoyed a hermit's life, they had never seen eye to eye on the subject. Ambrose had wisely given up after several attempts, and figured they'd just agree to disagree on the subject. After all, what was it to Cora if he enjoyed going out there? He looked at the old gris-gris bag in his hands. It had torn somehow, and looked a little worse for wear, and flattened. He couldn't remember putting it back into his pants pockets for the life of him, but, he reasoned, he couldn't remember much from the day anyway.

He looked up at Cora, and winced again. The buzz in his ears grew in strength as he leaned over, and dragged his boots from the end of the bed.

"Cora, you're a sensible woman. You don't believe in all this Sea-Island mumbo-jumbo. He's just a lonely old man, and there's nothing unnatural about the place at all. If you'll just come with me…"

He stopped talking. He'd been lacing up his boots, and when he looked over again as he was speaking, he saw Cora's expression, and wisely stopped short.

"I am a sensible woman. Thank you for noticing. But there is more on heaven and Earth, Ambrose, than perhaps is dreamt of in your philosophy—or something like that, anyway. I know this land. I know these people. You have to stop going out there now that this job is done. It will change you, and not for the better."

She stood up, and began to pace the small room, almost frenetically. Ambrose felt confused.

"I'm sorry, Cora. I hate to argue with you. I just don't see it, is all. It's just voodoo and legends and local gossip. He's fine, and this is frankly a little ridiculous."

She stopped pacing, and turned toward him.

"I am not ridiculous, Ambrose, but if you think so, then I will be happy to point you toward your car." Her jaw was set, and there was a fire in her eyes he hadn't seen before, that he would prefer not to see again.

"No. Cora, I'm sorry. I didn't mean to say that at all. It's just that, well, you see, sometimes I speak before I've fully thought everything out, and it's been a tough day. My head is killing me."

The buzzing was now so loud it was difficult to think straight, and his nausea was creeping back. Cora glanced at him stonily for a moment, as if she were thinking, before she exhaled slowly. She walked over, drew up her chair, and placed it in front of him. She caressed his cheek, and then took his hands in hers again. The buzzing died down. The nausea receded.

"Let me tell you something you don't know about Wellspring, Ambrose. I've been debating this almost since we first met, and it's been killing me, eating me up inside. But I think you got a right to know, and I hope you can forgive me for not saying something to you earlier. It's just that it was very clear you didn't know much of anything about your momma and your pops, and those old scars hurt. I didn't want to bombard you with all this until I thought you were ready."

Confused, his heart raced, and with his hands folded graciously within hers, his headache receded as he stared into her eyes, now moist with tears. Ambrose immediately felt sorry for distressing her, and for not taking her concerns—however unusual and irrelevant they appeared to be—seriously.

"What is it, Cora? What is it that would upset me about my parents?"

She leaned back in the chair a little, and closed her eyes. After a brief pause, she opened them again, and sat forward with a look of determination on her face.

"It's a long story, Ambrose, but here it is, nonetheless." She looked into his eyes. "As you are aware now, my mother and your mother were about as tight as two girls can be growing up. They met at school, down at Ashley Hall in the city, as I mentioned. I think they sat next to each other in homeroom, or something like that. Your mother's maiden name—I'm not sure if you were aware of this—was Lassiter. Ella Lassiter. And she was as beautiful as the rising sun, Ambrose. Her pictures don't do her justice, but my momma always said that everyone called her a 'four-alarm fire in August.'"

She smiled, and Ambrose couldn't help but laugh a little.

"I did not know that, Cora. I didn't even know her maiden name—Lassiter."

"Yes, Ambrose. Ella Lassiter. And she and Lucy Beaufain—my mother, of course—were joined at the hip in their school days. My mother would spend the school year with Ella's parents in Charleston, while breaks and summer vacations were spent primarily here on Edisto, at my grandparent's place down the road near Steamboat Landing—riding, shagging at the Friday-night beach concerts, spending time at the beach. They had a wonderful time together, and were thick as thieves."

Ambrose smiled at the thought of it, and reflected on the picture Cora had given him. The two women had certainly looked happy, dancing on that pier, now so many summers ago. He felt sudden unexpected angst as he—for perhaps the millionth time in his life, but for the first time in a while—wished that he'd known his mother. He looked down, and away from Cora as she continued.

"Well, the Thanksgiving before they graduated was to be another great holiday together. My momma was planning on heading to Clemson the following summer, and Ella to the great, white North, having been accepted to Princeton on an early admission. As I understand it, everything started out well, but very early on that holiday, the two of them went down to the Oyster Festival on the pier. As my momma told it to me once, she accepted a dance from David Wells' good friend, and Ella, to be kind, shagged with David Wells himself."

"Is that how they met?" Ambrose asked. "He never told me. At a beach concert?! Oh, Cora, I wish you'd told me all this before. I had no idea anyone knew anything about my mother.

I didn't even know her maiden name."

Cora squeezed his hands, and frowned. Tears welled in her eyes, and Ambrose was infinitely confused.

"What is it?" he asked.

"Ambrose, you gotta let me finish. There's a lot more to this history than you're aware of."

Ambrose hesitated, unsure how to respond.

"Okay," he said.

"David and Ella did hit it off pretty well. I mean, apparently she liked him all right, and thought he was a nice guy, not bad looking either. They started to see each other, and about that time is when my momma met my dad. They went on a few double dates that holiday season, headed into Christmas. They even came out here to Belleview, my pop's estate, and rode the land together, the four of them. My dad and David were from different worlds, but our mothers simply did not do things apart, and it was their friendship, I think, that brought them all together for a few beautiful weeks."

"Well," she continued, "about mid-December, Ella and Lucy went into town together on a simple errand. My momma couldn't even remember what it was they were trying to get at the store when she told me this story before she passed away. Apparently, they stopped at the Anhinga's dock to maybe get some fresh shrimp on the way home, and that was when they saw each other."

"Who?" Ambrose interrupted her, almost unconsciously.

"As my momma told it, Ella looked down the dock, and saw a tall, strange man briskly moving down the pier like he owned it. She told me—and I'll never forget these words, Ambrose, as long as I live and breathe—she said, 'That man walked like a king, and moved like the devil.' Ella met his eyes, and that was it. She would have no other. Poor Davey never knew what hit him. This man, your friend Mr. Grimball, walked right up to her, and just stared at her, like he'd seen a ghost, and your momma, well, your momma just stared right on back."

"Wait a minute, Cora. What are you saying? About my dad? What do you mean, 'poor Davey never knew what hit him'?"

Ambrose felt his head spinning. That damned insidious buzz had returned with renewed fervor, making his bewilderment all the more vertiginous. Cora looked down at their hands, still clasped together, and continued without missing a beat.

"He asked her what her name was, and reached out to touch her cheek, as if to see if she were real, and my momma slapped his hand away. This seemed to break both their spells. They'd forgotten my momma had even existed in that moment. My mother asked who he was, and he told them that he was Mr. Peyton Grimball, of Wellspring Island, a place of which my mother was vaguely aware. Mostly due to local whispers and gossip, more than anything else, and it was a place Ella Lassiter knew nothing about, other than that she wanted to go see it with this man. If there is love at first sight, Ambrose, I suppose that had to be it.

"He asked her out right then and there, and despite my mother's protestations, Ella accepted. She apparently shot my mother a rather unseemly look in the process. My mother went out with the two of them initially, but, as she put it, Ella and Mr. Grimball could not be kept apart that whole Christmas season. My mother had the less-than-enviable job of keeping

Davey Wells at bay, but she was falling in love herself, with my dad, and was spending time with him as well. It must have been a confusing time for all of them. Davey tried to see Ella, but she was hardly ever at my grandparent's place, and after only two weeks of seeing Mr. Grimball—a man considerably older than she was, I might add—she was running off without telling anyone. Well, you can imagine my grandparents were happy to see the Christmas holiday finished, and Lucy reassured Davey that all would be well when they got her back to Charleston, and this little egregious romance would be strangled in the cradle."

"I'm sure that's what happened then," declared Ambrose, but felt very unsure of this, and pulled his hands away from Cora's without realizing he'd done so.

"Ambrose, I'm just gonna put this out there, and promise me you'll stop and think it all through with me."

His head was truly spinning now, and he felt like laying back down. His unfortunate queasiness was beginning to return.

"I'll do my best, Cora. I just feel really badly again," he said. He continued to look away, his eyes shut tight.

"Well, in early January of that year, 1989, Ella stopped showing up in school so much. She would disappear for days at a time. Her mother was calling my mother's parents, and asking if they'd seen her, but nobody had. Lucy knew where she was, of course—being ferried out to Wellspring and back by that boozy old sailor who still deigns to call himself a shrimper. Sometime thereafter, maybe in mid-January, they had it out, and my momma begged her not to throw her life away for that man. They fought, and I think it hurt them both so bad that it scarred their souls. My momma cried telling me about it, as if

I was the first person she'd ever bothered to share such a story with. Shit, Ambrose, maybe I *was* the first one."

"She asked Davey to row out there during their spring break, in a final effort to win her back. When he returned, and my momma saw him the next day, she told me he was as broken as she'd ever seen a man. He never really smiled again, she said. She asked him once, years later when he came to work on the stable, what had happened. He told her that he'd rowed out that afternoon, and they'd seen him coming. She'd met him on the dock. According to him, she looked pregnant, but it was early still. He couldn't be sure. He begged her to get back in the boat with him, to come home with him. He cried out against the wind, for all the good it did him, and your momma kissed his cheek, and told him that she was home already. She said goodbye, and Davey Wells got back into that decrepit row boat of his, and spent his fury and his grief rowing across St. Helena Sound, never to see your momma again."

Ambrose moaned, and lay back down in the bed. He could hardly speak. His voice came out in a strange, sort-of-anguished whisper.

"What are you saying, Cora? What…is this? I'm David Wells' boy. I'm Ambrose Wells. I'm the last of the Wells."

Cora continued, though her voice cracked. She leaned forward, and took his left hand into both of hers.

"My momma never saw Ella again. Her mother, of course, was at first livid, and then distraught, at such a thing. She called Lucy into their house sometime in late March. Ella had been missing for weeks by then. Lucy knew where she was, and told her as much. What else could she have done? Ella's father had passed away two years prior from a massive heart attack, and her mother was never the same after Ella was gone. She called the police, but Ella was eighteen. She was an adult, and had made a choice. The cops went out to the pier anyway, and were met by that boorish sot of a captain, who informed them that he'd be happy to go and bring the couple back to shore for them—which he surprisingly did. At the pier, the couple arrived—Ella, a little more pregnant now—and informed the police of her willful decision. They were in love. She was expecting. She was an adult, and had made an adult decision. The cops left. What else could they have done? She was not a missing person; just a lost soul."

He moaned again, covering his eyes with his right hand, while Cora still gently held his left. Warm, salty tears rolled down her cheeks. Ambrose glanced at her. She looked reluctant to continue.

"Finish whatever this is you started, Cora," he said, gravel in his voice. She nodded in uneager consent.

"Ella's mother's heart was broken. So was my mother's. But Davey Wells' heart was shattered. He was never the same man. Throughout the hot summer he would sit at the bar at the Anhinga, and stare at Wellspring, sometimes from dawn to dusk. And then in late September, along came Hugo. Ambrose, were you not born on September 21, 1989 in the middle of a hurricane?"

Ambrose felt like puking. Or running far from Belleview. He sat up suddenly.

"I was born on the twenty-first, but forgive me if I don't remember the storm. Nobody ever told me about it until I read about the damn thing in fourth grade. I came running home and asked my dad, and he told me, of course, I was, and to go do my homework. And that's all I know, Cora! Apparently, I don't know a goddamn thing about myself! I didn't know that I was born in the middle of the biggest fucking hurricane to hit the Lowcountry in a century!"

He stood up, and walked toward the door in anger. He stopped short, his head spinning, miserably buzzing.

"But *you* did," he muttered.

"Ambrose, let me finish, and then you can run outta here, but you gotta let me finish."

"Well, finish then!" he yelled. He immediately felt badly about it.

She sighed, and her voice croaked intermittently in anguish.

"Hugo came down upon us, and though my momma tried to get him to, that miserable captain wouldn't send a message to Ella. Momma was evacuated with the rest of her family and most of the island, and didn't make it back until almost a week later. By then Davey Wells was taking care of a little baby boy with the help of Willie Dawes and some other friends, and everyone was back at work cleaning up the island. Amongst all the chaos, this fact almost went unnoticed, and by the time the ship was righted again, Ambrose, everyone just took it as a fact that Davey had a son. Papers were cleared, and people somehow didn't ask questions, but I don't know how, Ambrose. Mr. Grimball has a lot of power at his disposal."

"So am I Peyton's son, then? Or was she pregnant before they met?!" Ambrose was desperate, almost reckless with a fury he didn't know he had in him.

"I'm sorry, Ambrose." Cora sobbed, stood, and began to walk toward him. "I don't know. I don't know for sure. How could I—"

"Well, why tell me all this if you don't know, Cora? Why put me through it? I wasn't happy, but I wasn't unhappy. Now what the hell am I?"

"You're the same man, Ambrose. You're the same man I've been falling for since you almost killed me in that damned Bronco of yours. You're Ambrose Wells of Edisto Island."

"Am I?" he cried.

"Yes, you're Ambrose Wells of Edisto Island," she repeated, louder now.

He paused, and looked away from her toward the open door of the room.

"Tell me the rest, Cora."

She exhaled.

"Ambrose—"

"I think you know more, Cora. You told me this much. You have to tell me everything."

She walked toward him, looked up, and began touching his left cheek tenderly with her hand.

"I asked my momma what happened during that awful tempest. She told me that she didn't know for sure, but that she did ask Davey that time in the stable. Apparently, he told her that Captain Delacroix showed up at his place the morning after the storm blew through, before the National Guard had even made it out here yet. He told Davey that he needed him at Wellspring. Davey thought Ella was injured, and went in that old bastard's boat to help, which seemed to somehow weather the gale, but instead of the love of his life, he found a child. He wouldn't tell my momma about what happened between him and Peyton at that time, but he left with the boy, and to my knowledge, never returned to that accursed place for as long as he lived. If you want to know more, there is only one man who could tell you, but I am begging you, let the past go, and let the dead rest. There is nothing—nothing, Ambrose—that can change what happened out there, and you are a wonderful man, not despite it, but because of it."

She kissed him suddenly, and her hot tears rolled on to his cheeks. Ambrose felt his legs melt, and he leaned into the wall behind him, returning the sweet favor with unexpected, pent-up ardor. The concussive buzz of the metaphysical rang again in his ears with such fierce strength that he briefly felt he must pass out, overwhelmed by emotion and shock. He suddenly pulled away from Cora, and looked down into her plaintive eyes. With fear in his heart but conviction in his words, he spoke like a man who, for once, knew what to do.

"I have to know. I'm going back, but not forever. Forgive me, but I'll see you soon, Cora."

He turned, and walked out the door before he could hear her respond, and before he could be convinced of any other course of action.

Chapter Thirteen

Speeding out of the driveway, Ambrose kicked up a dust storm of red Carolina earth that slowly settled on the ancient oaks, standing like sentinels along the grand driveway into Belleview. This added a veneer of fine rouge to their impressive whorled barks, and coated the hanging moss with a dull, reddish gilt. He glanced at the clock in the Bronco, and saw that it was almost 2:30 p.m. He was supposed to meet Mr. Ben Legare, Peyton's consigliore–cum-accountant of sorts, at 4:30 p.m. in Charleston, but that had plummeted in importance behind seeing Mr. P.F. Grimball of Wellspring Island immediately. He rocketed down the road to Captain Delacroix's usual landing, before stopping the Bronco, and then running down the pier. Several grizzled shrimpers had returned from their early morning forays, and were beginning to unload their catch. The hot sun beat down on Ambrose as he almost frantically raced toward the *Flying Horse,* and he immediately jumped aboard—for the first time without asking permission—and yelled out Captain Delacroix's name.

"Captain Delacroix! Captain Delacroix! It's Ambrose Wells!" Hearing his own full name after what he'd learned caused him to cringe a little, which made him all the more upset. "Are you in there? I need to go to Wellspring immediately!"

He paused by the wheel, and waited. There was no answer but for the distant, lonely shrieks of seagulls, and the sound of the breeze whipping loose sails nearby. The horrendous buzz-saw that sounded between his ears was exacerbated by the heat of the sun that pounded down upon him.

"Shit," he muttered, mostly to himself, before he gingerly opened the hatch that led into the bowels of the old boat. The now familiar and awful smell of perspiration, booze, and mold seeped out, as if desperate to be free of the cabin, and was released into the breezy afternoon. It almost knocked Ambrose back, and probably would have had he not been prepared for it by now.

"Captain?" he cautiously called out into the dark belly of the ship. "Are you in there, Captain? It's Ambrose Wells, and I need a lift to Wellspring. I know we're not supposed to meet until tonight, but I could really use a ride right now. Are you in there?"

Silence ensued. He sighed, took a deep breath, and entered the dimly-lit, odiferous cabin. Everything appeared as it usually did. Empty bottles of Navy rum were seemingly everywhere, scattered amongst the hanging baskets, and on the ground and in the galley sink. The smell of rotten fruit tainted the air, and a low hum of flies competed with the concussive buzz in his head for attention. Ambrose resisted the urge to vomit in the sink, and croaked out another call for the captain. Nobody answered.

Determined to be sure that Delacroix wasn't passed out in the stateroom, he quickly passed down the central aisle through the main cabin, and opened the door to what was presumably the head. The stench from that sordid little room almost caused him to lose consciousness, and, it being clear that the captain was indeed not holed up in that filthy cesspool, Ambrose quickly slammed the door shut, cursing. He then proceeded on to the stateroom under the bow decking. This door was locked shut, but a little well-applied force, earnestly given, quickly released the flimsy lock, and the door sprung open to reveal nothing but a pile of cushions and grungy blankets—that looked like they had not been washed in years—several more bottles of rum, and, rather surprisingly, an old, flaking paperback copy of Moby Dick —that looked as if it had been flung into the wall on more than one occasion. There was certainly no sign of Captain Delacroix, and Ambrose cursed again. He turned to leave, when a flash of sunlight peeking through an exposed deck porthole, glanced off the metal of a small revolver that was hidden in the sheets to his left. Ambrose stopped, and picked up the antiquated, army-navy, Colt revolver. It had a nice feel; a pleasant weight in his hands. He turned it over several times, and opened the six-round chamber. It was loaded. Not knowing exactly why, he took the gun, and quickly escaped the awful cabin, armed, but still without transportation.

Back on deck, it was clear that the old Captain had abandoned ship, probably for some boozy port of call. Ambrose quickly disembarked, and jogged back up along the dock to another shrimping vessel that had returned from its morning efforts. Two men were wrestling with a large net on the main deck.

"Excuse me? Do you two know where I might be able to find Captain Delacroix of the *Flying Horse*?" He gesticulated with his thumb, pointing in the direction of the decrepit ship behind them. Both men laughed, and stopped working.

"Delacroix, I've heard of, but I was unaware he had designated himself with the sobriquet of 'captain'!" The larger of the two, sweating men had replied, dropping the net on to the deck with a certain finality that suggested disdain, more than the levity his laughter had suggested. The younger man behind him greeted Ambrose with a smirk that smacked of idiocy and inbreeding.

"Yes, the owner of the *Flying*—"

The larger man cut Ambrose off.

"I heard ya, son! If he ain't dead-drunk on his boat, then I figure he's probably just dead. I'd check the marsh for large and satiated gators."

The larger man paused as the smaller man behind him continued to hold the net and smiled with a shit-eating grin that belied absolutely nothing other than an alarming lack of intelligence. The larger, somewhat more erudite, man on the deck looked down at Ambrose, and noticed the almost-panicked look on Ambrose's face as well as the old revolver in his right hand, and frowned.

"He might be at the Anhinga. Spends a lot of time there, if ya know what I mean, but God knows how he affords to pay his tab, given his work ethic. Don't go killing anyone with that old six-shooter, now."

The young man behind him laughed at what he perceived to be a joke, but it was unclear to Ambrose if the young man fully understood what it was he was laughing about. Ambrose blushed, having almost forgotten the gun he'd picked up, and unconsciously hid it behind his back.

"No, sir, just need to talk with the man is all," he said, feeling silly for having taken the revolver. Uncertain what else to say, Ambrose sighed, and looked at his wristwatch. It was now almost three. In the emotional excitement of driving over here, demanding that he be taken to Wellspring, he'd made up his mind to reschedule with Ben Legare. But now, seeing as it was unlikely he was going to find the old captain, and given he was supposed to meet Delacroix to take him to Wellspring tonight anyway, Ambrose was slowly reconsidering his rash, initial impulse. Perhaps it would be a good idea to head into town, get his final necessary documentation, and put this whole job behind him, that way he could at least focus on the task at hand, and he could confront Mr. Grimball tonight when they met up later.

He thanked the two men for their time, and slowly walked back to the Bronco. The sun was beating down now, and to do anything quickly seemed altogether unnecessary. He decided to turn around, and go see Mr. Legare of Latitude Lane. Perhaps he would know something about what happened during Hurricane Hugo, and Ambrose could then see Peyton Grimball, armed with a little more knowledge than of what Cora had informed him. Could it be that Mr. Grimball was his father? If so, why hadn't he said anything? And where the hell had he been for twenty-six years? And what about his father? How did Davey Wells fit in? If Ambrose wasn't his son, why had he taken him in?

His head spun a little as he got back into the sauna his Bronco had become while it had been parked in the summer heat. Laying his head on the steering column felt good once the windows were open, and the breeze was allowed to flow through the car. He popped open the glove box, and gently placed the revolver in it before he set off, back in the direction he'd initially come from.

The drive into town seemed to pass quickly, though it took about forty-five minutes. All Ambrose could think about was his conversation with Cora, and its potential ramifications on his entire identity. It was almost too much for his mind to fully grasp. If P.F. Grimball was his father, did it change anything in the here and now? Was not Ambrose Wells still Ambrose Wells? If David Wells had raised him, was he not his practical father, for all intents and purposes anyway? These questions, and many more like them, ran laps around his conscious mind as he drove the beautiful, oak-lined highways that led out beyond Edisto Island, through Ravenel and Hollywood, and back into West Ashley on Highway 17. He quickly crossed the Ashley River, and drove around the periphery of the peninsula until he was downtown amongst the hustle and bustle of Broad Street. People were suddenly everywhere, and it took him by surprise that he should be annoyed by their presence, but after several weeks on the island he'd forgotten how the busy milieu and noisy commotion of the city jarred him. Horse-and-carriages full of tourists, bicycles, cabs and cops, cars and trucks, and egregiously loud motorcycles all competed for space on the road. The strong smell of horse piss wafted up from the hot pavement as a particularly large stream ran under his car at the intersection of Broad and East Bay Streets. Loud rap music could be heard rattling the windows of nearby businesses from a low-riding, Oldsmobile Cutlass Supreme, painted a brilliant jade green, that sat two cars in front of him at the light. It took him a minute to remember which direction to turn, but his memory of the bustling old peninsula—that oozed charm, sweat, and palmetto bugs from its subtropical, south-facing piazzas—slowly came around as he thought back to trips into town as a boy, and visiting while in college.

He found a parking spot on East Bay Street just before the Battery began, placed four quarters into the meter, crossed the street, and walked back up along the busy sidewalk. He came across Longitude Lane, and started down the very-narrow little path, nestled between the sides of homes before it opened up into a slightly larger footpath, with even the occasional gas light still standing. From here, he was much less certain, but Mr. Grimball had told him it was a little alley off of Longitude Lane that was perpendicular to it—hence the apt title. Ambrose slowly walked down the path until it opened up on the other side at Church Street. He saw no evidence of any offshoots that might resemble Latitude Lane. Checking his watch, he noted it was a quarter after four, so he was still a little early, which was a relief. The heat of the afternoon was approaching its sultry zenith, and he was beginning to sweat through his shirt as he turned, walked back up the pathway, and searched on both sides for a possible alley he'd missed on his first pass. He then noticed something he hadn't seen before.

In between two, high brick walls were several palmetto trees that had grown to a remarkable size. Their large fronds had obscured a small passageway that lay between the brick walls. He walked over, and brushed the fronds out of the way. Looking down, he saw an ancient, well-trodden flagstone with the words "Latitude Lane" faintly inscribed into the rock itself. In the narrow, dark space, the humid air seemed to shimmer in the heat, as if a raincloud might form within the alley itself, and he realized he'd have to almost walk sideways between the two buildings in order to squeeze himself through the cramped, tiny passage. *This guy must not have a lot of other clients,* Ambrose thought as he took a deep breath, brushing past the palmetto bushes into the steaming little alleyway—hard-pressed to even call itself a lane.

He slid down about twenty yards, catching his shirt on the rough and dirty brick several times, before he stopped at a small wooden door that looked as if it entered some space that must have connected to one or both of the buildings on each side of him some time in the distant past. The door was small and nondescript, with a ringed door knocker that had been placed about chest-high. The ring sat in the mouth of an iron bird rising from a nest of rusty ashes affixed to the door. There were no windows to peer into, and Ambrose was briefly unsure how to proceed. He looked up and down again, and saw yet another pale-gray flagstone, this one cracked and worn by the never-ending destructive forces of time and erosion. Ambrose got down on one knee to read it, and on it, barely legible, were the words "Benjamin Legare, CPA."

He knocked tentatively on the door, and waited for about thirty seconds. He was sweating clearly through his shirt now, and he could feel sweat dripping off his nose, and rolling down his legs into his socks. A mournful cicada started buzzing loudly, and the only relief Ambrose had was the natural shade of the cramped, little passageway he found himself in. With no reply, he went to knock again, and as he did, the door suddenly creaked slowly open, and his knuckles just grazed the door. It opened at such a languid pace that Ambrose wondered if a breeze had accidentally blown it open, though he certainly could not feel one.

"Hello?" he asked as the door gradually opened, only to reveal one of the most antediluvian, aged, old men he'd ever laid eyes on. The man standing in front of him was short and stooped, and stood maybe five feet tall on a good day. He had black skin that had slowly turned to a dark gray over the decades, like black leather that had been left in the sun. His eyelids practically hung over his eyes, which gave him the appearance that he was sleep walking, and his stubble was white, which gave his face a speckled appearance. His hair was mostly gone, but what few wisps remained were the same pale white color as the stubble on his face. His cheeks looked like they were falling off his skull, and the man had an overall emaciated appearance. His clothes seemed to hang off his body, as his skin did off his skeleton. He wore nice, pressed, gray pants with a white button-down shirt that had the sleeves rolled up. Ambrose could see every tendon in his forearms, and was afraid that if he shook the man's hand, it might snap off in a puff of ash and dust. His every breath rattled with inspiration and wheezed with expiration, and reminded Ambrose of a sleeping bloodhound with a head cold. So alarming was the stranger's appearance, that Ambrose reflexively stepped backwards into the stifling alleyway before he remembered his manners, and composed himself, extending his hand.

"Hello," he finally managed. "Are you Mr. Benjamin Legare? My name is Ambrose Wells. Mr. P.F. Grimball of Edisto Island sent me. I have a four-thirty appointment."

The man looked at him, and delayed speaking for so long that Ambrose thought he might be talking to an apparition. Finally, the old man smiled, revealing what he figured had to be a sparkling set of dentures, and he nodded in the affirmative.

"I am the man you seek, Mr. Wells. It is a pleasure to make your acquaintance. Mr. Grimball has said many kind words about you, and he is not a man to suffer fools."

His voice barely rose above a whisper, and it seemed to wheeze out of his lungs with just the requisite amount of carbon dioxide. Ambrose had to lean down to hear the man, especially given the loud cicada buzzing somewhere behind him in the alleyway.

"It's a pleasure to meet you, sir," said Ambrose. He shook Mr. Legare's extended hand, which was unnaturally cool to the touch, but the old man's warm smile made up for it, and Ambrose felt at ease despite the man's ghastly appearance.

"Come in! Come in, then, my fine, young friend," the older man said. He turned on a twisted cane that had a worn, silver handpiece he leaned on with his right hand. He slowly entered the dark, musty room, and Ambrose followed him in, shutting the door behind them.

"Please have a seat at my desk, Mr. Wells. This should not take long. I don't want to take up much of your time on this fine afternoon. I have found that it's always better to conduct business when seated and comfortable. When the body is at ease, the mind is free to think."

He nodded to a cracked leather chair that stood in front of a wide mahogany desk. As Ambrose's eyes adjusted to the light, he realized that he was standing in a room that was covered in dusty bookshelves. From floor to ceiling were books, most covered in the fine, gray, detritus of time, in some places, inches thick and connected with cobwebs. There were large stacks of them everywhere, and the only light in the room emanated from three small candles, two of which sat on Mr. Legare's desk, while the third sat in a holder that jutted out from the wall behind the desk. To his left there was nothing but aged tomes that filled row after row of neglected shelves, but to his right there was a small set of pocket doors open, revealing an equally dark room, and more, vast piles of legal proceedings and tax codes scattered helter-skelter. There were no windows in the place at all, as far as Ambrose could tell, and the only light was the weak candlelight that shimmered off the books and added to the stagnant heat. It felt like being in a tomb. The heat was almost oppressive, and Ambrose would have preferred to stay in the alley now that he was in Mr. Legare's office.

"I presume you are simply here to collect the final documents that the state requires to formally assess the property at Wellspring Island?" The old man wheezed as he slowly sat down behind the marvelous mahogany desk.

"Yes, sir," Ambrose replied, hoping to conclude his business quickly in the stifling office. He felt a little uneasy in the dark, hot, powder-keg of a little room they were seated in. "Mr. Grimball, for some reason, did not have copies of the most recent tax records in his library, though he certainly had most everything else."

Ambrose attempted a wan smile, but was not sure that Mr. Legare could see very well in the dim light of the room, or through the opaque cataracts that clouded his corneas; a different type of dust that settled with age.

Mr. Legare looked up suddenly from the documents he had removed from the desk drawer in front of him. He looked surprised, which in turn, surprised Ambrose.

"You don't think this is just a copy of his tax records, do you, son?"

Ambrose hesitated to speak. "Well, sir, I was under the impression…"

"This is Mr. Grimball's trust. We have only finished drawing it up this week. He had to know for sure, you see." The old man appeared to arch a white eyebrow up into the mountain chain of wrinkles that constituted his forehead.

"Know what exactly?" Ambrose replied. He loosened his collar in the oppressive darkness, feeling vaguely uncomfortable.

An airy type of punctuated expiratory effort emanated from the old man, and Ambrose realized he was laughing.

"Oh, my boy, but you haven't figured it out yet, then! Do you think your arrival on Wellspring was a happy turn-of-fate? A cheerful coincidence, perchance?"

He sputtered and gasped, and stopped talking. Ambrose feared he might have died all of a sudden, in paroxysms of mirth at Ambrose's expense.

"What do you mean, sir? What is this about? This trust? It's the first I've heard of it."

"Son," the old man said, looking up—thankfully still breathing in order to explain himself. "A man like Peyton Grimball doesn't need to have his property assessed by the state. The state of South Carolina had practically forgotten he existed, which of course has long been the desired goal. I had to remind them! And in so doing, I made a small request of your former employer that he send a very specific man for the job, one who was uniquely qualified for work on Edisto writ large, and Wellspring Island specifically."

He smiled, sphinxlike now, and Ambrose was beginning to feel his anger rise, like warm bread in an oven. He certainly felt as if he was in one.

"How did you know that I'd quit? Have you spoken to John?"

"Big John Connolly, you mean?" The old man cut him off. "An obtuse tool of a man, but a useful one for our purposes. Didn't ask many questions. Seemed to like the idea of sending a local down to get the job done. He seemed happy to have you out of the office, and very amenable to a quiet lining of the proverbial pocket, I daresay."

Ambrose shook his head, flabbergasted.

"Do you mean to tell me you set this up? This whole gig was your idea?"

"Not mine! Oh no, but my employer's, of course. I simply conduct the orchestra, but I do not deign to write the music," he said. He leaned back in his chair, and crossed his warped and gnarled fingers together like wild kudzu.

"But why?" Ambrose asked, the realization slowly beginning to coalesce in the back of his mind, like a word on the tip of the tongue, almost formed.

Mr. Legare suddenly leaned forward over the documents on the desk, and the candlelight illuminated his gray, and nearly completely opaque, corneas, which startled Ambrose.

"Why do you think?" he asked Ambrose.

Ambrose paused, afraid to speak for a moment.

"Because I'm his"—he paused again—"I'm his son? Is it true, Mr. Legare? Do you know? I need to know!"

"Only one man knows for sure, Mr. Wells, but when you close your eyes at night, what does your soul tell you? When your heart speaks to you, what does it say?"

Ambrose knew the answer, but avoided the question.

"I think you know what it says, Mr. Legare."

"I am too old to presume to know what lies in the hearts of other men. That is a young man's mistake," he replied simply, and pushed the leather folder across the dust-covered desk toward Ambrose. "If you must hear it aloud, then you must ask my employer. I believe tonight will be a good opportunity for you. He will be leaving soon thereafter, perhaps never to return, as I understand it."

The leather folder felt cool in Ambrose's hands. His heart was racing. Sweat was now dripping down his forehead, and collecting in pools along his clavicles and in his jugular notch.

"He is leaving for good? Where to? And when?"

"You didn't know he was leaving? He hasn't made this somewhat obvious? Is the *Bucentaur* now not loaded for a trans-oceanic voyage? Has he not been working on preparations for such a trip for at least a month? I'm sure Captain Delacroix could attest to the same."

"The trust then?" A wave of realization and understanding passed over Ambrose as he opened the leather folder, and looked at the title page to the trust.

"It is bequeathed to you, of course. The whole island, and all contents residing therein—except the *Bucentaur*, of course—the house, the library, the docks, and associated smaller structures have all passed to you as of midnight tonight," he said. "And, of course, the fountain," he added knowingly. "You must take great care of the fountain, Mr. Wells."

Ambrose's head was spinning in the torpid heat of the room. The candlelight began to blur and meld together. He found it difficult to read the words on the trust, but was able to make out his own name. He looked up at the ancient barrister. Mr. Legare was sitting back in his chair, his face covered in a black shroud of darkness. From this void, Ambrose heard him softly speak.

"My work is finally done. You will pass that on to John Connolly, and all will be well with the powers that be. I have arranged it as such. Ah…"

"What is it?" Ambrose managed to get out.

"There is one final letter. It is for you, and is supposed to be with the trust. It is just in the back. Let me procure it for you."

Benjamin Legare slowly—as if worn down like Atlas, but by the weight of time rather than the mass of the earth—and creakily stood, leaning on the desk as he did so for support. Ambrose laid the leather folder down, and stood to assist him, but was quickly waved off.

"Now, son, don't bother yourself. I will be right back, and then our business will be concluded."

He took a few hesitant steps, feeling the edge of the desk for assistance, and then turned, painfully hunched forward, and began to walk. Every step appeared to cause him agony in some used-up joint as he slowly padded off through the pocket doors into the other room. Ambrose waited in silence, and truly felt as if he were trapped in a mausoleum. The silence seemed to be interrupted by the occasional flickering of the candles, though they made not a sound. Yet the air was so still that even this silent nod to the passage of time was so infrequent that it seemed like an illusion.

Ambrose now felt certain that Cora had been honest with him. He realized the island, the fountain, the library even, was all his! He'd have a place to stay on Edisto after all. It was all like a dream come true, and yet he felt unsettled. The truth of his parentage had jarred his soul. He had to hear it from Peyton himself. He vowed to confront him before Peyton left—wherever he was going to—and to hear the words spoken from his lips. He needed that validation, and felt that it was owed to him. Suddenly he heard a thud, and a soft grunt, almost indistinguishable behind the sound of falling books.

"Mr. Legare?" Ambrose called out nervously, standing up. "Are you okay, sir?"

There was silence again, as if nothing had happened, and for a brief moment or two Ambrose thought he might have not heard anything at all. The interruption of his thoughts had been a reminder that time, in fact, did continue to relentlessly move onward, even in this still tomb of an office. He heard another soft groan, this time much more clearly, and throwing caution to the wind, Ambrose decided to check on the old man.

He walked through the pocket doors, and noticed one more candle lit that sat along the wall in the far corner of the room, casting the only light available upon the scene. He walked quickly, and stumbled on a small pile of books that he hadn't noticed were lying in front of him in the sepulchral twilight. Cursing, he caught himself, and walked forward a little further before almost stumbling on Mr. Legare, who was now lying on the floor, one hand clutching his chest, with the other at his side, a white envelope in its grasp.

"Mr. Legare! Are you okay?"

Ambrose thought him to be dead until another soft groan passed through his pallid lips. He knelt down to check on him. The older man was whispering something inaudible. Ambrose leaned forward to listen to him, and placed his right ear directly over the man's cracked, cyanotic lips.

"The envelope is yours. Take it now. It is all that remains to be done."

He continued whispering, even less audibly, and Ambrose looked up, over at the man's left hand. He took the envelope held within it.

"I have it. Don't worry. Let me call an ambulance for you, sir!"

He pulled out his cell phone. It glowed like a bioluminescent organism in a dark cave. It shocked him, as he quickly went to dial 9-1-1.

"Nine-one-one operator. What is your emergency?" he heard almost immediately.

"I'm with an old man who's collapsed. He needs help!" Ambrose practically shouted down the line, looking down at Ben Legare, whose very faint chest movements suggested he was at least breathing.

"Where are you located, sir?"

"Um, Latitude Lane?" he said, almost in the form of a question, unsure whether it existed on most maps of the city.

"Do you mean Longitude Lane, sir?"

"No, I mean Latitude Lane, ma'am," he replied angrily, worried that any delay could prove fatal for the old lawyer who was lying on the ground in front of him.

"Sir, that address does not exist. We can be at Longitude Lane in three minutes. Are you at that address, sir?"

Ambrose went to scream profanities into the phone, but stopped short. He realized he could just take the man out of his office, and be on Longitude Lane in a heartbeat.

"Yes, ma'am. I'll be there with him. Please come at once!"

He hung up the phone, not wishing to carry on the conversation further. He had to get Mr. Legare outside. He bent down to pick him up, and suddenly his aged hand reached up, and grabbed his sleeve, scaring Ambrose to no end. He stared down at the stricken man, whose cloudy eyes seemed to stare back, unblinking, through the darkness—through Ambrose even—penetrating his soul.

"Oh night, spread thy wings over me as the imperishable stars." The dying man spoke clearly, and Ambrose stopped trying to lift the man, and stared back at him.

"It's okay, Mr. Legare. Help is on the way. We just have to get you outside! I'm gonna lift you up and—"

Benjamin Legare inhaled rapidly and audibly, which caused Ambrose to stop his efforts once more. The ancient man suddenly smiled grandly. His opaque eyes widened as several tears streaked down his cracked, dusty cheeks, and as he exhaled the last remnant of life from his body into the stillness of the room, Ambrose heard him distinctly speak one last time.

"Oh! Oh! It is more magnificent than I had ever dreamed!"

Chapter Fourteen

THE SIRENS WERE ALREADY DISTANTLY wailing through the heavy purple dusk as Ambrose dead-lifted the old man out of the dark and dismal office. Even though daylight was receding, it seemed as if he'd been reborn when he'd stepped out of that dusty, crowded legal crypt. Mr. Legare seemed to have stopped breathing, and in a panic now, Ambrose had thrown his body over his left shoulder, and stumbled out into the humid gloaming, down the narrow alleyway onto Longitude Lane. The dying lawyer was surprisingly light, and Ambrose thought with a brief pang of guilt, *He's nothing but skin and bones, and dusty old clothes.* He turned left, and carried him down the lane to Church Street.

Stopping at the intersection of Church and Water Streets, Ambrose looked right, and saw the blaring ambulance carefully negotiating its way past startled tourists and parked cars. It stopped in front of him, and two men jumped out and quickly came over; one with a large bag of God-knows-what in tow, both grim-faced.

"What's goin' on?" said the taller of the two men as he knelt down, placing his left index and long finger over Ben Legare's neck.

"I'm not sure," Ambrose replied tentatively. "He just collapsed in his office, so I called."

"Is he breathing?" interrupted the stockier of the two men as he opened his bag, exposing a rather large device. Quickly unbuttoning Mr. Legare's shirt, the first man used his stethoscope to listen to his chest.

"He's not breathin', Mack, but he's got a weak carotid. You got an LMA on you?"

"Got it right here," the sturdy little companion said calmly. Ambrose took a step back from the stricken man on the street, and the efficient little warriors who had come to help. The second medic pulled out some type of clear, plastic tube that had a couple of strings hanging off it, and a large, plastic flange at the end that reminded Ambrose of photos of pitcher plants in Malaysia he'd seen in encyclopedias as a boy. He knelt by Ben's head, and using some type of curved metal object, he opened his mouth, and shoved the plastic tube into it. He then hooked it up to a purple bag that was itself hooked up to a small green oxygen tank. The little medic squeezed the modern bellows, and the first medic listened over Ben's chest as Ambrose watched it faintly rise with each squeeze of the bag.

"Nice job, Mack," the older, silver-haired man said. "Let's get him on the backboard and loaded up."

He looked at Ambrose as the younger man ran back to the truck, opened the back doors, and removed a large yellow backboard.

"What happened today?" he asked simply and directly.

Ambrose stuttered a little.

"He, well, you see, I was here on business, and I just met the man, and he went into the back of his office to get a piece of paper for me. Then I heard him fall. I went—"

"Okay. It's okay. He's still got a pulse, but he's sick as hell. We're gonna take him down to MUSC right away. You got a name on this guy?"

"Yeah, yeah," Ambrose said, trying to recover his senses. "His name is Legare. Ben Legare. He's got an office just over there on Latitude Lane."

"Longitude Lane, you mean? You from around here?" the tall man said. He continued to push on the purple bag every few seconds, causing Ben's chest to rise and fall. In between pumps, he slapped some cardiac leads on to Mr. Legare's chest that were hooked up to the machine that had been hiding in the blue bag. Ambrose could see the green squiggly line that anyone who watched medical dramas knew to be a heartbeat. That made him feel better as he tried to concentrate on the question.

"Am I…yeah. I grew up here, man!" He was a little offended. "Latitude Lane. Just there, down Longitude Lane on the right."

"Ain't no Latitude Lane, brother, and my family's been living here since before the Fall, if you know what I mean. Just Longitude Lane."

Ambrose, frustrated, decided not to continue the argument.

"Is he gonna be okay?" he asked.

"Not sure, friend," said the older medic. The younger one

plopped the hard, plastic board down next to Mr. Legare, and grabbed his neck. *Psst,* went another push of the purple bellows. His chest rose. His chest fell.

"One, two, three!" they shouted.

Both men slid Ben onto the backboard, and the younger man went about buckling him in while the silver-haired man squeezed the bellows again for good measure.

"What's his name?" the medic asked curtly, a second time, as he put medical tape around the tube sticking out of the lawyer's mouth, and plastered it to his sagging, dry cheeks.

"Like I told you, Ben Legare. He's a lawyer in town. Works for a client of mine. I was here on business. He just collapsed."

Ambrose spoke quickly, feeling guilty, as if he had somehow caused this to occur.

The stocky medic—Mack, apparently—looked up after securing the last buckle around his legs.

"You're not family then?" he asked Ambrose.

Ambrose shrugged helplessly.

"No sir. I just met him thirty minutes ago. I'm sorry, I—"

"Let's get him in the truck," the older man said brusquely. He placed the large blue bag that held the machine with the green line running across its screen by Ben's sorry-looking feet, both of which were still firmly ensconced in fading brown loafers, with completely worn tread. Ambrose had the peculiar thought that aging humans become more lined, while their shoes become less so.

"You're headed to?" Ambrose asked uncertainly, as if perhaps he should not be talking at all.

"MUSC," said the younger man now. "One, two, three!"

Both men lifted the backboard with Ben Legare clipped in on top, Mack at his head, with the older man at Ben's feet, keeping an eye on the wavy, little green line.

"Let's get a blood sugar once we're on the road. And call over to let 'em know we're comin'," he told his compatriot.

Before Ambrose knew it, the doors were shut, with stocky Mack and Ben in the back, and the older man hopping into the driver's seat.

"Should I follow you?" Ambrose asked, unsure how to proceed.

"If you could, that'd be great," the medic replied, looking over at him from the window. "ER doc might wanna chat with you, if you've got a minute."

"Sure," Ambrose said. "Of course."

"See ya over there, then," he said.

The sirens kicked back on, and the ambulance whooped and hollered down the cobblestone street as fast as the aged road would allow them to go. Ambrose watched as they turned right on Meeting Street, and disappeared, with only the loud sirens betraying their existence.

Several gawking passersby shook their heads and wandered off, and Ambrose headed back toward his car. He opened the door, and let the hot air dissipate as best it could into the almost-as-hot evening before he jumped in, and rolled down the windows. His heart was still racing a little, and after turning the engine over, he sat there for several minutes regaining his composure. The Wellspring Island trust, his sudden and unexpected inheritance, was now securely in his pocket. The remarkable confirmation, by two people now, of what he felt was true in his heart regarding his parentage was all quite shocking. He hoped the old man would live. His brief interaction with him, before his unexpected collapse, had been so interesting, and there were so many questions Ambrose had wanted to ask him, especially about Peyton Grimball and his mother. He felt the old man knew a lot more than he'd had the opportunity to divulge. *C'mon Mr. Legare, live!* he thought as he pulled out into traffic, and headed over to the city's main medical campus several blocks away.

It took him about thirty minutes to find a parking spot, and then wander over to the main emergency department waiting room. It resembled a melting pot of humanity, and he felt burdened with sickness and grief just walking through the room to the main desk. A man in the corner was vomiting with an alarming amount of body language, and a large volume of emesis was going into a little blue bag that he held in his left hand, most of which hit the mark, though a fair amount spilled over on to the floor. Several wailing babies made their presence known, and seemed to compete with each other in volume and ear-splitting shrillness. An old man with holes in his socks and ancient sneakers hiding beneath his seat, smelling strongly of body odor and rubbing alcohol, was actively removing his one remaining sock. As he did so, a shower of dead skin sprinkled down upon the floor, causing the well-put-together woman with pearls on to his right (owner of one of the howling infants) to get up quickly to escape to a far corner of the room by an empty water cooler. Electric-blue police lights flickered through the windows, reflecting off the glass that separated a very dour-looking matron who seemed to be in charge of this bedlam. Ambrose cautiously approached the window.

"Taylor! Charlene!" came a banshee shriek from his right as a nurse poked her head out, hollering into the cramped room like a Parris-Island drill sergeant. Ambrose almost jumped, not expecting such auditory violence, despite the general clamor of the waiting room. The matron in front of him continued typing into a computer as if he, the banshee, and the sea of humanity in front of her didn't exist. Ambrose cleared his throat.

"Taylor! Charlene!" yelled the nurse again through the open door to his right. This time a laughing young woman came barreling through the main door, several friends in tow.

"That's me, ma'am. Sorry, I was just having a smoke. Been waiting in here for a minute, you know?" She laughed with a familiar wink, and the nurse said nothing as she held the door for the young woman.

"Only one friend at a time, Ms. Taylor," the nurse said.

"Oh, okay," she said, and waved off three friends who immediately vacated the area—wisely, thought Ambrose, as a diminutive, very pregnant, fourth friend waddled after the other two women across the threshold, and into the main department.

"I hear you're worried you might be pregnant." Ambrose heard the nurse sigh as the door clicked shut.

"Can I help you, sir?"

Ambrose looked down, surprised to see that the elderly woman behind the computer was staring up at him now expectantly.

"Um, yes. I was told by the ambulance workers to follow them in. I'm"—he paused, unsure of his relationship to the stricken lawyer— "friends with a Mr. Ben Legare?"

The older woman said nothing in response, and instead began clicking on the computer again for several seconds. Ambrose wondered if he should provide identification or something.

"You mean the old guy they brought in about half an hour ago, son?"

"Well, I think so. His name is Ben Legare. He came by ambulance. He wasn't breathing." Ambrose didn't know what else to say.

"Yeah," she said, and sighed into her keyboard as if it were responsible for the lassitude in her soul. "He's back in here. You family?"

"No," Ambrose said, repeating himself, and silently wondering if anyone over the course of the last hour had bothered to look at he and Ben before asking that question. "I'm a friend, is all."

"Hold on a minute, hon," she said as she grabbed the phone to her right, and quickly began dialing a number. "Yeah, Michelle. I got a guy here says he's friends with the real old guy they brought here about thirty minutes ago." Pause. "Yeah, I figured as much. What do you wanna do?" Another pause. "Yeah, okay. Send Lily back then, would you?

She hung up the phone, and for the first time, looked in his eyes.

"He's here. Lily'll come, and bring you back to him. Just give us a second."

Before she could hardly finish speaking the door opened again, and a pretty girl with too much makeup, but a winning smile, stood on the other end. She looked over toward the main desk, past the homeless guy with the shedding feet, past the wailing children, past the unnecessarily loud vomiting man in the corner of the room, and nodded toward Ambrose and the matron behind the computer, as if to say, "Is this him?"

"That's Lily. She'll take you back," the older woman said, before returning to stare vapidly at the computer monitor.

"Thank you," Ambrose managed to mutter. She didn't appear to hear him, and he was relieved to walk over to follow Lily into the main department.

"Come with me, sir," she said, smiling and turning around to lead him through the department. She brought him to a small room with staid furniture and a clock that was an hour slow, and asked if he needed any water or anything at all. He declined, wondering why he was being placed in a room by himself. Lily left him there, and Ambrose sat motionless, thinking about the incredible series of events that had happened today. He checked his watch: 5:56 p.m. He still had time to get back to the pier on Edisto at 11:30 p.m. Whether Ben Legare was dying or not, Ambrose was not going to miss that ride out to Wellspring, and he knew Captain Delacroix wouldn't wait if he showed up late.

Suddenly he remembered the white envelope that Ben had given him as he lay dying in the gloom of his dusty office. He reached into his pocket, and pulled out the envelope, crumpled now after having been crunched in Mr. Legare's hand, and then folded in half and stuffed in Ambrose's pocket. He unfolded it, and straightened it out as best he could. The top left had a stamp on it that read "Mr. Ben Legare, Esq.," with no further address or information at all. The center of the envelope had Ambrose's name written in florid, black cursive, followed by

Wellspring Island written beneath it. Curious, he looked around the room to see if anyone else was watching, and immediately felt stupid for having done so. He gently tore it open, and pulled out a lengthy letter written in the same marvelous script.

My Dear Ambrose,

It is with much confidence and pride that I write this letter, so long overdue and yet, once you shall have read it, I feel as if you will understand my necessary silence and maybe even empathize with my sorrow, a sorrow that you must feel acutely, too, at times, and of which you are intimately a part.

"Mr. Wells?"

Ambrose looked up suddenly, and thrust the letter into his pocket violently, startled at having been disturbed caught reading this letter that he so badly yearned to study.

"Yes. Yes, that's me. Can I help you?" He stood awkwardly, and fished his hand out of his pocket to extend it toward the doctor who'd walked in with a nurse who followed behind.

"Well, yes, I hope so," the tall, bearded physician responded. He shook Ambrose's hand, and warmly smiled, yet there was sadness in his eyes. He gestured for Ambrose to sit back down. The doctor and the nurse sat down opposite him in the cramped little room, and Ambrose felt like perhaps he was going to be punished despite the warm smiles greeting him from across the carpet. An awkward silence ensued, and Ambrose was about to speak when the doctor beat him to the punch.

"My name is Dr. Shoffeitt. This here is Mindy. Were you

friends with the older man they brought in from Church Street?" he asked.

"Well, actually, sir, I don't know him well. He works for a client of mine, and we had some business to attend to this afternoon. He collapsed, and I called nine-one-one." He hesitated. "I'm not sure I can be of much help, but the ambulance driver thought I should come over."

There was another pause while the physician looked at the nurse, and then they both turned to look back at him.

"I see," the doctor said. "What do you know about what happened today?"

Ambrose shrugged for what seemed like the hundredth time in the last hour.

"I'm sorry, but that's it. I don't know anything else. The medics said he wasn't breathing, put some tube down his mouth, and packed him up and brought him here."

"That's right," the doctor said. "When he got here he still wasn't breathing, and only had a very faint pulse, which he quickly lost, unfortunately. We performed CPR, and gave him all the medications that we usually give to people to make their heart start again. We breathed for him through that tube you saw, but unfortunately we couldn't get his heart to start again, and he died tonight."

The doctor stopped talking in a well-rehearsed sort of way, and both of them looked at Ambrose expectantly. He felt he should say something.

"Well, that is less than ideal," said Ambrose. It was all he could manage, and the corners of the nurse's mouth curved up a little, as if suppressing a grin, and Ambrose blushed with embarrassment at the absurdity of such a statement.

"I mean," he said, trying to rectify the situation, "I just don't know him at all, and it's tragic that he's died. It's terrible. I wish I could help more. Have you called his family?"

"We're not sure he has any. We were hoping you might be able to help us with that. He had no identification on him of any kind, and, well…" the physician trailed off. He seemed confused.

"What's that?" Ambrose asked.

"Well, he's got scars on him that are…unusual," the doctor replied. "Would you mind just identifying him for us, for the record, as being the gentleman you were meeting with today? The police or the coroner may get in touch with you at some point, but you're not in any trouble. It's just a formality, really. We'll need your info."

Ambrose hesitated. He hadn't thought about the potential ramifications of being the last man seen alive with the deceased.

"Well, sure, I suppose."

"Follow me, then," said the doctor.

They both got up, and Ambrose followed suit.

"You said his name was…"

"I didn't," Ambrose replied. "But his name was Benjamin Legare. He was a lawyer in town."

"A lawyer, huh? Fair enough," Dr. Shoffeitt replied. Ambrose followed them out the door, down the hallway past myriad patients stuck in hallway beds, or in tiny rooms with families and friends and beeping machines and hospital staff. They walked into the main trauma bay, and in the far corner was a small area set apart by curtains that hung from the ceiling that had been pulled closed to give the deceased more privacy—more than the living seemed to have. Dr. Shoffeitt walked forward, and parted the curtains for Mindy and Ambrose to pass through.

Laying in front of him with a sheet over his waist but otherwise naked, was Mr. Benjamin Legare, Esquire. A plastic tube was still sticking out of his mouth. His chest was crushed inwards as if it had been sunken in by a great force, and he noticed bruising had already begun to develop along the dependent parts of his chest and abdomen. His feet were almost black, as if he was suffering from severe frostbite, but his face was gray and pallid. His eyes were staring through his foggy corneas, but it was as if they'd already sunk into his skull more than they had even been when he was still alive—perhaps not more than ninety minutes ago. He had an IV in his left arm, and there was blood oozing from around it, sticky and partially clotted, pooling on the stretcher.

"My God," he heard Dr. Shoffeitt whisper under his breath. Mindy exhaled sharply.

"What is it?" Ambrose asked. He was shocked as well, having never seen a dead body, but he figured the good doctor and nurse behind him—seasoned emergency department professionals they seemed to be—had seen their share.

"It's nothing. It's just—" he paused, searching for the right words. "It's just that he seems to be in a remarkable state of decomposition, but he can't have been dead for more than an hour. Right, Mindy?"

She nodded her head in agreement.

"Time of death was called at seventeen twenty-nine, sir."

"Oh, I see," Ambrose said. He figured all dead bodies would be this horrible.

"If you don't mind, Mr. Wells," the doctor said, "would you look at his back? It's just I've never seen anything like it. You said you know nothing about this man?"

Before Ambrose could answer, Dr. Shoffeitt and Mindy had walked over to Ben Legare's corpse, and rolled him onto his right side. Ambrose gasped. His entire back was scarred with large, crisscrossing cicatrices, so much so, there did not appear to be any normal skin left. Many of them wrapped around, and up toward his neck, then down along the buttocks only to peter out as faint, keloid disfigurements on his thighs and shoulders. The skin was tight in places and looked painful, and in others, where decomposition had already set in, there were pooling purple areas of softer, mottled tissue. A faint putrid scent arose from underneath the body as they had rolled it over, and Ambrose felt nauseated, stepping back.

"I'm sorry. I really don't know him. I don't know what—"

"It's like he'd been whipped as a boy!" Dr. Shoffeitt exclaimed. "I mean, I know he was an old man, but still…"

Dr. Shoffeitt and Mindy laid the cold body back down on the stretcher, and it made a sickening thunk. Ambrose felt awful. He wanted out of that curtained little room immediately. He had a letter burning a hole in his pocket, and wanted a quiet place to read it, far away from the dead and dying.

Suddenly, another nurse's head popped in through the curtains.

"Dr. Shoffeitt, we got a gunshot wound to the belly and left arm coming in hot. Three minutes out. We're gonna need this trauma bay."

"Shit," the doctor said. "All right. Mindy, call the morgue, and see if we can't move Mr. Legare down there immediately. Let's page a trauma out."

"Already done, sir," the other nurse said.

Everyone moved to leave the room except for Ambrose Wells and Ben Legare.

"Dr. Shoffeitt?" he asked tentatively.

"Oh...yes?" he replied, as if he'd just remembered Ambrose existed.

"You don't need me anymore, do you?" Ambrose asked, suddenly and thankfully feeling forgotten.

"Oh, no. You're okay. Just leave your name and number, and the cops may call you if they have any questions, but I doubt they will. They've got bigger fish to fry," he said, pointing toward the chaos and the noise on the other end of the curtains. The ambulance bay doors opened, and a stretcher rolled in with medics yelling, "We've got a GSW to the belly!"

"What happened to my three minutes?!?" Ambrose heard Dr. Shoffeitt yell.

Ambrose turned to look at what was left of Ben Legare, and felt bad for feeling sick to his stomach. He had seemed like a kind man. Ambrose had never seen a dead person before, and it spooked him, but he also felt guilty—as if it was somehow Ambrose's fault. The dead man's eyes stared vacantly up at the ceiling, and Ambrose thought that Ben Legare was definitely far away from this ugly place, and that scarred and horrid body. He turned to leave, passing through the way he came in. As he did so, he bumped into Lily who was running around a corner with towels in her hand.

"Sorry!" he exclaimed.

"It's okay," she yelled back, heading toward the gunshot wound victim.

"Is it always this busy here?" Ambrose called out.

She turned again, and smiled at Ambrose as she walked backwards, pointing toward the ceiling with her free hand.

"Well, it's usually a busy place, but especially tonight!"

"Why tonight?" Ambrose asked, uncertain what she was implying.

"Why? 'Cause it's a full moon, of course! It's always crazy around here on full moons!"

She laughed to herself a little, and half-walked, half-jogged back into the trauma bay where people were yelling. Ambrose briefly caught a glimpse of a young man sitting up in the EMS stretcher, desperately clutching his belly with dark, crimson streams of blood oozing through his clasped fingers, out on to the stretcher, and away on to the floor. As the door shut, Ambrose caught the young man's glance, and felt that they both knew that he would likely die—no amount of grasping could keep his life from trickling out of him. Ambrose fled the emergency department, clutching the unread letter in his hand.

Chapter Fifteen

THE WARM NIGHT AIR and the humid breeze felt especially nice after being in the chilly, air-conditioned emergency department, and Ambrose breathed it in deeply. Looking up at the globular, silver orb casting ethereal light on the city and every living soul within it, Ambrose felt as if he'd made a narrow escape from death itself. He turned a corner, happy to be headed away from the ER and back toward Edisto. He had so many questions he wanted answers to. However, it was difficult to know what to ask first. Grabbing the letter out of his pocket, he thought to himself, *Perhaps this will shed some light on everything that has transpired.*

He quickly opened his car door, placed his keys in the ignition, sat down, and opened the crumpled epistle again. He found that he could read the marvelous script with nothing more than the light of the moon. He tore into it, holding his breath unconsciously for the first two paragraphs.

My Dear Ambrose,

It is with much confidence and pride that I write this letter, so long overdue and yet, once you shall have read it, I feel as if you will understand my necessary silence and maybe even empathize with my sorrow, a sorrow that you must feel acutely, too, at times, and of which you are intimately a part. I suppose by now you have been made aware that Wellspring, and everything on it, is yours by birthright. I'm sorry for not simply telling you about our relationship directly; however, there were important considerations to take into account, and preparations to be made. I wanted to be absolutely sure you were who I thought you to be. However, all lingering doubts were immediately extinguished the minute you stepped on to the island's dock. It was instantly clear that you were my son. It was the first time I have had my breath stolen from me in many long years. You see, Ambrose, you have her eyes. When I see you I am taken back in time, and the heart has wounds that no geographic or temporal distance can fully mend.

It is with much confidence and pride, despite Mr. Wells' depression and neglect. I have enjoyed our brief time together more immensely than you will ever know, and more than I have a right to. Perhaps you will never find a way to forgive me for turning you over to your mother's old friend. I was hardly myself, and could not stand to look at you. I felt you had killed her, but I know now that it was I who should have left her alone. I shouldn't have succumbed again, but even a man of my not-inconsiderable knowledge can be ruled by the wilder passions of the tempestuous soul. If I can make amends in some small way, it is to give to you everything I have, except the Bucentaur, *of course.*

Benjamin will have told you that I am leaving. There are places I have not seen in centuries. I feel a poignant nostalgia that I thought had been buried too deep within my sturdy core to be recovered, and yet there it is. I would like to see the family's old estate. It is no longer in the family, of course—if it exists at all—but last I visited it still stood. I wonder if Hitler's bombs succeeded where Cromwell and his incessant Roundheads had failed, and where centuries of Saxons, Danes, and Normans failed before them. I wonder if the price of modernity has staked its claim on the old land. Are my parent's graves still there? My ancestors? My brother's? Perhaps his children, and theirs, and so on and so on? I wonder if a man of my age can even survive any longer in this most unusual of eras; "That all with one consent praise new-born gawds, though they are molded of things past, and give to dust that is a little gilt more laud than gilt o'erdusted," and so forth. The Great Bard knew what took me centuries to discover, it seems. I still do not know all the answers (what foolishness to think that I ever could have!), but I do know that I have done what I set out to do. It is your turn now. Wellspring is at once my greatest gift, my sincerest apology, and my familial bequest. If there was ever a time to leave, it must be now, now that I have a generation to pass it on to, and now that I have learned no amount of knowledge can replace love.

A few words on love: your mother named you Ambrose, after Bierce, of course, who was her favorite author, though I found his style somewhat lacking, and was never much in to short stories. "Good, but no Chekhov," I would say to her, teasing. I suppose you might have been Anton, had I been able to convince her of his superior talents. Spinoza was high on my list as well, but alas her veto was insurmountable. Ella was more stubborn than even old Ben Legare. Ambrose it would be, and Ambrose it was.

Hugo blew through like the 1885 typhoon that took out Edingsville. Wellspring took a beating, but came out on top, as always. As the wind battered the old house, your mother held my hand. Ben was there to help with the baby, having delivered many of them back in my old rice fields on Edisto, and Captain Delacroix was keeping an eye on the boats in the grotto below. Her cries quickened as the storm winds howled outside, and Ben looked up at me and shook his head. "Baby's coming feet first. Ain't no good." I'll always remember that look on his face. I yelled at him to get you out, and he just kept sweating, shaking his head. There was so much blood, and Ella grew pale as the full moon hidden behind Hugo's storm clouds. I begged her to drink from the fountain, to try and save her life—if not for me, then for you. She'd held out for months. "It isn't natural, Peyton," is all she'd ever said, and now she just shook her head.

I ran out into the gale, and grabbed some moonshine anyway. The rain pelted me, and I was practically picked up by the winds, body and soul, and blown off the island. Somehow I made it back, and I pleaded with her, Ambrose, on my hands and knees—how I pleaded with that woman—but she refused, and faded and faded. Ben shook his head, weeping, and finally pulled you out, blue as a heron and just as silent. I told her it was a boy, and she just smiled, too exhausted to speak, I believe. Ben slapped you good and hard a couple of times after cutting the cord, and then I saw all that blood again—soaked through the sheets, dripping on the floor, Ben covered in it. I put the glass of shine to her mouth, but she turned away, and as she did—a cry! Ben laughed, weeping still. "Here you come now, child. Welcome! Welcome!"

The house shuddered in a strong gust. Ben swaddled you in a towel, and gently placed you on your mother's breast. She could hardly open her eyes, but she looked at you and she looked at me and I will never forget the feeling. You see, I knew she wouldn't live, Ambrose. Ben had started to pack her with towels, but blood was pouring out like a river, and her life, as her labor cries had been, was swept away in Hugo's fury.

She died in my arms after whispering to you. "Hello my dear, dear Ambrose. You are as beautiful as I had dreamt." She then closed her eyes, and passed from the scene. You were still wriggling on her breast, and looking up at her in that shocked way that newborns do. Ben took you from her, and I screamed nonsense, and poured the shine down her throat. I heard you cry out, but she didn't move, and in an act of temporary insanity, I took her and picked her up. I took your mother, and I ran into the furious tempest, and I plunged us both headfirst into the moonshine. Whatever paltry faith in God and miracles I still had, died forever with Ella in that fountain. What good was a fountain of youth if the one you loved wouldn't drink from it? What good was a God who gave me the gift of life, only to take away the love that makes it all worth it?

She was already long gone, and I roared back at that storm as I held her. Finally the wind died down, and all of a sudden the eye passed over, and the full moon shone down on her face, illuminating her gentle, tender features, and I could have sworn she was still alive. For the second time in my life I wept bitter tears, and I don't believe the moonshine ever tasted as sweet as it used to afterward. Eventually Delacroix and Benjamin came and took me away. I learned two weeks later that they buried her at sea; that you had been given to Davey Wells. He did what he could, and I pitied him, too, over the years. He loved her as much as I did, the poor wretch. I think he died that night as well. They say time heals all wounds, but that is a fallacy that only the immortal could appreciate. Time anesthetizes the sting of old wounds—it is true—but they never really leave you. Those old scars become entwined with who you are.

A word on time: I knew that telling you the truth about your parentage would be a delicate task. I didn't think it could be done at the same time as telling you about the fountain. The captain, I should explain, calls its waters "moonshine," for that is when it works its nocturnal magic. The entirety of the month it is as regular a fountain as any, pretty enough in its way, and pleasant, but on the full moon, if you head down to take a look, something truly extraordinary occurs. I will not waste time to comment further. You will see for yourself in due course. It is, however, one of the most seductive and beautiful displays of the natural world that I have ever laid eyes upon—and I have seen a lot during my prolonged time in this mortal realm, Ambrose. I was not always a hermit. I once sailed far and wide on the Bucentaur, *with plenty of stores of moonshine on board. The world, for a brief moment it seems now, was my laboratory, and I had all the time in the world to conduct my experiments.*

You may still not believe me, and I admit that it is an amazing claim, and all amazing claims require substantial evidence—evidence you shall see for yourself soon enough. Let me add a note of warning: You may choose to divulge this information as you see fit; however, the outside world is full of superstitious men; some blinded by ignorance, some by religion, others by the very science they claim holds all eternal truths. The ignorant man is the poorest of souls. If it is a truism that knowledge is power, and I believe it is, he is not worth further consideration. The man of faith states it isn't "natural," but what could be more natural than a spring that percolates from the very Earth we all depend upon? Is Wellspring any less natural than any other body of water one may stumble across? It is the willful blindness of piety to suggest otherwise. The man of science, meanwhile, states that these things cannot be, because he cannot explain it, and yet here it is. He will ignore it altogether, or rail against it and call for its destruction, as if it is some apostasy of science, the modern religion. There is nothing more intolerable to the learned man than that which he is unable to understand. I should know. "Honi soit qui mal y pence." Guard it carefully, son.

I think I should tell you that, over the years, I've found that the water brings out the timbre of the man, and that is perhaps its real magic. Delacroix is no paradigm of wisdom, but what he lacks in cerebral acumen or simply natural curiosity, he more than makes up for in loyalty, discreteness, and the love of his long and sordid life. He drinks from the moonshine with relish, but from the well of life sparingly indeed. He will always be an important conduit between Wellspring and the mainland, and will keep you stocked with the sundry necessities of life. Remember, one red light means "come immediately." The usual white light means "all is well, and the usual morning run is all that will be needed." It is an old code, and he will respect your privacy otherwise with the exception of his "shiny nights" on which you can expect him to arrive at the spring around midnight with his old, copper cup, and his hat in his hand. It is his price for services duly rendered, and it is his thanks for a life once saved.

Ben Legare has been my most faithful ally but he has given up the shine. You will note his advanced age when you meet him. He has only given up our monthly toasts together several months back. The waters of life will preserve you at whatever place you are at in your life when you first drink them in. Once you stop, however, time quickly catches up, and takes what it is owed. I believe we all age at a rate that is acceptable to our conscience. To age rapidly would be shocking indeed, but Ben is a smart man of science, and a duly religious one to boot, who was torn about Wellspring. In the end, I think he chose death because he felt it was a part of life. Perhaps it is. I will miss him terribly. It will behoove you to find another who can help manage the affairs of the place for the unceasing, buzzing outside world. I leave it in your capable hands to determine how, and with whom, to proceed.

Finally, the fountain does not save you from all calamity. A bullet to the head is a bullet to the head. It doesn't bring people back, Lazarus-like. It is true, that non-fatal wounds will heal with astonishing rapidity, and that I have not been ill in centuries, but a quick, traumatic death would be just as fatal to me or Captain Delacroix as it would be to you.

I hope you will, as years go by, learn from my library, and continue to grow and develop into your full potential. I hope you can forgive your old man's abandonment, and know how I have thought, and will think, of you all the time. I will not likely return. I am beginning to think that Ben Legare—after all his preaching, and despite all of his natural and acquired intelligence—might have been on to something. Perhaps there is more to life than just living. Perhaps there are other worlds to explore. Perhaps.

With timeless love,
Your old man, P.F. Grimball

Ambrose sat in the car, dumbfounded, and stared down the street, unsure what to believe or feel or think, even. His mind ran in circles. Ten minutes passed before he moved stiffly, grabbed the keys that were still in the ignition, and turned the engine over. He felt he couldn't even begin to grasp everything, but that he had to get to Wellspring before Peyton left in the *Bucentaur.*

He quickly pulled into the quiet street, and wended his way back to the Savannah Highway, headed south. He crossed the Ashley and Stono Rivers without a thought, turned left to head through Hollywood and Ravenel again, and, speeding incessantly, reached Highway 174. As he passed the giant oaks that lined the road, and passed over the Intercoastal Waterway, he suddenly heard the easy chime of bells. Pulling him out of his intense single-minded pursuit to get to Edisto as quickly as possible, the bells reminded him of the outside world. He instinctively reached for his cell phone, and answered it without looking to see who the incoming call was from.

"Hello?" he asked. He spoke into the receiver automatically, still without thinking.

"Ambrose! Hey, Ambrose! It's Pete, man. You got a sec?"

"Pete? Pete who?" Ambrose asked, half-dazed and half-mystified as to who the hell Pete was.

"Pete! Pete Myers! From USC, you moron! How the hell—"

The reception was poor, and the phone cut off. It was spotty, and Ambrose suddenly remembered that he'd texted Pete weeks ago. About what though? The bird Ambrose had hit! He'd forgotten all about that, and frankly could care less. He was about to tell Pete that, when he remembered the connection had been dropped. He was approaching the top of the bridge over the Dawhoo Cut, and suddenly heard Pete patch back in.

"You there, man? Ambrose? It's Pete, about that bird pic you texted me!"

"Oh yeah, Pete! Hey, man. Sorry, I'm out in the sticks. Tough reception out here. Might need to call you back."

He immediately regretted answering his phone, but it was practically a reflex.

"Oh! Okay, man. Listen, though. Real quick! I gotta tell you! That bird you hit—do you still have it? It could be real important!"

Ambrose had to force himself to think about the bird and Pete Myers. He'd practically already forgotten again, his thoughts immediately drifting to his mother and Wellspring Island and the fountain, and he had almost unceremoniously hung up on Pete. He felt obligated to respond a second time.

"Oh yeah, Pete. The bird? No. No, I buried it. Why?"

Ambrose was irritated to be having this conversation at all right now. His car hit the top of the bridge, and he picked up an extra bar on his cell phone he knew he'd be losing immediately on the other side. He hit the gas pedal.

"Shit. That sucks, man, but not the end of the world! Listen, I had never seen it before, but I don't do birds. That's why it took so long for me to get back to you. I showed it to a friend here in DC. He's not a hundred percent, but he thinks—"

Pete cut out again. *Good riddance,* thought Ambrose, about to hang up for a second time.

"Keet! Did you hear me, Ambrose? It would be an incredible find! They're extinct. Been extinct for years! Nobody's seen one since the twenties!"

Ambrose's curiosity peaked.

"I hit a what? I'm sorry, Pete. You're cutting out!"

Ambrose's car swiftly moved down the far side of the bridge, and entered on to Edisto Island. "Edisto Island Welcomes You!" The sign flashed in his headlights, and Ambrose quickly caught the image of an egret and a sunset.

"You hit a fucking—" Silence.

"What?! I hit a what?"

Ambrose felt foolish for yelling into the phone. One bar. This was hopeless. Suddenly, by some miracle, Pete's voice came back, shrieking through the air like magic.

"A Carolina parakeet! They're extinct! Can you dig it up? Tell me you know where—"

He cut out again, and silence followed. Ambrose thought for a minute, and smiled. His smile turned into a low laugh, which turned into outright mirth. He threw his phone into the backseat, and laughed aloud, thinking of all those beautiful green parrots bathing at Wellspring Island in the fountain of youth.

Chapter Sixteen

AMBROSE SPRINTED DOWN THE DOCK using the bright light from the full moon looming overhead to navigate over the more-rotten patches of wood, and various pieces of fishing gear and rope that were strewn across the old dock. His now-worthless phone and keys rattled together in his pocket, and the antique revolver he'd pilfered from the old captain earlier in the day—years ago, it seemed now—dug into his lower back where he'd put it after grabbing it from the glove compartment. He had burst out of the rusted Bronco, dashed down the dock, and began to approach the *Flying Horse*, where he saw a figure standing in front of it, its back turned away from Ambrose, talking to Captain Delacroix who was standing on his worn-out vessel.

"Captain!" Ambrose cried out. "Captain! We have to head out now. I know I'm early, but we have to go before—"

He stopped short, almost tripping from such rapid deceleration. The figure in front of him had turned upon hearing his voice, and Ambrose was shocked to see Cora standing there.

"Cora! What are you doing here?"

"I came to chat with Mr. Delacroix in order to convince him to keep you from returning to Wellspring. What are you doing here so early?"

Ambrose paused to catch his breath, and was acutely aware of the captain standing above them both, eyeing him as if he knew Ambrose had stolen his weapon. He wondered how long it had been since the old salt had been short of breath.

"I came to head out early. I read the letter. I know about Ben Legare! I know about you, captain! I know the truth, and I have to speak to him before he leaves!"

"Not until eleven thirty, and not a minute sooner!" Delacroix said, laughing. "Those are my orders, and I'm sticking to 'em. I ain't leavin' early, but I'm leavin' when I'm leavin', and you better be on the boat, Mr. Wells! I made a promise to my benefactor, and I keep my promises!"

Cora turned, and the pearly glow of the moonlight on her face gave her an aura of unspeakable beauty, tempered with her usual melancholia. She took his hands into hers as he caught his breath, and he felt everything slow down; the wind on the sound, the passing stars, his heartbeat.

"There is nothing for you on that island but the interminable loneliness of purgatory. I came to stop you one last time, Ambrose, but I won't try to stop you again. It's a sweet seduction, and you won't know the bitter truth until you've drank of it."

"Cora, I have to speak with him." Ambrose started to protest.

"No! No, you don't Ambrose! You know everything you need to know! He's your father, and your mama's long gone. Fine! Your future is here. Here, Ambrose! There is nothing you can learn out there that will have any value to you if you don't have what I am offering you here and now."

Tears streaked down her lovely face, and Ambrose felt he was drowning in them, barely able to gasp a response.

"I have to ask him about her, and about me. I have to hear it from him."

The captain, sensing Ambrose's will slipping, quickly did a volte-face.

"It's fine. I'll leave now, if you'd like! Better to have you early than to arrive without you at all! It's almost time for the shine—for this old man, anyway. Don't matter to me if it's nine thirty or midnight. I'll take you and be glad of it. You'll be thanking me, young man. Yes, sir. Ain't nothin' like a little shine under the light of the moon to pick you up!" He cackled maniacally, and threw off a spring line.

"I have to speak with him again," Ambrose said quietly.

"You won't come back the same, Ambrose. Auntie Dawes and Willie know a thing or two between them. And so do I."

There was a pause.

"Is it real, Cora? Do you know?"

"As I told you once before, I know there is more on heaven and Earth, Horatio. I also know that this old bastard behind me should have died from alcohol abuse long before I entered this world."

She pointed with her right thumb over her shoulder toward the *Flying Horse* as Captain Delacroix started the engine, which coughed and sputtered out blue, foul-smelling smoke.

"Don't listen to her, brother. You come on out now, and I'll take you back tonight. It's just a nightcap, is all. Let the *Flying Horse* take you to the fair waters of Hippocrene!"

He laughed again, and threw off the bow line with the vigor of a much younger man.

"I really need to see him. I promise I'll be back. It's—"

"He loved your mother because she looked like her great grandmother, Ambrose. Like our great-great grandmother. Had she not, he would have walked right on by on the docks that day. I am sure of it. He lost her once so long ago. It must have seemed like a second chance—fate making amends, or whatever. I can't blame him, but it wasn't right. It wasn't natural. She wouldn't drink, or she wouldn't have died in that storm. She wouldn't have had to make that sacrifice for you. Your mother chose wisely. Ambrose, I'm begging you to choose wisely as well."

"Wait a minute. What do you mean, 'our great-great grandmother'? Are we…"

"Yes, we are. Distantly, though; so very distantly, Ambrose. Elizabeth Welch is our common ancestor. After she married into the Hampton family, she had two children. One of them was my great grandfather, and the other, her sister, is your great grandmother."

Ambrose had to pause for a moment while that fact kicked in.

"You coming?! Now or never!" Delacroix hollered down from the gunwale over the noise of the engine.

"Wait just a moment, Captain!" Ambrose yelled back. He thought it odd that just a moment ago the ancient salt hadn't wanted to leave until 11:30 p.m. on the dot.

"PG and EW then. On the oak behind Belleview?" Ambrose asked.

She nodded.

"Yes. He loved and lost, Ambrose. I don't know what happened at Sharpsburg, but he came home alive, and physically as healthy as ever, though with a broken heart. Generations passed, and then one day, there she was again, giggling on the pier with my mother. It must have been as if the last century had never happened, and he had to have her. He didn't love her, Ambrose. He loved the idea of her. She was his Elizabeth reborn, but she was not Elizabeth. He thinks he lost her twice, but he never had her at all. All that time, Ambrose. Don't you see what it's done? All that knowledge, and no perspective. He forgets what makes us tick, and then compounds the error by believing that he drinks it down every month. We're all on borrowed time, but what is that to a man whose got nothing but time? It's twisted him, and whatever he might have been—whatever he was—is so far gone now I'm not sure he even remembers. Please don't follow him down that rabbit hole. Don't go tonight!"

She released his hands as if to say she'd done what she could. He felt the loss of her touch acutely.

"I can't believe that. He loved my mother. He wrote this letter…"

Tears poured down his face.

"No, Ambrose. He loved Elizabeth Welch once, and since then he's loved nothing and nobody but himself. He couldn't even bear to raise you. What kind of man—"

"Stop!" Ambrose had heard enough. "I'll find out what kind of man!"

Jumping on the ship, he heard the captain roar his approval, and cast off the final spring line. Turning the wheel, the old boat started to drift away from the dock.

"Cora! It's the choice I have to make! I'll be back. You'll see! If I don't do this now, then I'll never know what type of man he was"—he paused, and then quietly finished—"or who I am."

She turned on the dock, and the moon shone in her eyes, giving them a luminous sparkle that surprised and astonished Ambrose, and forced him to catch his breath. It was as if the light revivified her, adding to her spectral beauty.

"This is what life is, Ambrose!" She shouted from the pier, and opened her arms, gesturing toward the windy bay with its glowing nightcaps and the radiant stars above.

"It's love! It's the full circle! It's birth and death and everything in between! You don't get to pick and choose!"

"I'll be back tonight, Cora! Just wait for me. I'll call on you!"

She just stared at him in the ghostly light of the moon as the boat pulled away, and Ambrose, in a brief moment of intense doubt, thought of jumping off into the sound and swimming back to the dock. But he felt the captain's sturdy, powerful hand on his right shoulder, and heard the words, "It's easier to praise death than to endure it, young man."

He turned to see the captain staring up at the fat moon as the breeze blew through his hair. He looked almost regal. Turning back to the dock, he saw Cora standing there, not having moved, watching the *Flying Horse* pull out of the harbor.

"Since when do you misquote Seneca?"

"I have a lot of time to kill," the sailor responded with a grand laugh. "*Ducunt volentem fata, nolentem trahunt.*"

Ambrose turned to the sailor, away from the pier.

"There's more to you than I would have guessed upon our first meeting."

"I could say the same," Delacroix said in response. He turned the wheel and took a long puff from the pipe that he'd pulled out of his shirt pocket, which he'd lit at some point when Ambrose had been talking with Cora. Smoke poured out of his lungs, and mixed with the fumes from the *Flying Horse* before it all disappeared into the steady breeze behind them both.

"But then I'd be lyin', college boy!"

He laughed, and Ambrose, feeling like he wanted to shoot the captain with his own pistol, repressed the urge, and turned away, looking forward to Wellspring Island as it slowly grew in size. There was no lonely silhouette standing on the dock as there usually was when the *Flying Horse* approached, and Ambrose prayed under his breath that he'd gotten there in time to pay Peyton Grimball one final visit.

The wind continued to kick up along the bay, and white, salty spray was flung across the bowsprit. The island grew closer at an infuriatingly slow rate, and Ambrose had the sullen thought that the Captain was slow-rolling their trip purposefully.

"Does she move any faster?!" Ambrose yelled.

Delacroix ignored him as he puffed acrid smoke out of his lungs, humming some ancient mariner's tune. Behind him the lights of Edisto Beach, the Anhinga, the Lusty Crab, the Piggly Wiggly, and hundreds of salt-worn beach huts twinkled in the night. Behind them, the lights of Belleview, Auntie Dawes' trailer, the Dawhoo Cut Bridge, and beyond were surely lit, keeping the light of civilization burning for yet another night. He had a brief thought of a picture he'd seen in a magazine, of Earth from Saturn's vantage point—a speck of light in a sea of darkness, just like any other. Feeling suddenly forlorn, he thought of Cora standing on the dock, and his loneliness morphed into inchoate guilt. He turned away in a physical effort to shake the feeling, and scanned the horizon ahead of the boat and beyond, past Wellspring. He didn't see any obvious sailboats off in the distance. Perhaps Ambrose would catch him yet, before the old man abandoned his ancient home.

After another five minutes of interminably slow cruising across St. Helena Sound, the *Flying Horse* eased up along the dock, and Ambrose threw the moldy fenders over the port side of the boat, grabbed a spring line, and quickly jumped out.

"I assume you'll be stepping off your floating home, Captain?" Ambrose yelled up from the deck. Delacroix cut the engine, and flicked the stubby ashes of his pipe into the bay.

"Ay, tie her off, and I'll grab the stern line! I've business to attend to. The old bastard owes me a drink!"

Ambrose threw the old rope insecurely around the cleat a couple of times, and started to dash along the long dock up toward the little path that led toward the main house.

"Take care of that little six-shooter you got there, Mr. Wells! Better men than you or Grimball have met the man in the little black suit after staring down her barrel!"

Ambrose ignored him, and heard his cackles blown away by the stiff, warm ocean breeze. He turned and practically sprinted up the steep, rocky path to the main plateau.

The sound of the parakeets in the fountain was much more raucous than Ambrose remembered from his previous visits, and he felt he could hear their frolicking in the fountain from halfway up the trail. Squawks and shrieks greeted him rudely as he pulled up on the plateau. Bathing in the moonlight, riotously splashing water and feathers into the air, were what seemed like a small army of the laughing birds. Several were perched on the old statuary, as if looking down on their friends and family, shrieking words of encouragement into the fracas below them.

Looking up at the main house, Ambrose noted that there were no lamps lit. He didn't think he could hear the low hum of the generators due to the cacophony of brilliant parrots fighting it out in the shallow fountain water. He looked left, and made a snap judgment to follow the trail down to the grotto. If Peyton wasn't there, but his boat was still, then Ambrose could search the house after.

His mind made up, he jogged, somewhat carefully now, down the steep path, and then carefully along the wet rock at the bottom that led into the claustrophobic tunnel. It quickly became almost pitch-black darkness, and he needed his cell phone light again, until, squeezing through the narrowest slot, he saw torch light illuminating the way ahead. As he wound the corner, the *Bucentaur* was still there, floating at her slip along the great rock wall. Silver moonlight cast luminous spotlights through the porous limestone roof and on to the water below, giving the grotto an otherworldly appearance.

From across the giant cavern, Ambrose could hear a man whistling, the sound echoing off the walls, obscuring the song's finer details. He hustled along the slick ledge that lined the grotto, passing by the hot torches that licked the sweat off his brow. He found himself alternating between near darkness and brilliant, flickering orange light. The cavern water to his right was an inky haze except for the fantastic lunar spotlights that beamed down through the massive holes of the natural ceiling.

As he approached the large boat, he realized he had no concept of what to say to the man he now believed was his father, and yet before he could even think, he heard his own voice reverberating off the limestone walls.

"Just where do you think you're going?!"

The cheerful whistling abruptly stopped, and the only sound was the flutter of the occasional bat landing or taking off from some unseen perch above them. Ambrose came up along the port side of the large schooner, and squinted in the flickering semi-darkness. Movement at the mid-ship caught his eye, and P.F. Grimball stepped out of the cabin, smiled grandly, opened his arms, and laughed.

"My son, I certainly did not expect to see you this evening!"

"Yeah, well, Captain Delacroix was obliging. You've placed his services at my disposal, or did you forget?!" Ambrose yelled. He was suddenly infuriated, waving the now-very-crumpled letter in the air.

"That I did, indeed! Although his service was not to begin for another hour or two. He has grown somewhat lackadaisical in his old age."

"Where the hell do you think you're going?!" Ambrose repeated himself, angrier now, as Grimball flashed his winning smile from the ship. "You write me this, this almost unbelievable letter, will me everything you own…tell me more about my mother than I've learned my entire life, admit to being my father—and then you disappear! You've been gone my whole life, and you just up and leave! I think I'm owed an apology, an explanation!"

Tears streaked down Ambrose's face. Looking at Peyton now confirmed everything in his heart. It was all true. Even the damn fountain.

"AND HOW OLD ARE YOU?!" Ambrose yelled.

Peyton stopped grinning, walked over to edge of the boat, and lightly hopped on to the ledge five feet from Ambrose, who was visibly shaking now.

"You've a right to know the truth. It's why I wrote you that letter. And yes, I'm leaving, Ambrose, but I'm leaving you well endowed." He sighed. "I knew you couldn't say no to this place, whatever charms Ms. Cora Hampton may possess. I have to admit, I am not a man that surprises easily these days, but this is the second time in a month now you've caught me off guard. I was unsure if you were the same little boy that Davey Wells took in, but when you stepped on to my dock a month ago, and I saw those blue eyes of yours…I knew immediately you were Ella's, and it stole my breath away." He walked toward Ambrose, and stopped in front of him. "And, Ambrose, I'm old enough to know when it's time for a change."

"Stop with the bullshit. You set me up. You had Ben Legare bring me out here under false pretenses. You've been planning on leaving since before I got here! You'd abandon me twice…" Ambrose trailed off

"I haven't the time or the desire to explain myself to you. Is this magnificent inheritance not enough? I may not be a father of which you can be proud, but everything you need to know is in that letter. Why do you think I gave it to Ben? You weren't supposed to be here again until I was long gone. So yes, I'd abandon you twice, if that's how you want to think of it, but live a couple of hundred years more, feel the pain of life amplified by the dusty, repetitive echo chamber of passing decades, and see if you still think of me with such ill will."

"Ben's dead, Peyton. He died in front of me, just like my mother did, but imagine not being able to even remember her face. God, for years I wished I could see her face just once in my dreams." Ambrose stopped talking briefly, unsure how to proceed. "I don't think badly of you, old man. I pity you. You can get on your boat and take off, but not before you tell me why you let her die here on this island, with immortality in your hands. Then I want you to explain why you left me to rot, and figure out life on my own. I demand an explanation and an apology."

Peyton laughed again.

"Demand away, Ambrose. You've got your mother's eyes and her stubborn temperament, I'll give you that. But other than that, you're all me." He turned to get back on the *Bucentaur*. "I'm all gassed up, and I have enough moonshine stowed away to last a good, long time—"

BANG! The sound of the ancient bullet striking the vessel to Peyton's left, caused him to stop, and slowly turn around to face Ambrose again, who was now holding the smoking revolver directly at Peyton's chest.

"I demand an apology and an explanation," Ambrose said, repeating himself with quiet purpose. "And then you can leave for all eternity, as far as I'm concerned."

"You just put a hole in the *Bucentaur*. You're lucky it's above the water line, you ungrateful—"

"The next one won't be lodged in your ship." Ambrose interrupted him. "An apology and an explanation, please."

Torchlight flickered behind both men, casting shadows over their faces as they squared off for what seemed like hours.

"You won't put a bullet in me, Ambrose," Peyton finally said, breaking the silence.

"How do you know what I will or won't do?"

"I know, because I know I wouldn't, and like it or not, you are your father's son."

"That seems a calculated risk. Are you sure?" Ambrose asked, cocking the hammer back on the old gun, his heart racing, knowing that Peyton was right. It was his only leverage though, and he knew he had to maintain the illusion that he very well might fire one off into the old man's unceasing heart.

"Yes, well I try to always be calculated, and I usually succeed." Peyton paused, and then hung his head in resignation. "But not always, I admit it. Do you want to know the truth, Ambrose? The truth is that I am sorry. I lost my mind the night you were born, and when I came to my senses you were already gone. I didn't have the courage to bring you back out here. My broken heart couldn't bear it."

Ambrose slowly lowered the pistol. Tears streamed down his cheeks.

"But this is the fountain of youth! You couldn't save her?"

"Did you read the letter, Ambrose? She wouldn't have it. She chose to die. Just like good old Ben Legare did. I will miss him dearly, and I admire them both for their courage; your mother for refusing the shine, and Ben Legare for quitting it.

I've been thinking I need to quit as well. It's just..." Peyton trailed off.

"Just what?" Ambrose asked. His quiet words eerily echoed off the rock over and over again, as if even the cavern wanted to ask the question, "Just what? Just what? Just what?"

"It's just that I need to go home first. I need to have one last grand tour. I have centuries of knowledge stored away, but what is it if it's not applied to anything of use?" Peyton paused, and looked down at his feet. "And I need some closure. It has been years since I've been home, and then, who knows, maybe I too can wean myself off the old shine. It is a seductive mistress though, and I feel weak. And tired. I am so very tired, Ambrose."

Peyton turned without another word, and limply climbed aboard the *Bucentaur.* Ambrose made no attempt to stop him. He felt exhausted as well, and couldn't have prevented him from leaving now if he wanted to. He'd gotten what he'd came for. Peyton walked to the wheel, and hit a button to his right. A low rumble kicked in from behind Ambrose, and he realized an engine had been started.

"See me off, will you?" Peyton yelled down. He intimated for Ambrose to untie the two spring lines, and throw them aboard. Defeated, Ambrose did so without another word. Peyton took the rope, and headed back to the wheel.

"You see, Ambrose," Peyton called down from the transom now. "We're all borne along our paths, but free will never dies. You make choices, and you accept their repercussions, whatever those may be. Your mother made hers. Ben and Delacroix made theirs. I have made mine. Your mother was a mirror image of her great grandmother. I was walking down the pier one day, and there she was—like a ghost, or a time traveler from the past; like Einstein's twin on the rocket ship, having come home to finally be with me. A century and a half ago Elizabeth chose to leave me, and a thousand years will not fully heal that old wound. Ella gave me a second chance at unrequited love, over a hundred years after the fact, and what did I know for all my book-reading and study? Not a thing about the inner sanctum of my own heart. Ella was lovely—beautiful, of course—kind, and wiser than her years would suggest, and I think she truly loved me, too, Ambrose, but deep in my heart I grieved for my Elizabeth when she died. You can't imagine the guilt, but I can tell you this: I still love her anyway."

Peyton paused, and turned the wheel, slipping the boat into forward gear. It slowly moved away from the ledge and toward the opening of the grotto, and the torchlight began to fade on Peyton's anguished face.

"The shame I felt, son. I couldn't raise you, and live with myself. Davey Wells, the man who loved Ella and deserved her, who was ruined by her death, took you in as a final act of selfless love. I hope you can forgive his insensitivity, and I hope you can forgive an old fool."

The *Bucentaur* began to pull away, and Ambrose realized he wouldn't be able to hear Peyton speak much longer.

"Will you return?" Ambrose croaked haltingly out to Peyton's back now. The old man turned to take a long look back at Ambrose.

"You were loved, Ambrose. More than you will ever know, perhaps, but your mother loved you deeply. Farewell, son! And think on the fountain! Remember, we are nothing more than the sum total of our choices."

"But will you return?!" Ambrose called out again, wondering if Peyton could hear him. The *Bucentaur* earned distance from the flickering stone pier, and approached the entrance to the grotto now, briefly flitting under a beam of moonlight.

"Twilight and evening bell, and after that, the dark! And may there be no sadness of farewell when I embark." He heard Peyton's ghostly voice echo off the limestone. *When I embark. When I embark. When I embark...*

Ambrose sighed, watching the wake from the boat ripple across the water, and lap against the ledge he was standing on.

"For tho' from out our bourne of Time and Place, the flood may bear me far, I hope to see my Pilot face to face, when I have crossed the bar," Ambrose quietly finished. The *Bucentaur* slowly moved around the hard curve that led out of the hidden entrance and into the main harbor. He watched until the ship was gone, until he was alone standing on the quiet ledge of the grotto, the torches flickering smoky, orange light off his brow. The small waves from the wake of the boat were still beating against the rock, one after the other, incessantly, each one affecting its neighbor, causing a chain reaction of smaller waves that crashed into other waves, giving form to where there had previously been nothing.

Chapter Seventeen

AMBROSE STOOD THERE FOR WHAT seemed like an eternity before he slowly turned, and began walking back along the ledge through the narrow, dark slot that led up to the main path. Stepping out into the moonlight and out of the grotto, he could hear the waves lapping against the rocks, and he turned to look off into the wide Atlantic Ocean. In the distance, the *Bucentaur* was headed due east, with all sails out and full of wind. The silver ship glowed against the dark horizon, and the ancient constellations sparkled overhead, as if watching her passage with distant, vague, and impersonal interest. Orion aimed his bow toward Taurus. The Seven Sisters twinkled in their customary spot in the firmament. Casseiopeia reigned with icy stillness over Andromeda, still chained to a cliff awaiting her fate. All seemed to be well in the world.

He slowly headed back up the path, and entered on to the main plateau. The parakeets had quieted down, and most of them were roosting in the trees above. The lamps in the old house remained unlit. A figure sat on the edge of the fountain, and hummed a familiar yet strange song from the past.

"Did you see the old wizard off then?"

The captain grinned happily, and was holding a care-worn copper cup in both hands. Drinking deeply from the cup, Ambrose could see his eyes light up in the darkness, and begin to glow a strange cerulean, and fiery blue.

"The shine is sweet as life itself, young man! Will you be havin' some then?"

Ambrose didn't reply. He walked past him, and stared, dumbfounded, into the old fountain.

"Suit yourself, college boy. I'll be waitin' for you at the *Flyin' Horse*. If you ain't back down in ten minutes, I'll just assume you're spending the night! You know the code. White, if you need me. Red, if you need me now. Don't reckon you will, though. Not with the shine to keep you company."

The captain laughed and laughed, lit a match that sparked intensely for a minute as he shielded it from the dying wind, and took a long drag from the old pipe that hung from his mouth.

"A good evenin' to you then, Mr. Grimball."

Ambrose ignored him completely, and stared into the fountain. Under the bright full moon, the water glittered and refracted the ghostly light off of a multitude of small silvery, translucent orbs. The orbs floated, sinking and colliding with each other, each small fleck of watery dust affecting the course of the next, and so on and so forth, creating a mesmerizing murmuration of suspended beauty. Standing over the waters of life, Ambrose thought of his mother. He thought of Elizabeth Welch and of Davey Wells, of Auntie and Willie Dawes and of Ben Legare, of Captain Delacroix and Cora Hampton, and of Peyton Grimball. Each one of them altering the path of others across time and space, each of them interconnected players in a vast drama affecting the course of everything else in the universe—all of them writing their way into the grand story as they should, affecting each other in ways known and unknown, sending ripples through the fabric of space-time. He thought of his own choices, and of those made by so many others. He thought of the reverberating motion of endless waves dancing across the waters of St. Helena Sound. He thought of the wind across the bay, filling the *Bucentaur's* sails, tussling his hair and evaporating Cora's tears from her cheeks. He thought of the life-giving black water of the Edisto River, pouring its heart into the greedy ocean. He thought of the beauty of the settling, red, South Carolina dust, illuminated by the dying light of an August sun.

About the Author

Andrew Ross was born in Toronto, Canada, but grew up in Cohasset, Massachusetts, and graduated from the University of Richmond in Virginia in 2002. After completing medical school in Norfolk, Virginia, he went on to complete a residency in emergency medicine in Charleston, South Carolina. He now currently lives in Savannah with his wife, Maggie, and their daughter Josephine, where he works as an emergency physician. A love of all things literary—especially history, biographies, and the classics—helped shape his interest in writing. Outside of literature, he enjoys traveling, mountaineering, skiing, scotch, and soccer. His goal for his novel, The Sweet and Bitter Taste of Moonshine, was to create a story that appeals to both those readers with an interest in history and philosophy, as well as to anyone who loves a good saga that spans the centuries and is set in the American South.

www.ingramcontent.com/pod-product-compliance
Lightning Source LLC
Chambersburg PA
CBHW030244200626
46816CB00002BA/504

* 9 7 8 1 9 4 4 3 1 3 1 7 3 *